Echoes of LOVE

Three romantic novellas

by

Patricia Simpson

Lucky Publishing
United States of America

Visit Patricia Simpson's Website
www.patriciasimpson.com

Note: This is a work of fiction. All the characters and events
portrayed in this book are either products of the
author's imagination or are used fictitiously.

Echoes of Love

Copyright 2013 Patricia Simpson

EAN 978-0-9840412-7-5

Reader Note

This book is a collection of novellas only previously available in digital form. This book is not available as an e-book. If you are interested in a digital version of these stories, please search for the original titles of the novellas:

LORD OF THE NILE
THE MARRIAGE MACHINE
GARGOYLE

When love finds you,
will you recognize it and act,
or will you hear only the echoes of love?

Table of Contents

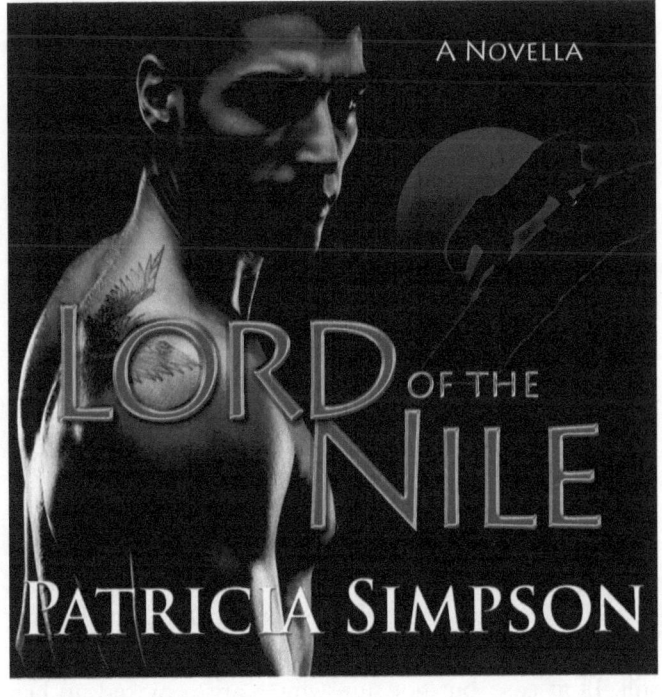

Sculptress Karissa Spencer is obsessed with
big black cats. And soon she'll know why...

Chapter 1

Baltimore, Maryland

THE BELL ON THE SHOP DOOR tinkled too soon. Surprised, Karissa Spencer looked up from the lioness she was sculpting. She glanced over the railing of the loft to the gallery below, wondering if her partner, Josh Lambert, had come back prematurely from his dinner run. The large gallery was bathed in shadows and the lights on the sculptures and paintings were nearly swallowed by the darkness. As far as she could tell, no one was there.

All was quiet, which was unlike Josh, who would have blustered into the shop, calling out to her and slamming the door behind him. Instead, the room remained suspiciously still. Ill at ease—but not sure why—Karissa picked up her sculpting knife and slipped off her stool.

"Who's there?" she asked, making sure her voice sounded clear and strong.

She stepped to the railing and looked down. A slight movement caught her eye and she glanced toward the pedestal that displayed a bronze of a panther. There in the shadows was a pair of golden brown eyes staring up at her, the same kind of eyes that had haunted her for more than a decade—the eyes of an Egyptian panther. Karissa felt a shiver of fear rush down her back.

Sixteen years ago she had come face to face with an Egyptian panther and had been obsessed ever since by the velvet power of the big cat. She had tried to capture its essence in clay, in bronze, in paint, and in marble, but the feral spirit of the cat had been elusive and her sculptures seemed empty and lifeless to her.

No one else noticed the missing element. Her pieces were popular and afforded her a decent living. In fact, her studio and gallery were going to be featured in an upcoming public television program called Women Artists in America. But Karissa knew something was missing in her work. Never once had she recreated the deadly power of the cat she had seen in Egypt. Had her prodigious memory failed her, just as it had failed to record a terrible night long ago? Or was she not gifted enough to capture the savage soul that smoldered in the eyes of the cat? And now here the eyes were again, just as she had remembered, as if to remind her of her shortcomings.

"Ebony," a voice declared in a soft sweep of baritone slightly tinged with a British accent.

"Pardon?" Karissa couldn't break away from the glowing eyes.

"If you would sculpt this in ebony, Miss Spencer, you would find satisfaction."

Ebony? She had never sculpted in wood. Ebony was dark brown, almost black, and the perfect medium to accentuate the sinuous lines of a cat. Why hadn't she thought of trying ebony? Karissa placed both hands on the rail and strained to see who was speaking in the darkness below.

"You seem to know me, sir. Have we met?"

"Once." The voice was smooth and rich, and she felt the tone vibrate somewhere deep inside her, as if to dislodge a memory long forgotten. But she did not remember this man. "A long time ago."

"Oh?"

"Perhaps you will not recognize me as I am now." The

man stepped away from the pedestal and into the light directed upon a freestanding bronze of three cats. He was dressed entirely in black—black shoes, trousers, and overcoat. Even his hair was black, swept off his forehead from a widow's peak and falling in slight waves to his collar. He was undeniably handsome, a bit older than she was— probably in his mid thirties—with a strong pointed chin and neat ears close to his head. She certainly would have remembered meeting such an attractive man, and knew without a doubt that she had never laid eyes on him.

Karissa never forgot a face, literally, because she possessed a photographic memory. According to her therapist, however, Karissa had chosen to put some of her Egyptian memories away because they were too painful to look at. Until she brought them out and faced the truth, she would forever be missing one of the most significant times of her life—the day her father disappeared.

Karissa cut off all thoughts of her therapist and looked back at the man in the gallery. If he belonged to the missing part of her life, she wasn't about to admit it to him or spend any time searching for his face in that exasperatingly blank spot in her memory.

"I'm sorry but I don't recognize you," she replied.

"It was many years ago. In Egypt." He bowed almost imperceptibly. "I am called Mr. Asher."

"Mr. Asher." She inclined her head slightly in return. "Is there something I can do for you?"

"Yes?" he replied. "But may I come up?"

"I'll come down."

Karissa clutched the sculpting knife tightly and descended the stairs, highly conscious of his regard. Mr. Asher was much taller than he first appeared, once she gained the lowest step. He was half a foot taller than she was, and she wasn't a short woman by any means.

He looked down at her and smiled, never once breaking

eye contact, and slowly raised the corners of his sensual mouth, appearing charming and provocative at the same time. Not many men had the confidence or self-possession to meet a woman's eyes for such an extended length of time. "What can I help you with?" she asked, making a pretense of brushing something off the nearby bronze so that she didn't have to continue to meet his intense eyes. "Do you wish to look at something in particular?"

"Actually, yes. But not one of your fine pieces of art." He stepped closer. "I have been looking for you, Miss Spencer. For quite some time."

"Oh? Why?"

"You might possibly be the only one in the world who can help me find something."

"Find what?"

"A tomb."

She gave a half laugh. "I'm afraid you have the wrong Spencer. My father is the archaeologist, not me."

"Your father is no longer available. You are. And I know you saw the lost sphinx."

The lost sphinx. Karissa felt something constrict her breathing as an overwhelming sensation of dread gripped her.

"No," she blurted. She turned away, fighting the urge to run back up the stairs and plunge into her work, just as she always did when bad memories threatened to descend.

"I know you remember the sphinx, Miss Spencer. The evidence is all over this gallery." He swept the air with a wave of his hand. He wore black gloves. "You do remember, don't you?"

"The only thing I remember about the sphinx is what people tell me."

"And what have they told you?"

"That because of the sphinx a curse was placed upon

my family, which is why my mother got sick and died when I was twelve. And why my father apparently ran off, never to be heard from again. But I don't see how the sphinx concerns you, Mr. Asher."

"It concerns me very much. On a personal level."

She rolled the handle of the sculpting knife against her palm, not really frightened of Mr. Asher, but experiencing a great deal of disquiet nonetheless. The topic of the sphinx was one she usually avoided. She decided to ask him to leave, but before the words could come out of her mouth, Mr. Asher continued.

"I have tried to locate you for many years, but you made the task very difficult. You changed your name for a period of time."

"I got married."

"Yes." His glance took in the rest of her figure and darted across the hand that clutched the knife. "But you are no longer married."

"My husband died four years ago."

"Was your marriage a happy one?"

"That does not concern you." She turned away so he couldn't see the emotions that rushed across her face. A stranger had no right to ask such a personal question. "I think you'd better leave, Mr. Asher."

"Have I offended you?" he put in quietly, coming up behind her. "I was simply curious."

"My personal life is none of your business." She pivoted to head back to the stairs. "Good-bye, Mr. Asher."

"I will go as you request," he replied. "But first, spare a moment to hear my offer."

She put a hand on the stair rail, paused, and sighed. "What offer?"

"I will pay you a small fortune, Miss Spencer, if you will come to Egypt with me and help me locate the ruins of the sphinx where you saw the panther."

He knows about the panther. She felt even more uneasy. Slowly she turned to face him. "Sorry, but I can't help you. I don't remember anything about that era in my life."

"You have a photographic memory, do you not?"

Karissa studied his handsome face, with its sharp elegant nose and wide lower lip. "How do you know that about me?"

"I know much about you. As I said, I have been trying to find you for years."

"What else do you know?"

"I know about the circumstances of your husband's death."

She felt the color drop from her face and her insides clench together. He couldn't possibly know about Thomas dying in bed with an eighteen-year-old girl. Karissa forced the hard knot inside to dissipate and vowed once again to avoid thinking about her philandering husband.

"Mr. Asher. I have nothing more to discuss with you." She motioned toward the door. "Now, please leave."

He moved toward the door, his footfalls soundless. Not many people could walk so quietly across oak parquet floor. At the door he turned. "Will you not consider my offer, Miss Spencer? It is very important."

"I don't accept offers from complete strangers. Especially offers that involve trips to foreign countries."

"I could make you a rich woman."

"By robbing graves? No thanks."

He stood in silence for a moment as if her words offended him. Then he put his hand on the doorknob. "My quest does not include stealing the possessions of the dead."

"What is your quest then?"

"To find a mummy of a certain woman and thereby repay a debt."

"That sounds noble, Mr. Asher, but highly suspicious."

"I assure you, my intentions are purely honorable."

"I'll bet." Karissa walked up a few steps. "Listen, Mr. Asher, I lost my father and mother to that sphinx. I have no desire to risk my life just to help your karmic credit rating."

"How may I change your mind?"

"You can't. Goodnight."

"You will find me persistent, Miss Spencer, for I must find the mummy as quickly as possible."

"If you harass me, Mr. Asher, you will find yourself arrested."

At that moment the door burst open, forcing Asher to step aside, and Josh Lambert breezed in with a bag of Chinese food. "Dinner is served!" he announced before he noticed the dark visitor near the door.

"Sorry! Didn't see you there!" In his haste to retreat, Josh bumped into the corner of a pedestal behind him. The pedestal tipped, sending the marble figure of a cat toppling through the air. In a streak of silver, Mr. Asher lunged to the side, caught the sculpture, and straightened, all in a single fluid movement.

"No harm done," Asher replied. He adjusted the statue until it was shown to its best advantage in the light. Karissa was impressed not only by his quick reflexes and elegant self control, but by his eye for the play of shadow and light on the stone.

Josh shot a questioning glance at Karissa.

Karissa paused, uncertain how to explain the visitor or his business. Not many people knew of her connection to Egypt, and she wasn't about to tell Josh of her troubled adolescence.

"If you will excuse me," Mr. Asher said, "I was just leaving."

He nodded slightly to both of them, and without making eye contact, walked out of the shop. Karissa watched him disappear into the night, as silently as he had come.

Josh raised his eyebrows. "Who in the heck was that?" he asked.

"Mr. Asher."

"Who's he?"

"I don't really know." Her voice trailed off and she found it difficult to concentrate on what Josh was saying as he trotted past her up the stairs.

"Karissa, did you hear me?"

"Pardon?"

"I said, did you want the Kung Pao Chicken or the Mongolian Beef?"

"Oh, I don't care, Josh. Let's just split them." As usual he had bought twice as much food as they needed. His over indulgence was not limited to food, but concerned every facet of their business—from decorating the gallery to buying the latest computer equipment. Josh called his extravagances "investments for the future." Karissa called them just plain extravagances, and knew the gallery could not sustain Josh's spending. The more pieces she sold, the more he spent, and she was tired of funding his spendthrift ways with her hard work. Josh had promised to cut back, but he was like a little boy with his lack of self-discipline.

Despairing, Karissa gained the top of the stairs, went over to her worktable, and gazed down at the clay lioness she had been working on for a week. Ebony. Perhaps that was the secret to capturing the spirit of the cat. She would buy some ebony tomorrow and see what might come of it.

Two hours later Karissa and Josh closed up and left for the evening. Karissa lived in a brownstone on Montgomery Street less than a half-mile away and was accustomed to walking back and forth to the gallery alone. Tonight, however, Josh insisted on accompanying her. She usually enjoyed the stroll along the avenues lined by sweeping hundred-year-old trees and equally old houses, but tonight Josh turned her peaceful stroll into a noisy parade, full of jokes and anecdotes about their patrons and clients.

At one time in her life she had needed the jokes and the laughter, and Josh had been a godsend. Her heart had been heavy and troubled then. Now she wanted more from a conversation than a good guffaw and more from a man than slapstick antics. But Josh had no other way of interacting with the world. The worst part of it was, Josh seemed confident that he was the man for her, and no matter how many times she gently turned him away, he always bounced back, more confident than ever that she would one day agree to a relationship.

More and more, Karissa found it impossible to work when Josh was around. She needed solitude, and Josh ignored her requests for peace and quiet. She knew it was time to sever their partnership in the gallery, but in order to do that she would need money to buy him out. And she just didn't have it. Most artists she knew did not make huge profits from their work—the ultimate sacrifice for having a career one truly enjoyed.

"As I was saying, Karissa—"

Suddenly Josh broke off his monologue and stopped in his tracks.

Karissa stopped as well and glanced at him in surprise. "What's the matter?"

"Them." He nodded to the path ahead of them where three men in European-style business suits stood in front of a sedan that had been pulled up to block the sidewalk.

Karissa surveyed the men in the light of the street lamp. They were dark-skinned and had black hair and moustaches. Two of them were broad in the shoulders while the third man was short and slight.

"They're watching us," Josh said out of the side of his mouth.

"Why would they do that?"

"Who knows? I kind of doubt they're waiting to give us a sweepstakes check. They just don't look the type."

"Let's cross the street," Karissa urged, "And see what they do."

Josh turned abruptly to head for the other side of the road, and Karissa hurried to catch up with him. She glanced over her shoulder at the men and saw one take a step toward them.

"They're coming!" she exclaimed.

Josh clutched her hand and set off at a quick walk. Karissa shot another glance backward and saw the thugs with the big shoulders trotting after them. Her heart pounded in alarm.

"Run," she cried.

She and Josh dashed back toward the gallery, sprinting along the sidewalk. Josh took a turn into an unfamiliar street and pulled her up an alley. They ran along the narrow lane, dodging garbage cans and parked cars. But they didn't run fast enough and soon Karissa could hear the labored breathing of their pursuers close behind them. Adrenalin shot through her system, overriding the sharp pain in her chest as she sucked in gulps of air, and forced her legs to go faster. Just as she thought she might outdistance the thugs, she tripped over a spade someone had left propped against a cement retaining wall. She landed on her shoulder and took the fall with a roll. But before she could scramble back to her feet, one of the thugs grabbed her arm. He wrenched her to her feet.

"Got you!" he shouted, panting. He had wide gaps between his teeth and wore a heavy cologne that reminded her of the bazaars of Cairo.

Karissa yanked her arm but he held fast. "Josh!"

Josh skidded to a stop and turned around, just as the other man grabbed him.

The gap-toothed thug squeezed Karissa's upper arm. "You are to come with us. And if you cooperate, I will not have to hurt you."

Karissa stared at him, baffled that anyone would run her down. "Why me?" she asked.

"No questions."

"But—"

He slapped her across the face. "I said no questions!"

"Hey now!" Josh exclaimed. "Don't go hitting her, or I'm warning you—"

"Shut up, American!" The gap-toothed thug pulled Karissa a few yards down the alley.

"What's it worth to you?" Josh demanded. "A couple hundred dollars? I can get you a couple hundred right now!"

"Shut him up, Shamir," the gap-toothed man ordered.

Karissa held the side of her face, frightened and alarmed by the man's brutal treatment. These men were dangerous. Were they connected to Mr. Asher? He said he was persistent. Would he resort to violence to get her back to Egypt?

The gap-toothed man dragged her toward the main street while Karissa struggled to see what Shamir would do to Josh. To her horror, she saw Shamir hit him over the head with a gun. Josh crumpled to the ground. Then Shamir picked him up, strode to the nearest dumpster, and heaved Josh into the container. The cover clanged shut. Karissa prayed someone would hear all the noise and come to their assistance or at least call the police. But no one seemed to take notice of the action in the alley. She felt sick with dread.

"Help!" Karissa yelled. Desperately, she dug her heels into the gravel of the lane and did her best to resist being kidnapped. Her captor clenched his nails into her flesh and drew a gun from his waistband.

"Shut up and quit struggling, or I'll do what Shamir did to your friend."

Karissa eyed the gun as it glinted in the darkness. Then she glanced down the alley where the big sedan waited for them.

"Let me go!" she twisted in his grip and ignored the flare of pain in her arm.

"I said shut up!" He raised the gun to strike her.

Suddenly an unearthly snarl ripped through the night, a sound so foreign that all three of them froze in their tracks. Goose pimples flooded the surface of Karissa's skin as she turned in the direction of the snarl. She knew at once that the sound came from a big cat. But what was a big cat doing in the middle of Baltimore?

"Abdullah!" Shamir gasped. His voice was pinched with terror. "It is Lord Azhur!"

"Shut up!" Abdullah ordered, but his tone was constricted as well.

Frantic with fright, Karissa glanced at the face of her captor and saw that he had turned pale with fear as well.

Before anyone could act, a dark shape leaped from a high wall beside them and sailed through the air toward Abdullah. Crying out, the man clutched at Karissa's arm and nearly took her down with him as he crashed to the ground. Karissa kept to her feet as she saw a streak of black land in the alley. The streak took the form of a huge cat as the animal pinned Abdullah to the ground and then shook him by the nape of his neck until his spine snapped.

Terrified, Shamir staggered backward, holding his

gun but shaking so badly that he couldn't pull the trigger. In one magnificent movement, the cat bunched its flank muscles and soared into the air, taking Shamir down by the throat. Karissa watched in horror as the panther lashed the man's chest open with a single swipe of his paw. Shamir's cries gurgled to silence as his feet thrashed the ground, and then he went still. The car at the end of the alley sped away, tires squealing, abandoning the dead men. Then all was quiet, and the cat turned around to face Karissa.

Her pounding heart lodged in her throat, choking her. Her knees shook with terror. She would be next. She met the unblinking gaze of the huge golden-brown eyes and knew she would be the next to die.

At that moment, a metallic noise rang out in the direction of the garbage dumpster. The cat turned at the sound and growled deep in his throat. Karissa glanced over her shoulder and saw Josh climbing out of the container.

"Josh, stop!" she cried.

He looked at her but didn't heed the warning. Perhaps he couldn't see the panther in the darkness. Josh slid down the side of the dumpster and dropped to the ground, holding the side of his head where he had been struck. "Jesus!" he declared. "What in the hell happened?"

He walked unsteadily toward her, still holding the side of his head.

"Josh, stop! There's a panther here!"

He paused when he caught sight of the shadowy form between him and Karissa. The big cat growled menacingly, lifting one side of its mouth to reveal sharp white teeth as it eased backward, closer to Karissa.

"My God!" Josh whispered. "What do I do?"

"Don't make any sudden moves. It just killed those two men."

Josh glanced at the dead men and then back at the

cat. He held up his hands as if to prove that he meant no harm and took a step toward Karissa. "Easy, buddy."

The panther growled again, more loudly this time, which convinced Josh to keep his distance.

"Okay, okay!" Josh sputtered. "I won't come any closer."

"Just stay there, Josh. Don't move. Cats are attracted by movement. Let's see what he does if we just stand still."

Josh stood as stiff as a statue, staring down his nose at the cat. The big panther slowly eased back until his long tail brushed against Karissa's shoes. The velvety tip of his tail flicked back and forth across her ankles, as if the cat were making sure she stayed put. She swallowed back a scream.

Minutes passed. Karissa felt a sheen of sweat between her skin and her silk shirt. Still the cat stood guard. Stood guard. Was he guarding her? Did he see Josh as a threat? Could the cat be protecting her? Karissa took a few steps backward. The cat paced sideways, positioning himself between her and Josh, but made no move to accost her. Heartened, she stepped backward again. The cat moved with her.

"He thinks he needs to protect me!" she exclaimed, dizzy with relief.

"Crazy animal! So what do we do?"

"I'm going to try to get to the end of the alley. Just stay where you are and let's see what he does."

"I wouldn't do it if I were you. Once you get far enough away from me, he'll probably jump you."

"I don't think so. He would have hurt me by now. I'm going to keep backing up, Josh. If you get the chance to make a run for it, call the police, okay?"

"Sure, but Karissa—"

"I can sense that he isn't a danger to me, Josh. I can't

explain how I know. I just do." Karissa gave him a brave smile even though she felt anything but brave inside. "If I get to the road, I'll try to make it to my apartment."

"Good luck."

Slowly Karissa began her journey to the end of the alley, talking softly to the cat the entire time. The panther snarled but didn't strike out at her. He seemed more intent on keeping his body between Karissa and Josh than impeding her progress.

Karissa heaved a sigh of relief as she reached the main road. Perhaps someone would see her and come to her assistance. Unfortunately at nine o'clock at night the avenue was deserted. She waved to Josh to assure him that she was still all right and he waved back. Then she turned around and headed for her apartment, trusting the panther would not attack her from behind. She looked over her shoulder and saw the dark shadow slink around the corner and pad soundlessly next to her at the base of the huge elm trees. By the time she reached the stone stairs of her brownstone, she had begun to think of the cat as a shadowy companion instead of a threatening beast.

She fished her keys out of her pocket and slid them in the lock. The panther watched her while his tail flicked back and forth.

"I'm going in now," she declared. "You must go away."

The cat ignored her with regal indifference.

Karissa pushed open the door and stepped into her foyer. She flipped on the lights and looked back at the cat. The panther sat down on the step and lifted its paw. She watched in amazement as the huge animal began to preen himself. Did the cat intend to stay? She hoped not. She didn't want a mankiller sitting on her doorstep.

Even though her life had been saved by the cat, she knew she had to alert the animal control center. The panther had killed two men and couldn't be allowed to roam the streets of Baltimore.

Karissa closed the door and hurried to her phone to call the police.

Chapter 2

AFTER THE POLICE LEFT KARISSA'S APARTMENT, and she had talked Josh out of spending the night on her couch to protect her, she fell into bed, exhausted. Still, she couldn't sleep. The police had listened to her account of the panther attack and begrudgingly admitted that the wounds on the dead men could have been inflicted by the claws and teeth of a big cat. But they couldn't find any evidence to support her story. Until they finished their investigation they urged her not to say anything to her neighbors about the supposed panther. Such talk could start a citywide panic. Karissa agreed and watched them go, feeling as if they had only half-believed her story.

Long past two in the morning she tossed and turned, and in her thrashing, knocked the framed photograph of her paternal grandmother onto the floor.

Blearily she turned on her lamp and fumbled for the silver frame. She held the photo toward the light to look at the picture she loved so well. In it her half-Egyptian grandmother, dressed in flapper clothes complete with cloche hat, was listening to a Victrola while smoking on the deck of a ship sailing down the Nile. The photograph represented everything her maternal grandmother hated: the Egyptian blood that was considered a blight on the family tree, a woman smoking or doing anything even remotely unladylike, faddish clothes, and people who defied convention by marrying out of their class. Had Karissa been raised by her Egyptian grandmother, she might have had a happier childhood. But after the death of her mother, she had been taken in by her blue-blooded Baltimore grandmother, and Grandmother Petrie had tried to wring every last ounce of defiance and individuality from Karissa's character through punishment and ridicule.

Karissa sighed and set the silver frame on the nightstand. No matter how much she had been punished for her spirited character, no one could take away her physical resemblance to her Egyptian grandmother. She had the same black hair and golden skin that had made her grandmother famous in her day. Karissa even had the peculiar birthmark at the base of her skull that her grandmother had been marked with as well. No one ever saw the red splotch, because it was hidden in her hairline, but Karissa often thought of the mark and was secretly pleased to be physically connected to Menmet.

Karissa lay back on her pillow. Now that her marriage was over and Thomas' death a faint memory, she was ready for something new—not the violence she had suffered that evening, but something like traveling to romantic lands and meeting people from different cultures. She was ready to take over where her grandmother had left off and pursue a life that truly fascinated her. Was that life here in Baltimore at the gallery? More and more she didn't think so.

In the morning, Karissa woke up late, only an hour before the gallery was due to open at ten, hurried through her shower, and skipped her usual morning coffee. Then she threw on a pair of black leggings, a black scoop-necked body shirt, and a new blanket jacket in a planets and stars motif that she had bought to ward off the fall chill. She grabbed her purse, opened the door, and nearly stepped on a pigeon lying on the threshold.

Karissa stared down at the bird and realized it was dead. Poor thing. Perhaps it had died and fallen from the gutter overhead. Karissa looked up at the gutter two stories above. How had a bird managed to fall at an angle so that it landed on her doormat? It didn't seem possible. Perhaps one of the neighbor cats had killed the bird and left it there. Karissa shrugged, went back into the house for some newspaper, and rolled the dead bird inside it. She carried it to the rear of the house and carefully placed it in the garbage can.

Still thinking of the poor dead bird, she set off down the sidewalk toward the gallery, keeping alert for any signs of the sedan from last night. The police had tried to convince her that the attack was random and perhaps even a case of mistaken identity. But Karissa was convinced that the men had some connection to Mr. Asher.

The autumn morning was overcast and breezy, and leaves scuttled across the walk and over her shoes. Karissa hugged her jacket around her slight frame and increased her pace. At the corner she spied a man in black standing near a newspaper stand. Could it be Mr. Asher? Alarm shot through her and she stepped off the curb to avoid him, but noticed that he had begun to walk at an angle to intercept her. Karissa looked around frantically, thankful to see a handful of people on the street. She could call for help if he accosted her. Still, she kept her walk brisk and ignored his approach.

Asher spotted Karissa Spencer at the same instant she caught sight of him If she had been surrounded by a hundred people he still would have recognized her in the crowd, for she carried herself with a certain aloof pride—a mark of nobility in his day. Karissa was also tall and slender, which lent a fluid litheness to her movements.

And there was no mistaking her hair either—the luxuriant black veil that hung to her waist. Yesterday he had almost reached out and stroked the shining ebony tresses, and was glad he had controlled himself, because he was quite certain that Karissa Spencer would have taken offense at such a forward gesture. Perhaps she didn't let any man stroke her. The possibility pleased him.

"Miss Spencer!" he called as she gained the other side of the avenue. She acted as if she didn't hear him.

Karissa saw Mr. Asher cross the road, and she increased her pace. Then he leapt from the curb to the sidewalk in an easy spring that she couldn't help notice out of the corner of her eye. The man was inordinately graceful.

"Miss Spencer!"

He strode up to her and matched her pace while he tried to get her attention. "You should not be walking unescorted."

"I can take care of myself, Mr. Asher." She glared straight ahead. She didn't like persistent people, especially persistent attractive men. Her husband had been attractive and she would forever regret the way she had succumbed to him.

Nevertheless, Karissa glanced to the side and let her gaze swiftly dart over Mr. Asher.

He wore his hair pulled back and tied at the nape of his neck. Both his ear lobes were pierced but sported no earrings. The collar of a black silk shirt showed beneath his expensive overcoat. Such dark clothing would make most men look sallow and pale, but the black wardrobe only intensified the deep golden tones of Mr. Asher's complexion, and highlighted the flash of his teeth and eyes. She couldn't imagine him wearing any other color except for pure white, which would produce the same effect.

Asher returned her glance, and she was struck by the warmth and intelligence of his expression. His golden-brown eyes were bordered by long dark lashes and attractive laugh lines—definitely not the hard eyes of a criminal. He broke off the glance and looked straight ahead.

"I heard about your trouble last night."

"Oh? How?"

"I saw an account in the morning paper."

"I'm surprised. The attack happened so late."

"True. It never ceases to amaze me how quickly news travels in this day and age, Miss Spencer."

"Or perhaps you know about it because you were there."

Asher stopped. "Do you think I had something to do with the attack?"

"Yes. Those men were Egyptians."

"They have no connection to me."

"I'll bet."

Asher frowned. "They were thugs who work for a man named Mustofa. He is a dangerous man whom I am afraid has followed me to your country."

"Why?"

"Come." He took her elbow before she realized he had even reached for her. "Let us keep walking while I explain. The sooner you get off the street, the better."

"Why? What is this all about!"

"The tomb I mentioned yesterday lies in a place called the Valley of the Damned. In the valley are many other tombs, most of which have probably gone undetected by grave robbers. There is a fortune to be found in the desert, Miss Spencer. Men like Mustofa will do anything to find those tombs, and they don't care whom they torture, kidnap or kill to meet their objective. They are excavating in an area that I believe is very close to the buried sphinx, and if they locate the tombs before I do, the mummy I seek will be lost to me forever."

"But how does this Mustofa character know about me?"

"His spies must have gained access to my files. But I am puzzled by how it could have happened. I have been extremely careful, especially where you are concerned."

She yanked her elbow out of his grip. "You have files on me?"

"Of course." He smiled slightly, showing the lower edge of a line of flawless white teeth. "I have been gathering information for years."

"Why?"

"As I said yesterday, you remain my only key to finding the tomb."

"And will you kidnap and torture me until I agree to help you?"

"My plan to elicit your aid is a nonviolent one, Miss Spencer. But as I said, I shall be persistent."

"You're wasting your time." She strode forward, hoping to outdistance him, but he kept up with her, effortlessly. "A television crew is going to be here next week to start filming a piece on my work. I have a ton of things to get done before then."

"I see." Mr. Asher's tone was heavy with disappointment.

By that time, they had reached the gallery. She drew her keys out of her purse and unlocked the door as Asher stood by and watched her hands. Karissa opened the door, just enough to let herself in and prevent his passage, and then looked back at him. "Now, if you will excuse me, Mr. Asher, I have some work to do before the gallery opens."

He raised his glance and leveled it upon hers. Whenever she stared directly into his eyes, she felt as if her self-control slipped a notch and found it very hard to look away. Even the soft low rumble of his voice was hypnotic.

He put his gloved hand on the woodwork just below eye level. "I have a story to tell you that may change your mind, Miss Spencer."

"I doubt it."

"Nevertheless, allow me to take you to lunch this afternoon, and perhaps what I have to say will help you see this matter in a new light."

Karissa gripped the doorknob tightly. She hadn't eaten lunch with a man—other than Josh or a client—for years, and never with a man as mysterious and attractive as Mr. Asher. Not until this moment had she realized what a social recluse she'd become.

"Name the time," he said, "and I will call for you."

"Really, Mr. Asher. I—"

"Grant me an hour. That is all I ask."

She sighed and studied his face for signs of deceit but could see only sincerity. "Well, all right. Come back at two. If I can get away, I'll have lunch with you."

"Excellent!" He smiled again, this time with a slow sensual slant of his mouth. Karissa could imagine the strength and passion of that mouth and how his lips might feel upon her mouth and neck, and her breasts tightened in a sharp twist of arousal. The sensation amazed her, not only because she was thinking of a man in sexual terms, but because she was responding in such a way to a complete stranger.

When she looked back into his eyes, she saw a knowing glint there, as if he had read her mind. She should have been embarrassed to have a man share her thoughts, but with this man she didn't feel embarrassed at all. In fact, his smoldering gaze only made her breasts ache for him more. Was it the blood of her Egyptian grandmother responding to this dark foreigner, or was it her own female instincts reacting to the presence of a strong, physically beautiful male? Whatever it was, she had the strongest urge to reach up and run her palm across his shining black hair, to stroke him, to kiss him—

"Until two then." He inclined his head again, and for a moment she thought he might ask to kiss her hand. Instead, he turned and walked noiselessly away.

Karissa sighed in relief and shut the door. She locked it with trembling hands. Her attraction for Mr. Asher was illogical and dangerous and it was best that she stay away from him. Before she took a step, however, she was grabbed from behind, her jacket was pulled halfway off, a hand was clamped over her mouth, and something jabbed her upper arm. Within seconds her world reeled into blackness.

When Karissa awoke, she found herself in a small room with plastered white walls and a peeling blue ceiling. The air in the room was so hot she found it hard to take a breath, and the white cotton shift she was draped in stuck to her in damp folds. Woozy and nauseated, Karissa struggled to sit up from the mat where she had been sleeping on the floor. At the movement, cockroaches scuttled across the tile and up the walls.

"Ew!" Karissa cried in disgust. She jumped to her feet, swaying as she fought for balance. Where was she? She blinked the stars out of her eyes and looked down at the long white nightshirt-like garment. Who had dressed her in an Egyptian galabia? And why was it so oppressively hot? She stumbled to the small barred window and stood on tiptoe to peer out. All she could see was an incredibly blue sky, with no hint of clouds, and the fringe of a palm leaf from a tree nearby. Karissa lowered herself from the window as a dark feeling of unease spread over her. There was no sky like the Egyptian sky. And no heat as dry and intense as the heat off the Eastern Desert. Somehow, she must have been transported to the valley of the Nile. She sank against the wall, stunned that she had been so easily kidnapped and taken to a foreign country. But by whom? Mustofa or Mr. Asher?

The answer wasn't long in coming. Soon after she awakened, a thin man with a gun opened the door and ordered her out of the room. She tried to speak to him, but he professed to know little English. Frustrated, Karissa stumbled through the door, still feeling groggy and clumsy. They must have given her a tranquilizer at the gallery and kept her drugged for days. A wave of rage passed over her. She detested the fact that she had been controlled, especially without her knowledge, and was still a prisoner. Reluctantly she walked behind the man across a dusty courtyard with a broken fountain and wished she had something to drink. She had a raging thirst.

She was taken into a yellow house on the other side of the courtyard. Somewhat relieved to be out of the heat, but still thirsty, Karissa followed her guide and was shown into a small parlor off the main hall. A short gaunt man with prominent brown eyes stood near the window, smoking a foul-smelling cigarette. He turned at her entrance and smiled, taking a long drag on the cigarette as he watched Karissa cross the floor toward him. He was balding and had a thin black mustache that traced the line of his full upper lip. His clothes appeared well-made, but his white jacket and trousers were slightly out of date. He wore expensive crocodile shoes but smoked cheap tobacco by the smell of it. The smoke nauseated her.

"Ah, Miss Spencer," he greeted.

"Mr. Mustofa, I presume?" She was so angry she could barely force out the words.

He smiled as if pleased that she knew his name and

nodded as he held his hands up, palms together, in front of his face. Though the gesture was one of respect, it lost considerable effect because of the cigarette poking through two fingers on his right hand.

"Who do you think you are!" she exclaimed. "Drugging me like that and taking me halfway across the world!"

"Had you not resisted so fiercely, I would not have had to resort to such tactics, Miss Spencer."

He stepped to a side table and lifted an earthenware pitcher. With great deliberation he poured a glass of water. "I would expect that you are thirsty, Miss Spencer."

"Yes." She wanted to snatch the glass from his hand, but she stood where she was, unwilling to be manipulated. Mr. Mustofa smiled and took a long appreciative drink. Her entire attention focused upon the sparkling glass and the slow bob of his Adam's apple.

When he finished, he let out a sigh of satisfaction and smiled. "You may have all the water you like, Miss Spencer. And it is bottled water, by the way. But first, you must promise to help me." He set the glass down on a nearby table and she followed the movement with burning eyes.

"Help you do what?" she croaked through parched lips.

Mustofa came around the table. "I want you to show me where a certain valley is, one you stumbled upon as a young woman."

"You expect me to help you, after you treat me like this?"

"You have no choice." Mustofa pointed the cigarette at her to emphasize his words. "You are my prisoner, Miss Spencer. And until you show me where the ruins of the lost sphinx are located, you will not have anything to eat or drink. Do you understand?"

"And if I can't remember?"

"I will know you are lying to me, because"—He tapped two fingertips on the side of his balding head—"I have been informed that you have a photographic memory."

"If you think I can remember everything, you're a bigger fool than you look!"

Mustofa's black brows came together in a scowl. Abruptly, he turned.

"Walaal!" he barked.

The door burst open and the thin man with the gun hurried into the room.

"Get this slut out of my sight. I do not want to see her until morning."

"Yes, Mr. Mustofa." The thin man grabbed Karissa's left arm but she jerked away.

"Keep your hands off me!" she said, realizing the guard had lied to her about knowing English. He had understood every word Mustofa had just said.

"And do not let her talk you into giving her food or water. She will have nothing until she learns better manners."

"Yes, Mr. Mustofa."

"Starving me will get you nowhere," Karissa retorted. "I am worth nothing to you dead."

He turned around, his bony face flushed with anger. "You are worth less if your memory is faulty. So use the coming hours to think, Miss Spencer. I am sure if you try, you can dredge up some childhood memories."

Karissa swept out of the room, shoulders straight and head held high. She was not about to cooperate with a bully like Mr. Mustofa, even if she could remember the lost sphinx. She would have to find some way of escape.

Asher hailed a taxi at the airport and jumped in the back. Though the car was air-conditioned, Asher felt sweat break out beneath his suit. Already the sun hung low in the

sky, which meant he didn't have much time in which to find
Karissa Spencer. Because of his worry for the American
woman, he had made risky travel arrangements and had
prayed the plane would touch down at the Luxor Airport
before the sun sank behind the western cliffs. He was also
praying that she was being held at Mustofa's compound,
because he could probably reach the place before sunset.
Still, to Asher, the traffic seemed to crawl through town.

The taxi rolled to a stop in front of a small yellow
house bordered by a high wall. Asher dropped a large bill
in the driver's hand and slipped out of the cab.

"Keep the change," Asher said, not wanting to take
the time to haggle over the fare.

"What about your bags, sir?"

His bags. In his haste, Asher had completely forgotten
about the three leather suitcases in the trunk of the taxi.
"Take them to this address, will you?" Asher slipped his
hand in his pocket and drew out a business card. He
dipped into his wallet for another bill. "And here. This
should cover it."

"All right."

The taxi pulled away from the cracked sidewalk just
as the ringing began in Asher's ears—the first sign that
the sun had melted into the horizon. Then all the noises
around him roared to life as a more primal, acute sense of
hearing kicked in.

In Karissa's prison cell the hours dragged on,
interrupted only by the scuttling cockroaches and the call
to prayer by the Islamic muezzin at sunset and then again
as the shadows of night crept into her small chamber. Cool
air off the Nile drifted in through her window, bringing
with it the aroma of street vendor food and the sounds of
people taking their evening strolls, laughing and talking
in the distance, too far away to hear the muffled scream

of a woman imprisoned on the outskirts of town. Karissa knew it would be useless to cry out anyway. She would probably be punished by the guard if she tried anything so foolish. Hopeless and frustrated, she stretched out on the mat and drifted in and out of sleep, feverish with thirst and weak from hunger.

Sometime during the night, Karissa awoke to the sound of voices. Her guard was talking with someone. She sat up and listened, trying to remember the Arab phrases she had learned as a child, but couldn't make sense of the conversation. Soon, however, she deduced that the thin man was being relieved by a new guard, whose voice was much raspier than the first guard's.

Karissa waited until Walaal left, and then she pounded on the door. "Sir?" she called.

She heard a rustling sound and a metallic clink. "Yes?"

"Please, may I have a drink of water? I am so thirsty."

"Well"—

She heard the lock turn over and stepped back as the door was pulled open. Standing in the moonlight was a burly man with a grizzled face and a dirty rag wrapped around his head. At the sight of her, he grinned and his eyes lit up.

"Well, well, well!"

Instantly, she regretted her request. The guard took a step toward her, but she held her ground, even though she wanted to stay far away from him.

"A drink, eh?" he chuckled. "That could be arranged, my little flower blossom—for a price."

"I have no money."

"I am willing to barter. That's the way we do things here in Luxor." His grin widened, displaying teeth stained by nicotine. Karissa blinked back her disgust. She calculated the distance between his large body and the open door. If she could entice him further into the chamber and switch places with him, she might be able to escape. But did she have the strength to run?

Still, this might be her only chance to get away from Mustofa. She brushed back a strand of hair and lowered her voice seductively. "What did you care to exchange?"

"What do you think?" The guard's eyebrows raised in delight as he ambled forward. "A taste of you for a taste of water."

She ducked away and turned, so that her back was to the door and he was no longer between her and the outside world. He chuckled, obviously enjoying the game.

"First, my drink."

"Oh, you are hard ones, you American girls."

She nodded and kept her distance as he chuckled and went back outside. He returned with an old plastic bleach container. The thought of putting her lips on the discolored rim of the bottle nearly made her retch, but her thirst overrode her disgust.

"There you go, my flower." The guard held out the bottle.

She tipped it to her lips and let the tepid water fill her parched mouth. In great gulps she drank, forgetting to take it easy, until the guard pulled away the bottle, laughing.

"Do not drink too much! You will be sick." He capped the bottle. "I do not want you puking all over me when I am"— He made a lewd thrust with his hips. Karissa wiped her mouth with the back of her hand and watched him. He leaned over to set the bottle on the floor and reached for his gun to lay it on the tile as well, and at that moment Karissa lunged for the door.

The water and fear gave her the strength to run. She dashed through the door and across the courtyard, hunting for a gate in the high wall that surrounded the compound.

The guard pounded behind her. Within seconds, Karissa knew her starved body was quickly losing power and she would never outdistance him. Frantically she ran along the base of the wall, praying she wouldn't step on a scorpion or snake in the darkness.

Suddenly the guard grabbed her from behind. She tumbled to the sandy ground on hands and knees. The guard pushed her hard in the small of her back, shoving her face down in the dirt, and then he pinned her rump and thighs with one knee.

"Get off me, you lout!"

"You are going to like this." He chuckled and fumbled with his pants. "American men are sissies. But we Egyptians are men. Real men."

He grabbed her elbow, lifted his leg from her rump, and wrenched her over onto her back. He grinned. "We take what we want and our women love it!"

"Like hell!" Karissa glared at him and kicked wildly, trying to hurt him.

He only laughed and clamped a dirty hand over her mouth. She pummeled him with her fists, but her blows seemed to have no effect on him. Then he reached for the hem of her galabia and yanked it up to her thighs. Karissa froze, stunned that she was about to be violated by a stranger. Then he reached for her panties and Karissa writhed, using the last bit of her strength to fight him off.

She glared at his sickening mouth and thrashed her head back and forth to avoid his kiss. His eyes gleamed in the darkness. She felt a wave of light-headedness overtake her but refused to give in to it. She couldn't faint now. She couldn't surrender to this disgusting man.

Suddenly a menacing growl rolled out of the shadows. The guard grunted in surprise and raised his head.

The growl came again, louder this time.

"Who is there!" the guard demanded.

A dark shape materialized from behind a clump of palms, and with measured footfalls, a huge black cat came toward them. The panther was in no hurry, as if he were certain his prey was incapable of escape. He padded closer, his shoulder blades flowing up and down like the well-oiled pistons of a killing machine, and his eyes were uncompromisingly cold.

"Lord Azhur!" the guard gasped. He scrambled out from between Karissa's legs, reached for his pants, and lumbered to his feet. "Please, Lord"—

The panther bunched his muscles and leapt upward.

Chapter 3

KARISSA SCRAMBLED TO HER FEET as the big cat lunged upon the guard. It looked like the same black panther that had saved her life in Baltimore. If so, how had the cat traveled to Egypt from the United States? Perhaps it wasn't a real cat at all. She half-expected to wake up from a nightmare and find herself in her house in Baltimore.

Yet the scrapes on her knees and the sand in her hair were very real, as was the body being dragged into the clump of palms near the wall. Karissa turned away in disgust from the sight of the guard's limp legs as the panther pulled his victim into the shadows. She didn't condone killing, but she was grateful to have escaped being raped by the guard. Yet where would she go now?

Her first concern was getting out of the compound. Karissa glanced up at the high wall that rose three feet above her head. She would never be able to scale it. She would have to find a gate. Fighting a ringing in her ears and the shakiness in her legs, she stumbled forward.

Within moments, she felt a presence behind her and glanced backward to see the panther loping toward her. Instead of walking alongside her as he had done in Baltimore, the panther padded ahead and guided her to a small portal. Karissa opened the wooden door and stepped into a lane that led to a littered alley bordered by tall apartments and shops strung together with clotheslines and electrical wires. She paused, having no idea what to do or which way to go, especially in the middle of the night with no money and no identification. The cat seemed to have an agenda of his own, however, and kept walking. After a moment, he paused to look back at her. He blinked, and his tail flicked back and forth as if he waited for her to catch up.

Karissa decided to follow his lead. After all, the cat had saved her life on two occasions. She walked after him as he moved stealthily through the quiet Luxor streets, past sleepy houses, darkened apartment houses, closed bazaars, and ghostly mosques. Karissa struggled to keep up with him. Other than following the cat, she had no alternative but to throw herself on the mercy of the U.S. Embassy, which she decided to do in the morning, should the panther lead her astray.

The city stretched endlessly along the river. Soon her steps were dragging, as she suffered from thirst and hunger. She had used her reserves to fight off the guard, and now she operated purely on determination and pride. But how many more steps could she will herself to take?

As if the cat read her mind, he led her to a shadowed alcove and sat on his haunches, waiting for her to catch up. Karissa could hear the musical tinkle of water and her spirits rose. The panther had led her to a small fountain attached to the side of a building. She could see the stream of water glinting in the moonlight. Karissa almost cried out in gratitude as she thrust her hands into the water and cupped mouthful after mouthful to her lips. Her mother's frequent warning to drink only bottled water ran through her thoughts, but in her desperation, Karissa ignored the voice and chanced illness.

Feeling much better after quenching her thirst, Karissa trailed after the cat. Soon the panther turned down a tree-lined street that took them south of town.

The city became a sprawl with the houses farther apart and here and there an irrigated field bordered the road. The cat veered to the right and padded down a smaller lane that headed toward the Nile, which gleamed in the distance. Karissa stumbled after him, sure that she would last only a few more minutes. She had never felt so weak or so desperately empty.

They passed between two pillars and continued down an avenue toward a two-story house surrounded by the graceful trunks and drooping fronds of date palms. She followed the panther to the front of the house, up the wide granite steps and onto the veranda. The cat took her to the front door and then sat down.

Karissa glanced at the panther. "Now what?" she asked, unsure why they were at this residence. Did he expect her to knock on the door?

Before Karissa could decide what to do, she felt a swirling sensation in her head and her vision sparkled and tipped. She staggered sideways and then she crumpled to the cool granite slab of the porch.

When she woke up, she was lying in a clean bed draped in a festoon of mosquito netting. Startled to be in unfamiliar surroundings, Karissa lurched to a sitting position and glanced around. She was in a large room tastefully decorated in brass and wood and potted plants. A half-empty glass of water stood on the bedside table. She couldn't remember getting into the bed, much less drinking the water. Had someone helped her do both things? Rays of morning sunlight slanted through the open doors of the balcony and poured across the blue oriental carpet. She must have been sleeping for hours.

Karissa slipped out of the bed and teetered for a moment, light-headed with hunger, and caught a glimpse of something white just beyond the French doors of the balcony. Holding her head, she walked across the thick carpet and looked down to see a dead ibis on the pale tile. She turned away in dismay that another dead creature had been left on her doorstep. But her hunger and curiosity concerning her whereabouts soon overtook all thought of the ibis. She was desperate for food and drink and hoped the master who ruled this house would be more accommodating than Mr. Mustofa.

Just as she decided to crawl back into the bed, she heard a light rap on the bedroom door.

"Miss Spencer?" A lightly-accented female voice spoke from the other side.

"Yes?"

"Would you like some breakfast?"

Would she? Her salivary glands leaped into action at the mere mention of food.

"Yes." She hurried to open the door. In the hall stood a small pudgy woman with black hair plaited in a braid that hung to her hips. She was probably in her fifties and had huge dark brown eyes that glistened with kindness. But what caught Karissa's attention and held it, was the tray of food the woman carried into the room.

"I am Eisha, the housekeeper."

"You know who I am?"

Eisha nodded and swept across the room to a small table.

"My master has told me of you."

"Your master? And who might he be?"

"My master will wish to tell you all himself. But he does not rise until midday. While you wait, you must eat and bathe and rest."

Karissa didn't appreciate the mystery surrounding her host and didn't admire a man who slept late, but she kept her views to herself. For now she would take advantage of his hospitality, if only to fortify herself for another escape. She stared ravenously at the plates of food Eisha uncovered: cold meats, pickles, savory foul beans and bread, and a mound of steaming scrambled eggs. Out of a silver coffee carafe drifted the wonderful aroma of strong Egyptian coffee, flavored with cloves. The smell nearly made her swoon.

"I am not accustomed to American breakfasts," Eisha said, setting a place on the table. "Is this satisfactory?"

"It looks wonderful!" Karissa smiled shakily. "Thank you."

Eisha straightened. "When you are done, just ring the little bell." She gestured to a brass bell on the tray. "I will prepare a nice bath for you."

"Thank you." She pulled off a piece of bread and consumed it without chewing it more than three times. Next came a pickle and a forkful of egg. While Karissa ate, Eisha carefully poured her a cup of coffee. Karissa tried the spicy beans and washed them down with a long sip of the fragrant coffee. In only moments she felt the empowering effect of the food. She turned to the housekeeper.

"Eisha, I need to get back to the United States. Is there a phone somewhere that I could use?"

"Yes. But eat first and then you may make your arrangements. I am sure my master wants you to stay until he has a chance to speak with you."

Karissa wasn't sure if she had exchanged her miserably hot cell in the middle of Luxor for a more extravagant one. But she decided to finish the meal first and ask questions later.

At half-past noon, Karissa walked down the hall toward the garden, where the master of the house awaited. Eisha had helped her make arrangements for money to be wired to a hotel in Luxor. Then Karissa had phoned Josh to tell him where she was and give him the phone number and address of the house in which she was staying. But Josh wasn't at home or at the gallery, and she was forced to leave a message on the answering machine. When she was done, she decided to wait for the master of the house to stir before she thanked him and went on her way.

Since her Western clothes had been stripped away by Mustofa, Karissa had been given a linen dress by Eisha to replace the dirty galabia. The garment was a lovely wrap of the finest gossamer, more filmy and feminine than anything she had ever worn. It was pleated in a way that concealed her intimate areas while at the same time afforded the barest covering in the heat. Instead of feeling awkward in the foreign attire, Karissa experienced a strange sensation of deja vu, as if she had worn such a dress before, when she knew very well that she had not.

She walked toward the door that opened onto the garden. Near the door was a cage filled with chattering finches. A few steps beyond was another cage that contained two falcons. More cages were scattered throughout the garden, all filled with birds native to Egypt, from hoopoe birds to swallows. Karissa's heart went out to the creatures. Though they lived in a beautiful garden and were obviously well cared for, they were still prisoners, just as she was. In the garden beyond, she could barely make out the figure of a man through the leaves of the trees. She stepped toward him intending to offer her thanks and then leave immediately.

Asher heard a light step behind him, turned around, and was struck speechless by the sight of Karissa Spencer in the linen gown. She walked toward him and he was lost. All he could see was the woman he had loved thousands of years ago. Senefret. Through the branches of the sycamore-fig trees came a mirage from his past—a tall, fine-boned, exquisitely beautiful woman dressed in purest white. He stared as his heart leapt in his chest. Ah, beautiful Senefret! She was even more lovely than his memory of her.

For a long moment he let himself succumb to the vision and slipped into the past where he had known a woman he had loved with all his heart. But as Karissa drew closer, he pushed the vision from his thoughts. It was unfair to himself and to Karissa to invest the American woman with the traits and history of an Egyptian beauty long since dead.

Long since dead but not forgotten, Asher's heart reminded him. Until that moment he had been able to ignore the anguish buried inside him, but one look at Karissa and the heartache roared up like a wall of flame. The pain in his chest nearly sent him to his knees.

When Karissa drew closer and recognized him, her expression changed from open interest to dark suspicion, and the mirage vanished.

"Mr. Asher!" she exclaimed in disgust, stopping at the fountain a few feet away. "I should have known!"

"Miss Spencer," he replied, ignoring her angry remark. "Good afternoon." His tongue tripped over the English words that never came naturally to him, no matter how many years he spoke the choppy language. He rose from his seat.

Karissa's scowl deepened, shadowing her luminous dark brown eyes and wrinkling the flesh above her delicate pointed nose. He had the wildest urge to press his lips to the wrinkle and smooth it with a kiss, but knew such a gesture would only infuriate her.

"You had this planned all along!" she continued, stepping forward in anger. "The thugs, the kidnapping, the rescue by your trained panther"—

"Trained panther?"

"Yes! The cat that kills people and leaves gifts at my

doorstep. You could be arrested for manslaughter, you know, owning a dangerous pet like that."

"I have no such pet, Miss Spencer, I assure you."

"Then what brought me here last night?"

"Whatever it was, it was no pet."

"It seemed to know where you live."

He shrugged off the insinuation and smiled, mesmerized by the soft sloping curve between her nose and lip. Her mouth moved enticingly whenever she spoke, drawing down the tip of her nose. He wanted to touch that nose with his, to feel her lips upon his skin, to discover the taste of her neck. His loins stirred, almost painfully. In the sixteen years he had been in Luxor, he had never encountered a woman who could make his blood race like this one. He forced himself to glance away.

"Are you rested?" he asked, changing the subject. "Did you get enough to eat?"

"Yes, but don't think you can buy my cooperation with the bed and breakfast routine. I appreciate the hospitality, Mr. Asher, but I've made arrangements to leave. Tonight."

He sighed. "Even so, can I not interest you in lunch? You agreed to meet me for lunch in Baltimore and to hear what I have to say. Will you not honor that agreement here in Luxor?"

"Why? It's useless." She swept away from him, turning her back.

"Useless? In what way?" Asher's gaze traveled down the shapely curves of her hips and legs as he imagined how it would feel to press against her slender length. His loins quickened again and he breathed in sharply.

"Nothing you say could bring back my memory. Half a dozen doctors have done everything they know to induce me to remember. But I just can't."

"You can't or you won't, Miss Spencer?"

Slowly she turned to face him, and her expression was as cold as marble. "What are you implying?"

"That you don't want to face the truth. That there is something about the sphinx that you don't want to remember."

"Well it's easy to see why, isn't it? My mother died from the curse of the sphinx and my father vanished off the face of the earth."

"Oh?" Asher crossed his arms and tilted his head. "Did your father really disappear, Miss Spencer?"

He studied her face, searching for the truth in her reaction. She stared at him, her eyes wide. For an instant a tense silence hung between them, and then she whirled around and stomped to the fountain. Asher rushed after her, determined to help her remember. He would have reached up for her bare shoulders, but she turned and glared at him.

"Leave me alone, Mr. Asher!"

"I only want to help you."

"So I can help you find the sphinx. What a sterling motive, sir!" In disdain, she presented her back to him again.

"I may be the only one who can help you remember, Miss Spencer."

"And why are you so special?"

"Because." He leaned forward, closed his eyes, and breathed in the perfume of her hair. Every particle in his body wanted to reach for the woman standing so tantalizingly near to him. "I was there that night."

He saw her entire body go rigid.

"Yes," he went on, "I was there. And I think I can guess what happened to your father."

"You are wrong," she finally replied in a thick tone. "No one else was there. Just me and then later my mother."

"Perhaps you were not aware that I was there."

"No!" Karissa shook her head vehemently. "I saw nothing! No one! It was the middle of the desert. I would have noticed."

"Some things are not what they appear to be, especially when seen through the eyes of a child."

"I wasn't a child. I was twelve years old!"

"A child, nevertheless." He softened his tone. "You were a little girl who saw something she could not fit into the definitions of her world. And so you chose not to define it or examine it, ever again."

"I don't know what you're talking about!" She glared at him and he realized she was about to bolt away. He grabbed her wrist to stop her.

"Let me go!" she shouted.

"Not until you look at the truth. You know what happened at the sphinx, Miss Spencer. Admit it to yourself! Take back that missing part of your life."

"No!" She yanked her arm, but he held on tightly.

His heart ached to see the pain in her face, but he pressed on, determined to finish what he had begun. "You saw something that you simply cannot face."

"No!"

"Yes, Miss Spencer."

She shook her head and then covered her face with her free hand. Huge sobs heaved in her chest and she hunched over, miserable. Was the truth finally reaching her?

"You have it all wrong"—

"How was it, then?" he inquired gently. "Tell me."

"I can't. I can't!" Tears streamed down her cheeks. He released her wrist and she covered her face with both hands as if ashamed to be seen crying.

An overwhelming surge of compassion washed over Asher. He couldn't let her stand there alone, suffering, so he reached out and surrounded her in a gentle embrace, tucking her against his chest until her tears subsided. To his amazement, she let herself be drawn to him. Asher sank his hand into the thick mass of her raven hair and urged her to lean her head against his chest while he slowly stroked her back. His body sang to her surrender as she placed her small palms on his torso and let her weight sway into him. He breathed in her scent and slowly increased the pressure of his embrace. He couldn't help himself. Though his aim was to offer her comfort, he couldn't deny his need for her.

Isis, how he longed to kiss her! He lowered his head and brushed the tip of his nose across the hair at her temple. At the movement, she turned her head, and his jaw grazed her cheek. Asher's breath caught in his throat as her smooth skin passed over his. For a heart-thudding instant, she allowed her cheek to linger against his, and a tiny sigh escaped her lips.

"Karissa!" he said, his voice rough with passion. He pulled back to look at her. She glanced up at him in surprise, with tears clustered in her black lashes.

For a moment he stared down at her. He had no wish to denigrate her grief and remembrance by initiating intimate physical contact between them. And he had no intention of forcing himself on a woman who wasn't interested in his attentions. But for an instant he saw the light of desire flicker in her glance and knew that he had not misinterpreted her sigh.

With a low moan born of loneliness and hunger, he gathered her up in his arms and bent to her tear-streaked face.

Chapter 4

THE KISS BEGAN AS A GENTLE PRESS of Asher's lips upon hers, but once he tasted the lushness of her mouth, he couldn't hold back. Karissa's lips were like a perfectly ripe plum—dark, luscious, soft and wonderfully sweet. As he pulled her even closer, he heard her sigh again. The wistful sound set him on fire. Asher pushed his hand into her hair, reveling in the way the silky strands slipped between his fingers. The women he had known in the ancient days had worn ornate braided wigs, perfumed by cones made of animal fat which were placed on the tops of their heads. A man could not caress such coifs with the freedom afforded by Karissa's naturally luxuriant hair. He cradled her head with his palm as she leaned back to accept him. Then he slanted an intense kiss upon her, using his tongue to stroke the line between her lips until she allowed him entrance to her warm mouth. She opened to him.

It was Asher's turn to sigh this time, and the raggedness of the sound shocked him. What kind of hold did the American woman have on him, that he was eager to give himself to her already? Yet he wanted her more than he had ever wanted a woman, even more than—

Asher broke off the thought and slipped his tongue into Karissa's mouth. He felt her exploring him, tentatively at first and then with a boldness that inflamed him. The kiss grew harder, hotter, wilder. Karissa's hands released their grip on his white cotton shirt and slid up his torso. She curved her arms around his neck and hugged him fiercely, grinding against his mouth as if she had hungered for him for thousands of years. Her passion took him completely by surprise. And yet, one night long ago Senefret had reacted to his kiss in just this way.

Karissa's breasts pressed against his chest and he could feel the hard buds of her nipples. The thought that she was already aroused made him grow as hard as granite. He closed his eyes and the line blurred between this woman and the woman from his past, as he let his body surge to life for the first time in over a decade. Then he slowly slipped his hands down the graceful slope of her back and cupped her rump, pulling her against him and leaving no doubt as to his desire for her. She pressed into him, perfectly formed to fit against him, which only made him ache for her more. Karissa sighed at his ear, driving him mad with her sweet warm breath, until he couldn't resist lifting her up slightly, just enough to ease her over his burgeoning flesh. He sucked in a long and tortured breath and fought the urge to make love to her right there in the garden. He had no right to ask that of her. He barely had any right to kiss her and hold her like this.

Sighing, he let her slide back to the ground. He pulled away from her mouth and gazed down at her, surprised that he could have reacted so strongly to her. After a moment, she released his neck and let her hands slip down the front of his shirt as she glanced up to meet his gaze. The plum of her mouth looked delightfully crushed.

Off in the distance someone called to him, but the summons barely registered. Asher drew his hands away from her back and lightly grasped her elbows, denying himself the pleasure of kissing her again. If he tasted her mouth once more, he knew it would be impossible to let her go.

"Are you all right now?" he asked lowly, not sure whether he referred to her emotional outburst—which seemed to have occurred hours ago—or to the passion that had just flared between them.

Karissa nodded and blushed, and then stepped away from him. "Isn't that Eisha calling you, Mr. Asher?" she asked in an endearingly uneven voice.

Asher glanced at the garden entrance where his housekeeper stood, holding a tray of food, and then returned his attention to Karissa. He ran the pad of his thumb along her cheekbone in a gentle caress.

"To you my name is Asheris." He put the accent on the middle syllable, which made a sound like the wind in the desert.

"A-share-iss." She let the name slip softly through her teeth.

He smiled quietly, pleased to hear his real name on her lips. "Come," he said, guiding her forward with a light touch on her lower back. "Take the midday meal with me so that we may at last talk."

Karissa strolled beside him to a secluded table near the fountain. There she spent the late luncheon in a strange state of disquiet, worried that by kissing Mr. Asher—Asheris—she had lost her objectivity in regard to him. She was also concerned that he would bring up the lost sphinx again, and she couldn't bear to think about it. He had taken her dangerously close to the edge of remembrance and she wasn't ready to advance any farther. Compounding the other two concerns was the fact that though she was physically and mentally distracted by the man sitting across the table from her, she could not afford to waste her time gawking at him. She intended to listen to his story and get back to Baltimore.

Karissa ate sparingly, too keyed up to be hungry for

food. As she nibbled, she couldn't help but recall the passion she had just experienced in Asheris' arms. But how serious could a man be about a woman he had known for a mere few hours? She had learned to be wary of men who displayed deep passion for no apparent reason, and had vowed never to fall for a charmer again. It seemed to be a family weakness to succumb to handsome men, and she was determined to break the chain.

She peeled a pomegranate with deft fingers as she worried about her feelings for the graceful, elegant Egyptian across from her. There was more than shallow attraction for him in her heart, so much more that she experienced a sudden swell of tenderness whenever she glanced at him. The undeniable attraction was intensified by a curious feeling of familiarity—that she already knew Asheris as an old friend, that she was accustomed to the width of his shoulders, the intelligent tilt of his head, and the slow sensual slant of his smile. Yet it was silly to think she already knew him. Such thoughts were for foolish romantics who believed in love at first sight, soul mates and previous lives. As far as Karissa was concerned, such ideas were ridiculous.

As if he could read her thoughts, Asheris looked up from his plate and gazed at her without speaking, his eyes full of warmth. She returned the gaze, wondering why she wasn't nervous when staring at a man for minutes on end. She had never understood the words "falling into someone's eyes", but now she knew precisely what the phrase meant, for she felt herself plunging into Asheris' soul and had no power to hold herself back.

"I am supposed to be convincing you to help me," he declared at last, tearing apart a piece of flat bread and giving half to her.

She accepted it. "Yes. You mentioned something about a story."

"Indeed." His smile faded as he tore off a piece of bite-sized piece and chewed it slowly. For a long moment he stared at the line of acacia trees in his garden but she could tell that his eyes weren't seeing the trees at all. He was contemplating the telling of his story as if to choose the right words, and from the look in his eyes, the story was not a happy one. Perhaps nothing connected to the lost sphinx was pleasant.

"Is it a true story?" she asked.

"Yes. From long ago." He set down the bread. "It concerns my—ancestors."

The pause made her wonder if the story was connected to something or someone much closer than Asheris' ancestors. But she said nothing and waited for him to begin.

He sighed and raised his incredible eyes to meet hers. "A long time ago there was a beautiful priestess named Senefret. She had been raised by the worshippers of Sekhmet, the lion goddess, to become the Great Royal Wife of the pharaoh, but she did not want to wed the pharaoh. He was an ugly misshapen man given to bouts of insanity, which I have learned from modern science, was probably the result of intermarriage. You know, do you not, that pharaohs often wedded their sisters?"

"Yes, I've heard that."

"Unfortunately, the practice weakened the stock in many cases. So it was for the pharaoh. And Senefret did not want to spend her life married to such a monster, even though it would bring her glory and wealth."

"To some people, glory and wealth don't mean all that much," Karissa noted, thinking of Grandmother Petrie and her sterile life.

"Agreed." Asheris chewed another bite of bread and went on. "So Senefret decided to take her fate into her own hands. She was a brave woman with a bold spirit, and she decided to run off to the northeastern border where her brother, who was a general in the Egyptian army, was fighting nomadic invaders. She was certain her older brother would help her escape her marriage. But when she got to the border, she found her brother suffering from a mortal wound. He died in her arms. Grief-stricken and knowing she had lost her only supporter, Senefret decided to die fighting. The following morning she donned her brother's battle gear and rode to war next to the commander in chief of the army, who was half-brother to the pharaoh and a great favorite of the people. During the course of the battle, she saved the commander in chief's life, and in turn, he snatched her out of danger just as she was about to receive a fatal arrow. They rode back to camp in the commander's chariot. A bath was drawn and wine poured, and the commander insisted that the young general join him in a toast while he bathed. The commander stripped, unknowingly revealing his well-conditioned soldier's body to a virginal priestess. Instead of turning away, Senefret decided to find out what it would be like to have a real man before she died in battle or was shipped back to Thebes. She removed her male attire and offered herself to him.

The commander did not know who she was or where she had come from, and she refused to tell him. She asked that he kiss her, not question her, and the commander willingly granted her request, for she was a beautiful woman and her bravery on the field had mightily impressed him. For an entire night they made love. Then, before the camp awakened, Senefret slipped out of his tent to return to her brother's. On the way she was captured by an agent of the Temple of Sekhmet, who had sent a spy to follow her."

Karissa stared at him, mesmerized by the story and completely forgetting about the pomegranate on her plate. The tale seemed so familiar to her. Had her father told her the story long ago when he used to tuck her into bed?

"So then what happened?" Karissa asked.

"Senefret was dragged back to Thebes. There it was discovered that she had been deflowered and was no longer fit for the pharaoh. This was an abomination to the gods. She was executed and entombed in the Valley of the Damned, forever barred from entering the Afterworld."

"That's horrible!

"Yes. And Senefret's body"— He paused and for a moment he seemed to have difficulty in speaking. —"Her body is the one I must recover and re-inter, so that she may find peace in the Fields of Iaru where she belongs."

"Fields of Iaru?"

"The equivalent of your heaven."

Karissa studied Asheris' face. While telling the tale of Senefret, he had expressed genuine emotion. Either he was a good actor he was connected to the characters in the story on a personal level.

"How does this story pertain to your—ancestors?" she inquired.

"My family is related to the commander in the story."

"Oh." She felt let down by the easy explanation.

"But there is more to tell of the commander." Asheris poured a glass of wine and offered it to her. "The story is not yet finished."

"Then please continue." She took the glass and savored the brush of his warm fingers against hers. "Thank you."

"My pleasure." He poured a goblet for himself and slowly took a sip. "As to the commander, he had fallen madly in love with the mysterious Senefret. But he was caught up in his dreams of personal glory and bound by duty to finish the campaign in the north before he pursued a woman and declared his feelings. Half a year later, the commander returned to Thebes as a war hero.

When the commander made inquiries about Senefret, it was discovered that he was the man responsible for deflowering the priestess meant for the pharaoh. The High Priestess of the Temple of Sekhmet accused him of the crime. In those days the priests and priestesses were very powerful, almost as powerful as the pharaoh himself. When they demanded the life of a mortal they usually got it, especially if that mortal had offended the king or committed a sin. On the day of his "death", he was told of the fate of his beloved, and he was devastated. Then, for that one night with Senefret, the commander's life was forfeited—but not, I might add, in a conventional way."

"What did they do to him?"

"They mummified him alive."

Karissa froze in disbelief with the wine goblet pressed against her lip. She lowered the glass. "They what?"

"They mummified him alive. It was a practice known to them, a secret now lost."

"Mummified alive? What does that mean? How?"

Asheris took a long draught of wine. "Many of the secret rites have been lost over the centuries. But the fact remains that the commander was buried alive and cursed by the Temple of Sekhmet to be a living mummy until released by a woman who loved him. The priestesses were certain the curse would hold forever because they knew the only woman who loved the commander was Senefret and she was already dead."

He heaved a sigh and pressed on, his eyes dark and troubled. "And because the commander was still alive in his tomb, his spirit or ka could never leave the earth and go to the Underworld where it belonged. The Lioness cult therefore damned him to eternal hell, just as they had damned Senefret."

Karissa reached out and slipped her hand over Asheris' right wrist in a gesture of compassion. "This story is very sad."

"Yes." Asheris nodded and covered her hand with his left. "But Osiris, the God of the Underworld, took pity on the lovers. He knew what it was like to be forever damned to remain in one world. So he lifted the curse, as much as it was in his power to do so. Since he was Lord of the Underworld and Ruler of the Night, he released the commander's ka by allowing it to wander free, but only during the night hours. And only in the form of a cat."

"A cat?" Karissa felt a shiver race down her back. "A panther?"

Asheris nodded and silently regarded her as if waiting for her to make more conclusions.

"Not the panther I saw at the lost sphinx!"

He raised his eyebrows as if to encourage her to reconsider.

"But the panther would have to be thousands of years old! How could he live that long?"

"He is no ordinary beast." He squeezed her hand and then reached for his wine. "He is the spirit of a damned man."

Karissa sat back, trying to take in all that he had said, and fingered the stem of her glass. If what he said was true, she had been saved twice by a mythical panther. If the cat were supernatural, its unearthliness would certainly explain how it had traveled from Baltimore to Luxor. She glanced at Asheris.

"So the panther spirit was the cat who saved my life?"

"Quite likely."

"But why? Why me?"

"Because you are very important to him."

"Because I know the location of the lost sphinx? What has that to do with the mummified commander and the panther?"

"The man was locked inside the sphinx, Karissa. You let him out."

She paled. "When the sphinx collapsed?"

"Yes." Asheris finished his wine. "The sphinx guarded the entrance of the Valley of the Damned. But as everyone knows, the Valley of the Damned is in a barren desert that is constantly altered by wind and sand. No one knows for sure where the ruined sphinx lies buried. No one but you, Karissa. You are the single living soul who holds the key to finding Senefret's body."

"But I can't remember!"

"I think you can." He reached for her hand again and surrounded it with the warmth of his. "If you are willing to relive that night, Karissa, to face whatever troubles you about it, you could redeem the soul of a woman whose only sin was to choose personal freedom."

"I can't," Karissa replied in a low voice. She couldn't bear to think of two people trapped forever because of her. Yet the pain of examining the night at the sphinx would be even more acute. Besides that, she had no time to get caught up in Asher's fantasy. She had her own problems and her own schedule to consider. She jumped to her feet, knocking back the chair. "I can't! I simply can't remember!"

In contrast, he rose to his feet with elegant gracefulness. "But will you try?" he asked softly.

She stared at him, wanting to run far away from him and into his arms at the same time. Was she losing her mind?

He placed his napkin on the table. "Will you at least agree to drive out to the desert with me and take a look? I will make it worth your while."

Karissa raised her chin and studied him. Money would enable her to buy out Josh and break away from his disruptive presence. That in itself would give a welcome amount of peace of mind, perhaps enough to make up for the craziness of arriving in Baltimore a day or two behind schedule.

"How much money are you willing to pay me if I decide to go with you?" she asked after a long pause.

"Thirty thousand in U.S. funds, plus expenses."

The sum staggered her, but she didn't show her surprise. "I already made a plane reservation for eight o'clock this evening, though."

"I will buy a new ticket for you."

She swept back her hair and noticed that his eyes followed the movement. For thirty thousand dollars, she could be persuaded to spend one more day in Egypt. "All right, then, Mr. Asher. Let's go."

Chapter 5

ASHERIS DROVE HIS LAND ROVER through the outskirts of Luxor, effortlessly dodging trucks piled with grain and easily passing overloaded buses. Karissa wondered if Asheris did everything with quiet competence. She glanced at him, appreciating the sleek way he looked in his dark glasses with his hair pulled back to the nape of his neck. Her gaze traveled across his sharp jawline accentuated by the white collar of his shirt and down his arms where the rolled-up sleeves revealed his tanned forearms. She liked the way the fine black hair lightly shaded his sinewy arms and could imagine his chest was similarly shadowed. Asheris shifted into a lower gear and swerved around three camels while Karissa's gaze dropped to his lean thighs draped in a pair of khaki pants. He had long, well-formed legs and narrow aristocratic feet that manipulated the pedals with authority. She could imagine that Asheris did everything with authority. A vision of him moving over her in bed— making love to her with a maddening amount of self-control—flashed through her thoughts. Where had that vision come from?

To get her mind off the image of Asheris in bed with her, she stared out her window. She had been here only a short while and already was falling in love again with the lush green valley and the stark golden cliffs that bordered the Nile. She loved the contrasts of Egypt, a place where skyscrapers rose beside pyramids, where British cruise ships sailed past feluccas used by fisherman since ancient times, where camel caravans loitered in the parking lots of gas stations. The delightful mixture of the sights and sounds of her childhood came rushing back, filling her heart with a joy so sharp she sighed out loud.

"What is wrong?" Asheris asked, shooting a sidelong glance at her.

"Nothing." She smiled. "It's just good to be back, that's all. I didn't realize that I missed Egypt."

She looked at him and saw the corner of his mouth rise in that slow lop-sided smile of his. The sight made her heart do a crazy flip-flop. What was it about this man that could make her react so strongly, just to his smile? Whatever it was, she was in danger of falling under the spell of Egypt again, but in an entirely new way.

Within forty-five minutes they had climbed through a steep pass in the cliffs and wound up an arid canyon until they reached the desert above. Instantly the Land Rover was hit by a blast of gritty wind. They rolled up the windows and turned on the air conditioning. Asheris dropped into a low gear as the road dwindled to a sandy track. Karissa surveyed the expanse of dun-colored sand dunes but saw nothing she recognized. Asheris continued the drive and after another hour, they passed through a vaguely familiar outcropping of sandstone.

"I think I remember that," she declared, nodding at the banded plateau. Her tongue, suddenly dry, stuck to the roof of her mouth.

"What do you remember about it?"

"The sphinx was near here. To the left, I think. Over there." She pointed to a sheltered cleft in the rock. Asheris steered the four-wheel drive to the cleft but found the passage barred by a boulder the size of a small sedan, as if someone had purposely blocked the path. He turned off the engine and put his right hand on the door.

The sudden silence closed in on Karissa, allowing the haunting wail of the desert wind to seep into her soul, reminding her of the night so long ago when her world had fallen apart. She suddenly regretted coming with Asheris.

"Shall we get out and look?" he asked.

"I can't."

"You can, Karissa."

"I'd be an idiot to go near the sphinx again. What about the curse?"

Asheris sighed. "The only real curse was invoked by the High Priestess of Sekhmet and involved the commander in chief of the army. No one else."

"But what about my mother's death?"

"A coincidence, surely."

"And my father?"

"You tell me, Karissa."

"How can I when I can't remember?" She passed the back of her hand across her damp forehead.

Asheris turned to her. "Is there anything you recall about the sphinx? Anything at all?"

"It was night. That's all I remember."

"That is all?"

Karissa glanced at him. "Didn't you mention that you were there that night, too? Don't you remember anything about the sphinx's location?"

"No. I was"— He glanced away as his voice trailed off in a vagueness that wasn't in keeping with his usual definite manner. —"I was not myself at the time."

"What do you mean? Were you ill or something?"

"I wasn't myself, that is all." He sent her a hard look that warned her not to press the issue. She glanced away, perplexed, and decided to ask him later what he meant.

He reached for her arm. "Please, Karissa, you must

trust me when I tell you there is no curse. If you will only walk a while and look around, something might spark your memory. It is important that we find the lost sphinx as quickly as possible."

She pulled her arm away. "Can't you get it into your head that I don't want to remember?" Her voice was sharp with anger.

He paused, as if he possessed infinite patience even after such an outburst, and stared into her eyes for a long moment. "To remember is to start to recapture yourself. To heal."

She glared at him. Would the man never give up?

"If you cannot do it for yourself, then do it for Senefret."

Her resolve to stay in the Land Rover faltered. Why did he have to remind her of the tragic priestess? Protecting her sanity was one thing. Refusing to help a stranded soul was quite another. She let out an exasperated breath.

"All right! But I can't guarantee anything." Karissa snatched her hat from the back seat, opened the door, and jumped out, prepared for the unforgettable searing heat of the sand. Though Asheris was maddeningly persistent, at least he had sent his manservant to purchase hiking boots and cotton clothing for her before they left Luxor, to make sure she had protection against the inhospitable desert. She plopped the hat on her head and looked up to find Asheris studying her.

He smiled at her as he slipped the keys in his pocket, obviously approving of the way she looked in her khakis. Trying not to think of his magnetic eyes or the way he had just twisted her around his finger, she stomped off toward the narrow cleft in the rocks. He walked beside her without making a sound.

Karissa plodded through the sand, squinting in the bright sun, and hoping she would see something familiar so she wouldn't have to review the events that took place when the sphinx collapsed. But the longer she stared at the rock outcropping and the dunes beyond, the less certain she became that she had ever set foot in the area. At the edge of the outcropping, where strewn rock gave way to the endless desert sand, Karissa stopped and pushed back her hat.

"Are those backhoes over there?" she asked, pointing to the outlines of yellow machinery about a half-mile away.

"Yes. Mustofa has brought equipment out here to search. And should he find the entrance to the Valley of the Damned before we do, he will take everything without regard to ownership, and sell it on the black market to the highest bidder."

"Maybe Mustofa knows something we don't. And that's why he's digging over there."

"No. I am fairly certain that Mustofa knows very little. He has just made a good guess."

"Well, I don't recognize anything," she declared, looking back out to the dunes.

"Nothing?"

"Nothing." She turned and was surprised to find Asheris directly behind her. Was he trying to block her return to the Land Rover? Karissa glared at him. "Excuse me," she announced, taking a step as if to plow through.

"Wait." He reached for her shoulders and enclosed them in a gently restraining hold. "Just for a moment."

"It's almost four o'clock. I could still catch my plane."

"You can get a flight in the morning."

"Maybe I want to leave now."

"After you have come so far? Come into the shade and talk to me for a moment. Over here." He urged her to walk toward a shady crevice in the rock. Karissa spied a metallic glint at the base. Could there be water? She would love to dip her hands in some water.

"All right," she followed him. "But just for a moment."

There was indeed a small pool at the base of the rock and a patch of grass. Karissa hunkered down, untied the scarf from her neck and dipped it in the water. She used the wet cotton to wipe her face and neck.

Asheris sat on a nearby rock and watched her. "Tell me of your mother," he said.

She glanced up in surprise. "My mother?"

"Yes. Was she sick for a long time before her death?"

"No. She died unexpectedly from a strange fever that baffled the doctors."

"Were your parents happy with each other?"

"My mother hated Egypt. She gave my dad a hard time about having to live here. They argued about that a lot."

"Did your father love your mother?"

"Yes...oh...I don't know." His questions made her nervous. She had asked herself the exact question a hundred times and wondered why she could never bring herself to examine her memory for an answer.

"Did your mother love him?"

"It was hard to tell. Grandmother Petrie often said that my mother rushed into marriage because of my father's good looks and charm, and warned me never to repeat the mistake."

"Marry in haste, may we repent at leisure, as they say?" Asheris remarked.

"Perhaps." She suddenly wondered if she were in danger of doing exactly what her mother had done by falling precipitously in love with the attractive confident man who sat near the edge of the water.

Asheris picked up a pebble and tossed it into the pool.

A series of rings blossomed outward and then drifted away to nothing. "Did you ever think that your father might have had a lot in common with his colleague, Dr. Raeburn?"

"Her?" Karissa pulled at the brim of her hat, mostly to hide her pinched expression. She didn't like discussing her parents' relationship. "Gracie Raeburn was plain and dowdy. Why would my father be interested in her when he had someone like my mother? My mother was a beauty, you know."

"It may have been that your father valued Dr. Raeburn's mind and not her face. Your father may have enjoyed talking about his work with a woman who shared his love of archaeology."

"Why are you bringing this up?"

"So that you will consider what was going on between your parents and Dr. Raeburn when you were twelve years old."

"What are you implying?"

"Nothing. Perhaps if you think about your parents and Dr. Raeburn, you will begin to remember."

"There's nothing to remember!"

Asheris took off his dark glasses and slipped them in the pocket of his shirt. He turned his intense gaze upon her, and she wondered if he intended to use his hypnotic eyes as a weapon.

"Karissa, you are fooling no one but yourself. There is a reason why you have let that night slip into blackness. And I believe you saw something that highly disturbed you."

"I saw nothing!" She jumped to her feet as she pushed away a flashback, like a strobe light blinking on the sight of two people embracing, and then blinking off again. "I remember nothing! And don't try to put ideas in my head!"

She glared at him over her shoulder. The vision of the embrace in the sphinx flashed into her thoughts again, this time more slowly, giving her enough time to see the expression on her father's face. She heard the echo of her own voice screaming in her thoughts. No-o-o-o! She saw her father glance in her direction, saw Gracie Raeburn twist in his arms. And then Karissa heard the ominous thud above their heads. Her heart twisted in her chest. She slammed her hat on her head and cut off the memory before it could rush to its horrifying climax.

Karissa dashed out of the tiny oasis, trying to outrun the memory. Just the notion that she might relive the moments inside the sphinx made her desperate with fear. She couldn't endure seeing it all again, couldn't bear to think that she had been responsible for—

She broke off the thought and ran through the slipping sand. Her hat flew off, but she didn't care. All she could do was run blindly into the desert , hoping that if she went far enough and fast enough, she might outdistance the truth.

But she couldn't outdistance Asheris. He loped behind her, easily catching up with her, and grabbed at her arm to stop her. The movement knocked her off balance, and she fell, which sent her rolling down the slope of a dune. She slid to a stop at the bottom, but before she could scramble to her feet, she was pinned to the ground by Asheris, who forced both wrists to the side of her head as he straddled her legs.

She struggled to get away, but he held her firmly. After a few moments she surrendered and glared up at him. Only then did she realize her face was caked with tears and dust.

"Stop running, Karissa." His voice was much softer than the grip on her wrists. "It is time to see things for what they are."

"No!"

"Your father did not run off with Gracie Raeburn."

"Yes he did. They were having an affair!"

"Who told you that?"

"My mother! She suspected it for years!"

"And you believed her?"

"Yes!" Karissa stared into his golden eyes. Damn those eyes. How could she escape the power of those eyes and the way they could pull her thoughts right out of her mouth. Her heart pounded in her chest, her neck, and her temples as the truth welled up inside her. She ran the tip of her tongue over her parched lips and saw Asheris watch the movement.

He bent down.

"No," Karissa began to whimper but his mouth closed over hers and cut off her protest.

"I am here now for you," he said against her lips. "Open your soul to me." Then he kissed her in a lingering, thorough manner that set her heart racing all over again. Slowly he lowered himself until he sank down upon her, his firm chest to her breasts, his hard abdomen to her soft trim torso, and his lean legs stretched alongside hers. The weight of him made her body flare into full arousal, and the sheer size of him made her wonder if he might cover and consume her like a dark falcon. And his tongue! His tongue drove her mad. The surface of his tongue was quite raspy, which heightened the erotic sensation of every stroke. No man had ever done to her with his tongue what Asheris was doing now.

Karissa melted into the sand as Asheris moved over her in the first step of the sinuous dance between a man and a woman. She could feel the mark of his arousal, and when he surged against her and groaned, she felt her woman's blossom open, spreading its nectar deep inside her, preparing for the seed it ached to receive. She wanted to respond to him, wanted to wrap her arms around his muscular shoulders and pull him down to her lips. But he held her wrists above her head, and all she could do was gasp and moan as he bit her breasts through the cotton fabric of her shirt and bra, and arch upward as he kissed her throat and ears.

Open her soul to him? What did he mean? Did he want her to trust him enough to tell him everything she could remember so that he could drag even more memories to the surface? Or did he want her to open to him physically, and let him make love to her, here on the desert sand? How could she do either? She had known Asheris for less than a week. How could she succumb to a man with such certainty? Yet she knew she could trust him. And she knew she wanted him. There was no doubt in her mind that she wanted Asheris—in her arms, in her thoughts, and in the deepest place inside of her. This need of him was elemental, undeniable, like breathing or eating. She had never felt so certain, not even with the man she had called her husband.

"Tell me now," he said, his voice husky.

"Tell you what?" she closed her eyes as he kissed her brow.

"Why you cannot face what happened that night."

An image as sharp as a knife blade sliced through her desire for Asheris. In the vision she saw her father look up, saw Gracie Raeburn slowly pull her arms from her father's shoulders.

"No!" she gasped.

"Tell me." He urged, rising to his knees. "What are you seeing?"

"Them together!"

"Who—your father and Dr. Raeburn?"

"Yes." She felt tears burning in her eyes. "I saw them embracing. I saw the look on my father's face."

"What kind of look?"

"It was"— She glanced at him and felt the corners of her mouth pulling down uncontrollably. She didn't want to break down, couldn't break down. Not in all her therapy sessions had she come this close to cracking.

"It was what?"

Karissa blinked through her tears and knew she was losing control. Something about Asheris' eyes induced her to spill her guts, to bare her soul. She sighed raggedly and then whispered. "It was ecstasy."

Asheris' grip eased on her wrists. "Ecstasy because of Dr. Raeburn?"

"Why else?" her voice was flat.

"There are joys other than that between a man and woman," he put in gently. "There is the joy of discovery."

"Joy of discovery?" She had never once considered her father might have been embracing Gracie Raeburn for reasons other than sexual intimacy, especially after hearing her mother's views on the subject. Could she have been mistaken? Could she have seen ecstasy on her father's face and attributed it to love or lust, when all the time it had been out of the sheer joy of finding a grave site intact after years of searching? Ah, God—

"What else do you remember?" Asheris asked, leaning closer. "Keep going!"

The vision came again, like a wave of nausea. She saw her father look up again, saw Gracie Raeburn once more slowly pull her arms from her father's shoulders as the sound of thunder filled the burial chamber, as the thunder filled Karissa's mind, choking out the hammering of her heart. She couldn't look any more, couldn't bear to hear the screams.

"No!"

"What do you see, Karissa? What is happening?"

"I screamed. I couldn't believe he would betray

Mother like that. So I started to yell. No-o-o!" She sank back, exhausted, as the words died on her lips.

"What did he do then?"

"Nothing. There wasn't time." She closed her eyes and tears dropped down her temples and into her hair. "If I hadn't yelled, they might have had time. They might have been able to save themselves."

"From what?"

"From the block, the granite block that came down. Oh, God!" She turned her head and wept openly, unmindful of Asheris. She longed to cover her face, but he still kept her wrists trapped.

"Karissa." He kissed her left temple. "It was not your fault," he said. "You must know it was not your fault."

"It was! If I hadn't yelled, if I hadn't distracted them—"

"Many burial chambers were booby-trapped. Surely you knew that."

"But if I hadn't yelled, they might have had time to get away!"

She shut her eyes, trying to blot out the image of the huge granite block, as big as a boxcar, which had come roaring out of the darkness. But this time there was no stopping the sight or the sound. This time she heard the horrified shattering scream as the block of granite crushed her father and Dr. Raeburn, and then set the entire disintegration of the sphinx in motion. Karissa watched it all again and realized she was screaming and screaming and screaming.

Then she was lifted to her feet and surrounded in the warmth of a loving embrace. She let her head be held against a strong shoulder, let her waist be supported by the link of a powerful arm, for she could neither stand nor speak, or stop the flood of tears that poured from her eyes. Then that someone enfolded her to a human heart and murmured the words no one had ever said to her—words she had desperately needed to hear when she was twelve years old and had just witnessed the gruesome death of her father.

Karissa, let it go. It was not your fault. You could not have known. It would have happened anyway. There was nothing you could have done to stop it. You are not to blame. Karissa, my sweet, let this darkness out of your heart. Let it go.

For sixteen years she had hidden the truth from everyone, including herself, that she had been responsible for the death of her father in the sphinx. For sixteen years she had lived with guilt so awful that she couldn't even look at it. And for sixteen years she had hung in an emotional limbo, frozen by the brand upon her child's heart that had damned her to a lifetime of unworthiness and self-recrimination. No one had been able to see the brand, but she had known it was there, every day, and the invisible scar had crippled her in so many ways.

But with each moment in the strong arms that held her, she felt the scar dissolving, each jagged edge smoothing out and uncoiling, while all the pain and anguish drained out of her as she wept. No one had ever held her or comforted her like this. Her grandmother had never even guessed she had a dark secret, and had been too uninterested or afraid to examine the source of Karissa's rebellious tirades and black silences. So who held her now? Who cared enough about her to hold her like this? She glanced up through her tears, half-surprised to find herself not in her grandmother's house in Baltimore, but in the arms of an Egyptian man on the edge of the Eastern Desert.

He gazed down at her, his golden-brown eyes full of compassion, his expression intent with concern. And suddenly she heard his words again in her mind. He had called her his sweet. No one had ever murmured an endearment to her like that and truly meant it. And even if they had, she wouldn't have felt worthy enough to accept it. Now, however, she could. Asheris had helped her see that she was not to blame for the tragedy so long ago. Her heart swelled with an almost painful surge of gratitude.

"It has gone, the darkness?" he asked gently.

She gazed at him, stunned that Asheris could have walked into her life and started her on the road to healing just like that. She tried to smile, but the expression only reached her eyes. Wordlessly, she wrapped her arms around his torso and clutched him with all her strength. He had given her what no one else had offered. He had shown her the way to look at the past and forgive herself. New tears came, tears of release and relief this time, and he held her until the sobs subsided.

"Karissa?" he asked at last, pulling away to take a look at her face. "Are you all right?"

She reached up and stroked his cheek with her right hand, cherishing the man who had just guided her through the gates of her trauma and beyond. "I think so."

He turned his head and kissed her palm.

"Who are you?" she asked in wonder, reaching up with her other hand. Her eyelids felt hard and scratchy from crying. "How did you ever find me?"

"It was you who found me," he replied. "But that story is for another time."

"Why not now?"

"The light is fading. I must get you back to Luxor before nightfall."

"But what about the sphinx?"

"We will have to look for it another day." He stepped away. "Come. We must hurry." He held out his hand to help her back up the slope.

Karissa reached for him and took a step, but dragged her feet because she was in no hurry to leave. Why was he suddenly so pressed for time? There was plenty of light to search for more clues. They might end up arriving in Luxor after dark, but why would that matter? His behavior was at odds with his insistence that they find the sphinx as soon as possible. She didn't quite know what to make of it. With her second step, her boot hit something hard in the sand and she looked down. The corner of a piece of red granite stuck out of the dune.

"Wait!" she exclaimed. Karissa drew him back down the slope and then knelt on the sand. "Asheris, look!"

Chapter 6

ASHERIS DROPPED TO HIS KNEES beside her and brushed away the sand to expose a block of pink granite. Nearby, Karissa toed through the sand, searching for another block and quickly finding one. She glanced up and met Asheris' gleaming eyes.

"Could this be the lost sphinx?" she gasped.

"It might be! I am going to establish the bearings of the location." He scrambled up the dune and pulled a compass out of his pants pocket. Keeping the rise of the rock formation directly behind him, he held out the compass and noted the direction of the exposed granite blocks. Karissa joined him at the top of the dune and reached down for her discarded hat. The wind was harsher at the top of the dune, and she hoped they would leave soon.

"I will bring men out here to dig tomorrow," he declared. "And we will see if the blocks are truly part of the sphinx."

"And if so, then what?"

"Then we will find the underground corridor that leads from the sphinx to the necropolis of the Valley of the Damned."

"The necropolis is underground?"

"Yes. The sphinx was built to guard it."

Karissa smiled. Though she was emotionally drained,

she was still highly aware of Asheris' excitement. "That would be something, if we've really come across the lost sphinx just like that, by accident."

"Not by accident." He smiled down at her and dropped the compass in the pocket of his pants. "You brought us here."

"You had a hand in it, too," she countered. "If not for you, Asheris, I would still be running out in the desert. You helped me find the part of me that was lost, and in so doing, found these blocks."

"That part of you was there all along." He reached for her elbow and the gentleness in his voice turned to briskness. "Come. It grows late, Karissa. And I must be back before nightfall."

"Why?"

"I have business to attend to. And much to arrange."

"What do you do for a living, anyway?" she asked as they hurried toward the Land Rover. It was easier to talk of his life and interests than let her mind drift back to the night the sphinx collapsed.

"I am an antiquities dealer. I also lecture at the university here in Luxor and in Cairo, as well as in Europe." He pulled open the door of the vehicle and held it for her.

She got in and glanced at him. "As an expert in Egyptian artifacts?"

"Partly. I am considered an authority on the history of the Middle Kingdom." He closed her door and walked around to the other side of the Land Rover.

"My father would have enjoyed talking with you."

"And I would have enjoyed talking to him." He backed up the four-wheel drive and made a wide turn to head out to the main road. "I would have asked him what naughty things you did when you were a little girl."

"Me?" She smiled, feeling lighter than she had in

years. "Naughty?"

"Yes, you." He cocked an eyebrow and looked over the top of his sunglasses at her. "You kiss like a naughty girl."

"Oh, really?" She tried to repress an outright grin.

"Like you know what you want from a man."

"That isn't being naughty, Mr. Asher, that's being honest."

"Oh? And what truths do your kisses tell?"

"I think you know, because you kiss like a wicked little boy."

"Ah." He smiled his slow smile when he realized she had thrown his taunting words right back at him. The smile broadened as he turned his attention to the road. His teeth were very white against his skin.

Something warm and wonderful twisted inside her. Karissa gazed out the window, emotionally depleted but aware of a tantalizing prospect of happiness lurking at the edge of her exhaustion. Perhaps tonight, after she had rested and he had concluded his business, she could spend some time with Asheris before she left for Baltimore the next day. She could suggest celebrating the discovery of the lost sphinx and let the evening develop from there. She couldn't imagine leaving Luxor without telling him how much it meant to her when he had held her in his arms and given her comfort, and without spending her last few hours in Egypt with him.

The only lover she had known had been her husband, and to define his perfunctory rituals in bed as lovemaking was to defile the very essence of the word. Thomas had been an indefatigable partner, determined to last as long as humanly possible before reaching a climax. But in his obsession with his own performance, he forgot the importance of touching, of exchanging whispered words of love, of conveying rich emotion through kisses of exquisite tenderness—the kind of kisses Asheris had already given her.

Instinctively, Karissa had known there could be much more between a man and woman than the mechanical coupling she had experienced with Thomas, but until meeting Asheris she had never desired to explore her theory. Now she thought that she would wither away in abject desperation if she missed the chance to make love with the man beside her. With Asheris, it truly would be making love, because her feelings for him grew deeper and broader with every kindness he showed her, every way in which he touched her, every time he kissed her. She felt herself opening to him simply at the rumble of his voice or the lift of his smile. Surely he must be falling in love just as quickly, the way he held her and looked at her with such warmth in his eyes. A person couldn't hide the truth that shone in their eyes. No one could fake such a genuine expression.

She sighed and crossed her arms over her chest. She would be a fool if she left herself fall for a man who lived a world away from her home in Baltimore. She was crazy to think a man from another culture could be a good choice for her. But did she have a choice? Her heart knew no boundaries, geographically or culturally, and it was begging her to have faith in Asheris. She had spent a lifetime ignoring her inner voice. Perhaps it was time to listen.

Soon after they arrived back at Asheris' walled estate, he left to tend to his business. Karissa called Josh to tell him of her change in travel plans, but once again was forced to leave a message on his answering machine. She wondered if the man was ever home. She hung up the phone, realizing she hadn't given a definite date for her return. Was she secretly hoping Asheris would ask her to stay for a few more days? She really couldn't stay, no matter how badly she wanted to get to know Asheris. She had spent the last sixteen years totally devoted to her sculpture. She couldn't throw it all away by being unprepared for the PBS special, even though she suspected her life was quickly taking on a new dimension because of Asheris, and that never again would she be completely satisfied with just her work.

Now that she thought about it, she felt even more driven to spend the last few hours with Asheris. To pass the time, Karissa took a long bath, luxuriating in the large sunken tub and savoring the foreign sensation of well-being that had begun to flicker in the center of her soul. She emerged from her bath, dressed in another of the delicate linen sheaths Eisha had laid out for her, and slipped on the armbands and necklace that had been placed there as well. The jewelry seemed to be very old, crafted of gold-colored metal and colorful gems, probably paste imitations of carnelians and emeralds, and real pieces of lapis lazuli. The wide colorful collar suited the dress and set off her complexion. Karissa glanced at herself in the mirror, and was slightly shocked to see how closely she resembled the female figures she had seen painted on the walls of tombs. Her Egyptian blood had never been as obvious as now when she was dressed in the garments of another age.

Karissa continued to stare. The garment felt right on her body. The jewelry draped perfectly across her shoulders and breasts. Even black hair was cut in a blunt style across the middle of her back and above her eyebrows, just like the hair of the ladies she had seen in her father's books. Sekhmet, Senefret, Asheris, Osiris. Why did the unusual names ring with such poignant familiarity? Was it because her father had been an Egyptologist and she had grown up on stories of the ancient world? Or did the familiarity spring from some fountain much deeper than her childhood? And why had Asheris provided her with these items of clothing? Was if for her pleasure or for his?

And if his, whose image did he see when he looked at her?

Perhaps Asheris was obsessed with a vision from the past. He didn't seem like the type of man to be possessed by a fantasy, but why else would he want her to dress in ancient clothing? She'd lay odds that the image from the past was Senefret. But why such an obsession for a person so long dead? Couldn't he be satisfied with a real life and blood woman?

Frowning, Karissa slipped off one armband, and was infused with a strange melange of hurt and resentment for his disinterest in seeing her for herself. But she refused to let the hurt eat away at her. She would demand the truth from Asheris as soon as he came back for the evening.

Shaken and angry, she walked to the table near the door, picked up the brass bell, and rang it sharply. "Eisha!" she called.

Moments later, Eisha bustled through the open door.

"Yes, Miss Spencer?"

"Where are my clothes?" she asked.

"What clothes?"

"The galabia I was wearing when I came here the other night."

"That?" A confused expression passed through Eisha's dark brown eyes. "But that was just a rag."

"What did you do with it?"

"I threw it away, Miss Spencer." She glanced at the linen dress Karissa wore. "Do you not wish to wear the dress?"

"No. What about those khaki pants I had on this afternoon?"

"They are dirty. They must be laundered."

Karissa's frown deepened.

"Is there something wrong with the gown?" Eisha asked, tilting her head.

"Yes. I feel as if I'm dressing in someone else's wardrobe. Who does this dress belong to?"

"I don't know." Eisha wrung her hands, obviously worried that Karissa was upset. "Mr. Asher selected it from his collection for you to wear."

"What collection?"

"His artifact collection."

"Is the collection in the house?"

"Yes." Eisha looked over her shoulder as if afraid of being overheard.

"Would you take me to see it?"

"Mr. Asher likes to personally show the collection to guests."

"I don't think Mr. Asher will have enough time. And I would really like to see it before I leave tomorrow. Please."

Eisha glanced at her and then sighed. "All right, Miss Spencer. Follow me."

The housekeeper led her down a corridor, into a darkened wing of the house on the other side of the garden, and down a few steps. She selected a key from a ring on her belt and turned an ornate lock. Then she opened the door, flipped on the subdued lighting and held the door open for Karissa to pass by her.

Karissa stepped into the room, awestruck. In pools of light, much like the arrangement of her gallery, she saw polished statues of granite, tables of ebony and ivory, boxes of all shapes, chairs with lion feet for legs, alabaster chalices, and ancient instruments that looked like simple harps. But what caught her attention the most was a glass case at the end of the room in which a life-size figure of a woman stood bathed in light. Karissa flowed closer with Eisha at her heels.

When she got close enough to make out the features of the woman, she stopped abruptly, shocked by the resemblance between the figure and her own appearance. The woman had long black hair, a slender face with wide dark eyes, delicate nose, and full lips. She was dressed in a fashion identical to the one Karissa was wearing.

"Who is this?" Karissa inquired, her voice hushed.

"A statue of an ancient one," Eisha replied. "The master had it carved by a French sculptor years ago."

"But who is she?"

"She was known as Senefret, a priestess of the Temple of Sekhmet."

Karissa stared up at the beautiful haughty face of the priestess. Asheris was obsessed with the woman, and the only reason he was attracted to her was because of her similarity to Senefret. Her heart wrenched painfully. Karissa glanced down at the dress she wore and then back up to the housekeeper. "I am dressed exactly like her."

"You look much like her," Eisha observed. "Strikingly so."

"Is this dress something she might have worn?"

"Yes. As I said, it came from this collection."

"So I'm wearing a priceless artifact?"

"Yes."

She held up her arm and stared at the golden band. "And what of this? Is the armband real, too?"

"Yes, Miss Spencer."

Karissa felt a chill pass over her, even though the evening was still balmy. "This jewelry is probably solid gold!"

Eisha nodded.

"This is crazy!" Karissa slipped the golden ring down her arm and off her hand. "Do you have something practical to wear, Eisha? I don't care if it is one of Mr. Asher's shirts. Please, just get me something practical until the khakis are laundered."

"As you wish. This will not make Mr. Asher happy,

however."

"Mr. Asher won't be happy if I ruin these, either."

She reached for the strings of the necklace where they were tied together at the nape of her neck. The sooner she got out of the ancient garments, the better. She wasn't certain why she was driven by the need to take off the clothing, whether because of the Asheris' peculiar devotion to Senefret or the claustrophobic feeling the ancient dress and jewelry invoked in her. She looked up to find Eisha staring at her.

"I'm going back to my room," Karissa said. "Would you please find me something else to wear and bring it there?"

"Certainly. At once." Eisha ducked out of the room to do Karissa's bidding.

Karissa found her way back to her chamber and waited until Eisha appeared with a shirt and a light cotton robe, both masculine attire. Then she left, allowing Karissa to dress, and returned a few minutes later with the evening meal and a babble of apologies.

"I thought you might like to eat in here," she explained, carrying the food to the table, "since you don't have proper attire for the dining room."

"Thanks." Karissa saw the single plate on the tray and wished she didn't have to eat alone, even though her sentiments regarding Asheris had taken a sudden turn. "Isn't Mr. Asher dining at home this evening?"

"No. Mr. Asher is never home in the evening."

"Oh." The comment deflated her even more. But she quickly replaced her disappointment with anger. Anger was a much less vulnerable way to deal with a man like Asheris. "Does he usually stay out late?"

"Quite late."

So much for her plans to ask him about the clothes. It was obvious he would not grace her with his company this evening. It was for the best anyway. Whenever Asheris was close at hand, she fell under his spell. It was better for the both of them that they kept their distance.

Karissa sat down at the table. The clothing Eisha had brought her smelled faintly of Asheris. She tried to ignore the light musky fragrance, but his scent made her pause for a moment and think of his kiss and his arms. Then Eisha put an aromatic plate of rice, lamb, and vegetables in front of her, and the smell of the food brought her back to her senses. A folded newspaper lay on the tray.

"Would you like to read the paper?" Eisha asked, holding it out. "It is an English version."

"Yes. Thank you."

"I thought you might like to read while you eat, as Mr. Asher has no television in the house."

"Thank you, Eisha." Karissa took the paper. "That was kind of you."

A minor headline at the bottom of the page caught her eye. Man mauled by cat. She scanned the article and realized she was reading an account of the panther attack on the man who had tried to rape her. The succulent lamb caught in her throat as she continued to read. The article mentioned the name Lord Azhur, partially attributing the death to him. Who was this mysterious lord and what did he have to do with the panther?

Karissa glanced up from the paper to find Eisha carefully folding the linen dress near the bed.

"Eisha," Karissa began. "Tell me, do you know anything about a person named Lord Azhur?"

"Lord Azhur?" Eisha's hands paused for a moment but she didn't look up from her task.

"Yes. I've heard that name twice now, and here it is in the paper. Who is Lord Azhur?"

Eisha picked up the golden armband. "He is a character in our folklore."

"In your folklore? But why would someone being attacked by the man-killing panther call out the name of Lord Azhur?"

"Because Lord Azhur is said to be half-man and half-panther. And that is whom they believe is attacking them."

"That sounds far-fetched."

"Not to an Egyptian. Many of our ancient gods had the bodies of men and the heads of birds or animals. Perhaps they were half-man and half-beast as well."

"But we're not speaking of ancient gods, here, Eisha. We're talking about a panther attack in modern day."

"I know." Eisha nodded. "It has been rumored that Lord Azhur walks the earth again as he did thousands of years ago. There have been reports such as that one in the paper for many years now."

"And no one has caught the cat?"

"No." Eisha took the dress and jewelry to the door. "But no one has tried very hard to capture him, Miss Spencer, for it seems those who are killed by Lord Azhur are unsavory characters, criminals—all evil men."

Karissa chewed thoughtfully.

Eisha continued. "Lord Azhur does what our police sometimes fail to achieve."

"But isn't anyone curious to find out who or what this Lord Azhur really is?"

"He is a spirit, Miss Spencer, doomed to walk the earth for eternity. The Arabs named him when they first came across him in the desert. They soon learned to fear him. In fact there are places that no man will go after sunset in the Eastern Desert."

"Why?"

"Because Lord Azhur haunts the desert there. Some say he guards ancient tombs, and that he will kill all who venture close to the valley where the tombs are said to be."

"But he is the one who brought me here. It must have been him. A panther saved my life and led me to this house."

"A panther?"

"Yes. I followed him for miles. He was in the United States too, I'm sure of it. And he never once threatened me."

"I do not know how to explain it."

Karissa stirred her rice with her fork. She recalled the story Asheris had told her of the commander who had been cursed by the High Priestess of Sekhmet, mummified alive, and then partially redeemed by Osiris. If the panther was more than just a simple creature, he might be the same cat Asheris had mentioned in his tale. And if the cat was the wandering spirit of the man buried alive, of course he would have wanted to protect the single human being who knew about the lost sphinx. And he would have brought her to the house of the modern man who was intent on finding the sphinx as well. It all made sense. The only part that wasn't easily explained was Asheris' connection to the sphinx and his uncommon loyalty to a woman long dead.

Karissa decided not to brood upon the subject. She would ask Asheris point blank about it in the morning.

The next day she rose and padded across the tiled floor to the balcony. Just as before, she looked down to find a dead bird, this time a hoopoe bird. Karissa glanced around the sunny garden, even though she was certain she would see no sign of the cat that had left her the gift. She assumed the panther had brought the bird to her, just like the other times. Cats often gave their owners presents such as this as a symbol of love and respect. Did the panther have such feelings for her? She hoped not. She wasn't too crazy about the possibility that a man-eating cat considered her part of his "family." Karissa turned away and went back into the bedchamber.

Eisha came in a few minutes later with her clean khaki pants and cotton shirt and a promise to send someone out to buy her more suitable apparel later that morning.

Karissa took her breakfast in the garden, surrounded by the caged birds, who were all singing and chattering. The air was still and pleasantly warm, and held a shimmering promise of the blessed day to home. Karissa tipped her face to the sky and savored the moment. The mornings and evenings were her favorite times of the day in Egypt, both far different from any she had enjoyed in the States. She felt a wave of homesickness, not for Baltimore, but for her days in Luxor, when she had been a child. How she had loved it here! And how she would hate to leave.

Long after ten o'clock, Eisha came back to clear away the breakfast dishes. She chatted brightly about the garden as she put the plates on a tray, and Karissa listened, half amused. She wondered if Eisha had been longing for female company, for she was never in any hurry to break off their conversations. She didn't mind, though, because she had to wait for two hours until Asheris emerged from his chamber, and those two hours seemed days away.

Suddenly, however, Eisha cocked her head. "The doorbell," she declared. "Mr. Asher must have a visitor. Excuse me."

Karissa nodded and looked at her watch as Eisha hurried out of the room. Ten-fifteen. Who could be visiting Mr. Asher at this early hour?

She finished her coffee just as Eisha returned.

"Miss Spencer?" she said, "There's a gentleman to see you."

Chapter 7

"A MAN?" KARISSA QUESTIONED, rising to her feet. Would Mustofa have the audacity to come here? "Did he give his name?"

"He said his name was Mr. Lambert."

Josh? Karissa couldn't believe Josh had come all the way from Baltimore after having received her first message. He must have been traveling nonstop ever since, and paid a premium for tickets in the process. She was relieved that her visitor was Josh and not Mustofa, but she wasn't too pleased that Josh had dropped everything to fly to Egypt when it wasn't necessary.

"Shall I show him in?" Eisha added.

"Yes. And bring some coffee, please?" Karissa motioned toward the empty carafe. "I'm sure Mr. Lambert will be in need of refreshments."

"Certainly." Eisha hurried off and returned with a slightly disheveled, stubble-cheeked Josh.

As soon as he caught sight of Karissa, he strode forward in haste, swiping palm fronds out of his way and tripping once on the uneven tile of the old garden.

"Josh," she greeted. "What are you doing here?"

"I was worried." He grabbed both her hands and held her out in front of him. "Are you all right?"

"Yes." In fact, she was better than she had been in a long while, but decided not to mention it. She slipped her hands out of his grasp. "I'm fine."

"So what happened? Did that Mr. Asher snatch you out of the gallery?"

"No. I told you on the answering machine that a man named Mustofa kidnapped me. Mr. Asher has been very accommodating."

"But why? Why were you kidnapped?"

Karissa briefly explained about the lost sphinx and the buried tombs, carefully omitting any reference to Asheris' story about Senefret.

"So how did you get away from Mustofa?"

"Believe it or not, a black panther rescued me."

"A black panther? You mean like the one we saw in Baltimore?"

Karissa nodded. Eisha swept forward with a tray of coffee, dates, and sweet breads. Karissa introduced Josh to the housekeeper and then motioned for him to sit down.

"The locals believe the cat is part of Egyptian folklore, a half-man half-panther named Lord Azhur."

"So what was he doing in Baltimore? Vacationing?" Josh popped a date in his mouth.

Karissa glanced at him, wanting more than anything to bounce what she was feeling and what she had learned about Asheris off someone who knew her, someone she could trust. But though Josh was a longtime friend, he just wasn't the type of person she could confide in. While Karissa knew he could be endearing, she still wished he would be less like a basset hound tripping on his own droopy ears, and more like a man of thirty-two. So she sighed and decided to keep her own counsel. Besides, she should trust her own judgment.

"Everyone thinks I can remember the location of the lost sphinx," she explained, "including Lord Azhur. That's why he protected me, I assume."

"Hmmm." Josh took a long swig of coffee. "So what

are you planning to do?"

"I was planning to fly back to Baltimore, either today or tomorrow."

"Oh."

"There really wasn't any need for you to come all this way, Josh."

"I was worried about you." He reached across the table and put his hand over hers. She let her hand remain but all the while wanted to pull away. "I couldn't sleep thinking my favorite sculptress was in danger."

"I appreciate it, Josh, but I'm in no in danger. And you shouldn't have gone to so much expense on my account."

"There are times when money is no object."

He gazed at her, with a crazy smile on his lips that made him look like a lovesick puppy. Karissa slipped her hand away, wanting to ask him if money was ever the object with him, but not wishing to hurt his feelings. That would be too nasty after all the hours he had spent traveling to her side.

She was about to suggest that Josh freshen up and take a nap, when she saw his smile freeze and his gaze travel upward to somewhere above her head.

Karissa turned, just as she felt two elegant hands slip around the corners of the back of her chair. Asheris had come up behind her, and yet she hadn't heard the slightest sound of his approach. She glanced up at him, struck by his dark handsomeness and bemused by the way he stood behind her, as if laying claim to the space between her and Josh.

"I thought I heard a stranger's voice in my garden," Asheris said.

"This is my business partner, Josh Lambert," Karissa remarked, turning back to the table. "Josh, this is Mr. Asher, whom you may remember from the gallery?"

"Sure." Josh pushed to his feet, forgetting his napkin,

which fell to the ground. Flustered, he reached down, picked it up, and then offered his hand to Asheris, realizing too late that he still held the linen. Blushing and grinning, he transferred it to his other hand.

"How do you do?" Josh asked.

Asheris didn't move from his stance behind Karissa, which forced Josh to step forward and lean into the handshake. The subtle power play was not lost on Karissa. She sat back, allowing her weight to sink against Asheris' left hand. His long slender fingers pressed into her shoulder.

"Mr. Lambert." Asheris paused as if judging Josh in some way. "What brings you to my country?"

"Karissa, actually."

"Oh?" Asheris returned his right hand to the back of her chair.

"I was worried about her. I wanted to make sure she was all right."

"It is my hope that Karissa consideres herself well taken care of."

"I do," she put in. A warm flood passed over Karissa. She was being taken care of, better than anyone had cared for her in her entire life. Though she had never lacked in the physical needs department in the home of Grandmother Petrie, she had never been given understanding and compassion, both of which Asheris offered in abundance.

"Even so." Josh put his napkin on the table. "I still want to accompany you back home, Karissa, to make sure that Mustofa character doesn't threaten you again."

"Until she leaves, you are welcome to stay here as my guest, Mr. Lambert."

"Really? That would be great."

"In fact, you must be tired after your long journey. Would you care to rest for a few hours and refresh yourself?"

"As a matter of fact, I would. I'm dog tired!"

Asheris slipped his hands free and clapped them. Eisha appeared a few moments later. "Would you show Mr. Lambert to a guest room, Eisha," he said. "He will be staying with us temporarily."

"Very good, Mr. Asher." Eisha turned to Josh. "Would you follow me, sir?"

"I'll catch you later, Karissa," Josh said, taking another date from the tray. "And thanks, Asher."

Asheris nodded slightly.

Josh strode after Eisha while Asheris lowered his hands, but this time his palms came to rest on the tops of Karissa's shoulders. She thrilled to his touch. Before she could say anything, however, he lowered his head and pressed a tender kiss near her ear. Goose bumps burst on her arms and across her back.

"You are unquestionably," he said, "the loveliest creature in my garden."

She flushed with pleasure at his words. "Thank you," she murmured.

"It was nice to awaken to the sound of your voice." He brushed back her hair and kissed her neck, and she couldn't resist inclining her head to allow him room for more kisses. His lips ventured across her neck as his hands slid down the front of her cotton shirt to caress her breasts. A sigh escaped her and she tipped her head back against his shoulder as he hovered over her.

"Asheris," she gasped, almost forgetting her intention to question him about his control of her wardrobe. "You're up early, aren't you?"

"Yes. I am up," he murmured in her ear. "Very much so."

She flushed again, wishing the back of the chair was not there to separate them.

"Was I talking too loudly?" she asked, trying not to succumb to his mouth, but having little success. She was about to melt against the chair. "Did I wake you?"

"Exquisitely." He eased a warm hand into the opening of her shirt, slipped his fingers into her lacy bra, and pinched her nipple, which sent a delightful spiral of sensation right down to her womanhood. "And do I not awaken you as well?"

"Yes!" She couldn't bear the one-sided embrace for another instant. Twisting around, she stood up and rose into his arms, and he took her in a fluid motion.

Hungrily their mouths came together as her arms went around his neck. He slid his hands down her back and pulled her hips to his. In a moment she was fused into him, her breath coming fast and hard as he crushed her against his straining body. Their kisses turned into a frenzy of tongues and lips, of passionate nips and ragged sighs. Karissa wanted him so fiercely that she didn't care if they sank to the tile and made love right then and there, in broad daylight. She longed to consume him and be consumed in return, and the sharp need for him made her moan out loud.

"Karissa," he gasped. "I ache for you."

She half-opened her eyes, nearly overcome by the need to join her body and soul to his. But she could not forget the clothes and the doubt that nagged her, making her wonder about Asheris' motives. She couldn't give herself freely as long as doubt held her back.

"Is it me you ache for," she murmured, "Or another?"

He pulled away from her mouth and she felt his body tense.

She glanced up, anxious to read his expression before he could hide his initial reaction. Asheris' face was full of surprise and then wariness. His wariness was all she needed to answer her question and cool the flames of her desire.

"I do remind you of someone," she said, her voice breaking. "It isn't me you want, is it?"

"Yes it is!" He tried to pull her closer, but she pushed against his chest.

"Let me go," she demanded miserably. "Please, Asheris."

"Karissa, do not pull away from me!"

"I have to!" she stepped back and he reluctantly loosened his hold on her. "I knew by those dresses you gave me to wear that I reminded you of someone else. But I'm not playing second fiddle to anyone again. Not ever!"

"You are not playing second fiddle, Karissa. I do not know how to explain it, but there is something about you—"

"That reminds you of that priestess, right?" Karissa wrenched out of his grip. "That's why you came on to me so strong, so quickly!"

"It is much more than that. You must believe me."

"Why should I? You're just like Thomas, looking at me and wishing you were with Senefret. Maybe all men are like that. Who knows! And who gives a good God-damn!" She broke into a sob and whirled away, stumbling blindly through the garden. Men could go to hell. Thomas, Josh, and Asheris—all of them.

He loped up behind her. "Karissa, please, you must listen to reason."

"Go to hell!" she cried. "I'm leaving!"

"Do not do this. You must not leave me like this!"

"Why not?" She turned at the door. "I have better things to do with my life than serve as a stand-in for other women. How do you think that makes me feel?"

He paused, struggling for something to say to convince her to stay. The look on his face was so desperate that for a moment she almost believed he truly cared about her. Then logic and pride brought her back to her senses.

"I thank you for your hospitality," she said. "But I'm taking the first flight out of Luxor. If the blocks turn out to be the lost sphinx, you can mail me a check. I assume you have my address in your files."

Asheris sighed. "There are reasons for my conduct," he declared. "I am not able to tell you everything about my life. I only ask that you have faith in my actions and trust in what you feel for me."

"I've been fooled before, Mr. Asher, and it just isn't worth it."

"I am not trying to fool you, Karissa. What I feel for you is unbelievably real, unbelievably good. Surely you can see that."

"No. Sorry."

"Then you are lying to yourself again."

"Who has been lying to whom!" She glared at him, her emotions roiling, unable to trust her feelings or the motives of a handsome man.

"You cannot go!" Asher reached for her arm just as Josh appeared in the doorway.

"Keep your hands off her!" Josh demanded, lunging for the Egyptian. He would have knocked Asheris to the ground but for the Egyptian's finely honed reflexes. Asheris quickly stepped to the side and out of Josh's path. Josh stumbled through thin air, but didn't lose his balance. He spun around, angry and breathing hard.

"I knew there was something funny going on around here!"

"Josh!" Karissa exclaimed. She didn't want him getting involved in her personal affairs with Asheris and hated to see the Egyptian have the chance to make a fool out of him. She dashed to Josh's side and took his arm. "It's okay!"

"No it isn't okay! This asshole thinks he can push you around. And I don't like it."

"I have not make Karissa do anything against her will," Asheris put in calmly.

"I'll bet. I saw the way you just grabbed her and heard what you said. She doesn't have to stay here another minute. She can damn well leave whenever she pleases!"

"Yes." Karissa raised her chin. The best solution was to leave Asheris' house and go to a hotel downtown. From there she could make travel arrangements, leave Asheris and Egypt far behind, and get back to her own life—what she should have done long before succumbing like a little fool to Asheris' charm. "Get your bags, Josh. I'll call a cab." She turned to Asheris, "If I may be permitted the use of your phone."

"Of course." His eyes glittered at her. "You know I can refuse you nothing."

For a moment their eyes locked and held and Karissa had her first glimpse of Asheris' wrath. The warmth she was accustomed to seeing had vanished. In its place was a cloud of stormy topaz, so cold and unemotional that she shuddered at the force of it.

Without another word, Asheris brushed past her and strode into the house.

As impossible as it seemed, Karissa couldn't get a flight out of Luxor that day and was forced to make reservations for the next afternoon. She and Josh got rooms at the Blue Palace Hotel and spent the rest of the day cruising the bazaars. When the merchants took their afternoon break, Karissa retired to her room to work on her interview presentation. She didn't emerge until dinner, which she and Josh had agreed to share at the hotel restaurant at eight o'clock.

Josh was late, leaving Karissa to while away the minutes drinking a glass of wine and gazing across the glistening expanse of the Nile. She sat in the outdoor section, which was built of white stone overlooking the river. A balmy breeze drifted through her hair and ruffled the gauzy skirt she had purchased at a market stall. The evening air was a perfect temperature, the view was gorgeous, and the spicy smells of lamb and chicken coming from the kitchen were heavenly. Even though she brooded over Asheris, she still enjoyed the ambiance of the hotel.

"Sorry I'm late!" Josh declared as he strode up to the table, startling her out of her thoughts. "I had an important errand to run." He wiggled his eyebrows and opened his suit jacket, just enough to permit her a quick view of a handgun stuck in his waistband.

Karissa watched in concern as he rebuttoned the jacket. "Why did you get that?"

"I have a feeling we aren't through with your Egyptian friend yet. And the next time I confront him, I'm going to have a little firepower to back me up." Josh plopped down in his chair. "You wouldn't believe how easy it was to get the sucker. And how cheap it was!"

"I don't like guns, Josh."

"Well, neither do I. But I'll feel a whole lot safer with it." He picked up the menu. "Have you ordered?"

"No. I was waiting for you."

They ate dinner and chatted about the upcoming PBS special. Karissa couldn't help thinking about the lunch she had shared with Asheris, and how he had captivated her with his story. All Josh could do was crack jokes about flight attendants and complain about the airline food, claiming he had been served a roll that was as hard as a dog biscuit. When Josh got up to pay for dinner, Karissa wandered over to the edge of the balcony and leaned upon the warm stone, remembering the way Asheris had touched her and kissed her. She had almost been fooled into thinking he actually cared for her.

Josh wanted to check out the nightlife in Luxor, but Karissa declined, worried that she might be seen by Mustofa or Asheris. She wanted to turn in early anyway, because of the big travel day ahead of them, so she walked back to her room and got ready for bed. She slipped on the khaki shirt, making it do double duty as a nightshirt. Then she made sure the door connecting her room with Josh's was locked, tucked her room key into the pocket of the shirt, and slipped between the cool sheets.

The bed smelled of heavy cologne, pine-scented air freshener, and cigarette smoke, a far cry from the freshly laundered scent of the bed linen at Asheris' home. The two days she had spent in the luxurious environment of his home had spoiled her. She sighed and lay back, wanting to forget the man, but knowing it would take a long time before her mind would be clear of him.

Karissa drifted off to sleep and didn't awaken until close to dawn, when a strange clicking sound brought her back to consciousness. She rose to her elbows, listening for the unfamiliar noise, and then saw the dark shape of a man outlined against the open doors of her balcony. Someone had come into her room by way of the French doors.

"Josh!" Karissa yelled.

At the sound of her voice, the dark shape bolted toward her. She scrambled out of the bed, tripping on the sheets, but caught herself to keep from falling to her hands and knees.

"Josh!" she screamed.

The man grabbed for her. She glanced at his dark face beneath a mop of black hair and a huge moustache but didn't recognize him. Was he a common thief or another of Mustofa's thugs? Whoever he was, now that she had seen him, she was probably in serious trouble. For a moment she hesitated, unsure of where to go or what to do. The intruder's stocky body blocked her way to the main hallway, so she dashed to the balcony, praying that Josh had heard her.

Dressed only in the khaki shirt and her panties, she grabbed a hotel robe from the bed and she raced through the French doors. She flung a leg over the side of the baluster and looked down at the one-story drop below. She would have to jump over the side and into a garden area that bordered the outdoor pool. With luck, however, she might run into someone to help her down below. Without much thought to personal injury, Karissa sat on the rail of the baluster and pushed off, just as the intruder burst onto the balcony. She landed with a hard thump in the sandy earth below, and felt as if her knees had just jammed into her thighs.

She yanked on the robe and limped off, headed for the shadows along the side of the hotel. Behind her she heard the thud and gasp as the man with the moustache hit the ground. She had only seconds to dash around to the front of the hotel, find the lobby, and ask for help.

Just then Josh hollered from above. The man with the moustache stopped and looked up, which gave Karissa time to race down the gravel path toward the front of the hotel. Then in the dawning light, she saw the locked gate in the wall. It made sense, since the path led to the pool, that the gate would be closed and locked to prevent accidents in the water. Karissa's heart sank. The wall was too high for her to scale. And now the intruder had turned and was running toward her. She backed against the wall, trapped in a wrought iron box canyon.

Her heart leapt in her throat as the man ran up, a cruel smile on his face.

"Nowhere to run, American?" he asked.

She refused to answer him and wished she was wearing more clothing. If this man were anything like the last thug with whom she had dealt, he might attempt to assault her.

Karissa crossed the robe over her body, just as a black shape sailed through the air.

The black panther had come to her rescue again.

The cat hit the intruder dead center in the chest and knocked him to the ground. The man yelled and he struggled with the big cat. He even managed to lumber to his feet and stumble into the bushes, but the panther leapt after him.

Josh careened around the corner, brandishing his handgun. "What's going on?" he cried.

"Lord Azhur went after the intruder!" Karissa pointed in the direction of the tangled undergrowth. Josh peered into the bushes, which were still quite shadowed even though light was slowly climbing in the east. In a few minutes the sun would show above the cliffs of the Eastern Desert.

"Stop!" Josh yelled. Still the man crashed through the shrubbery, sniveling in terror at being chased by a huge cat. A blood curdling snarl rent the air and the man broke free, mere feet from Josh.

Josh reacted without thinking and squeezed off a shot.

The bullet buried itself in the man's leg and sent him toppling to the ground. Over the body of the fallen man soared the panther, paws outstretched, headed for Josh. Aghast, he staggered backward and took another shot, hitting the cat before he fell onto the sand.

"No!" Karissa screamed.

The panther plunged to the ground and collapsed in the sand, panting heavily and trying in vain to regain his footing. Karissa watched him struggle and was filled with compassion for the beautiful animal that had saved her on three occasions.

"Josh!" Karissa cried, appalled that he had hurt the panther. She ran toward the cat.

"Watch it," Josh warned. "It might be dangerous!"

"You shouldn't have shot it!" she exclaimed, sinking to her knees beside the animal. "How could you!"

"I thought it was going to get me!"

By that time, two men from the hotel came running around from the back. Karissa recognized the bellboy who had been on duty that evening and another man she had never seen, probably the night manager.

"What is going on?" the manager asked.

"I caught this guy breaking into my colleague's room," Josh explained, training his gun on the man with the moustache. "He needs to be turned over to the police."

"I will call them," the bellboy said, turning on his heel to return to the hotel.

"Bring him inside," the manager pointed at the bleeding man. Then he caught a glimpse of the dark shape in the shrubbery behind Karissa. "Is there someone else over there?" He stepped closer.

"No." Karissa shielded the panther from view. "Just my garment bag," she lied. "The thief tried to steal my things."

The manager stroked each side of his mustache with the curl of his right index finger, as if deciding whether the disturbance could be covered over easily, thereby restoring the decorum of his hotel. "Very well." Then he reached down and yanked the intruder to his feet. "Come along, you," he demanded. "You have much to explain."

Josh kept his gun trained on the intruder and guided him toward the back of the hotel, leaving Karissa to deal with the cat for the moment.

She glanced up to watch Josh disappear around the corner of the building and felt the first rays of sunlight on the back of her shirt and the calves of her bare legs.

What could she do about the panther? Call a vet? And what would the veterinarian do once he discovered his patient was none other than the mankiller, Lord Azhur. Would the vet demand that the panther be put to sleep? She couldn't take the chance. And yet who else could help dig a slug out of a panther's shoulder?

Struggling with the dilemma of what she should do, Karissa pushed back the branches of a shrub so she could take a good look at the cat, only to find that the panther had vanished. In its place was a tall slender man lying face down, his black hair tumbling over the crook of his arm, long lean legs splayed in the sand, and his shoulder bleeding profusely.

Then he moaned and turned to face her. For a moment Karissa couldn't speak, so great was her shock at seeing the familiar features of a man she recognized immediately.

Chapter 8

"Asheris!" she exclaimed.

His eyelids fluttered. Then his eyes opened and found hers. "Karissa."

"It can't be! You"— She broke off, too shocked to complete the improbable thought. "You and the panther are"—

"A tale for later," he gasped. "Please, help me."

She jerked back to reality, back to the sight of the blood on his arm and in the sand and the ashen tint to his skin. Now was not the time to ask him about the panther and what she thought had transpired a few moments ago. There was a real flesh and blood man on the ground in front of her who needed medical attention.

"Can you get up?" she asked.

"With your assistance."

She got to her feet and reached for his uninjured arm, leaning backward to pull him up. Slowly and shakily Asheris rose. As he stepped from under the shrubs and out of the shadows she realized with another shock that he was completely naked. Though Karissa was worried about his condition, she couldn't help noticing the sculpted beauty of his torso and hips, and the dark hair that feathered from his belly and spread out at his loins. He was uncircumcised. She had never seen a natural man before.

She flushed at the sight of him and stripped off the white hotel robe she was wearing. She was dressed only in her shirt and panties, but the long shirttails were sufficient covering for the time being.

"Here," she said. "Let me put this on you." She eased the robe over him, taking care not to hurt his injured shoulder. He put his right arm through the sleeve and she tied the belt around him.

"Thank you," he said.

"Come up to my room and I'll call a doctor."

He reached for her forearm. "No doctor."

"The police then."

"No police. Just you."

"But you've been shot!"

"I will be all right." He closed his eyes for an instant, as if fighting off a wave of pain.

"Come on then." She slipped her arm around his waist. "The back door must be open."

He draped his right arm over her shoulders and leaned heavily upon her, as if most of his strength had drained away with his blood. She staggered for a moment until she found a rhythm in the way they walked together, and then guided him toward the back of the hotel. She prayed they wouldn't run into Josh, because she didn't want to have to explain Asheris' presence or the possibility that the Egyptian had transformed from a panther into a man.

They slipped in the back of the hotel and headed for the elevators. From across the lobby Karissa glimpsed Josh and an officer of the law walk into a room accompanied by the manager. Relieved that Josh was occupied at least for a while, she pushed the button for the elevator. Perhaps she could get Asheris out of the hotel before Josh found out he had been there at all. She felt compelled to protect Asheris' secrets from everyone, even Josh.

Asheris was silent all the way to the room. Luckily

Karissa had put her room key in the shirt pocket the night before. She unbuttoned the flap on her pocket and pulled out the key while Asheris stood beside her, pale and quiet.

"You need a stiff drink," she remarked, pushing the door open.

"Yes."

She shut the door and led him to the bed. He sank down on the mattress.

"Lie down and I'll have a look at your shoulder," she said.

Asheris lay back, his raven hair stark against the white pillow. Karissa loosened the robe and gently drew back the left side to reveal his shoulder.

She grimaced. "I'll have to clean it before I can see anything. But I'll get you that drink first." She rose and hurried to the bar near the television where small bottles of liquor were lined up by inverted glasses. She unscrewed the lid of a bottle of Jack Daniels and poured it into the glass. Then she returned to the bed.

"Here, Asheris." She handed the drink to him. Asheris took the glass in his left hand and rose up just enough to sip the bourbon.

"Thank you," he murmured.

"I'll get some soap and water," she said, heading for the bathroom. She was glad to have something important to do, because the sight of Asheris wounded was highly disturbing.

When she returned to the bedside, she could see the liquor had already affected him. His cheeks had more color in them and his eyes were open and clear. She flipped on the lamp and sat down beside him, acutely conscious of the nearness of his body and the slightly spicy scent of his skin, as if he had dusted himself with coriander.

Carefully, she dabbed his shoulder with a wet washcloth

until the ragged edges of the wound were visible. Asheris had been shot at such close range that there were powder stains on his shoulder.

"You're lucky," Karissa observed. "It looks as if the bullet just grazed you."

"Good. Just wrap my shoulder."

Karissa made a patch with a clean folded washcloth and tied it in place with strips of a torn pillowcase.

"Good," Asheris commented when she finished.

"Now what?" she asked. "Do you want to go home?"

"Yes. And I want you to come with me."

"I told you, Asheris, I have to go back to Baltimore."

"I must show you what was found yesterday." He looked into her eyes and she felt the familiar hypnotic sensation melting away her resolve. She broke away from his gaze and stood up, determined to resist him, but his rich voice followed her. "Karissa, please come back with me."

"I'm not going anywhere with you until you explain some things first."

"Such as?"

"Such as who you really are!"

Asheris sighed and lay against the pillows she had piled in back of him. The robe fell open above the belt to reveal the taut suppleness of his abdomen. Karissa glanced away from his body and looked into his eyes.

"So?"

"So," he repeated tiredly. "Surely you must have guessed who I am."

"I think I have, but it's too outrageous to consider."

"Why?"

"Eisha told me about a legendary man who could change back and forth into an animal. But, it's just a folk tale. It isn't possible!"

"How do you know?"

"I've never seen it happen! No one has!"

"No one has seen your God, yet many believe in him."

Karissa stared at Asheris, unable to refute his reasoning. He reached out and gently drew her back down beside him. She acquiesced and sat near his hip with her hand still in his.

"Karissa, there are powers possessed by some people that would astound you, especially in the days long ago when the mind of man was more open to possibilities than it is now. In my day, man was obsessed with the unknown and the fantastic. In this day, man is obsessed by facts and data." He paused and closed his eyes for a moment, as if gathering his strength, and then continued. "Unfortunately, while looking for proof and applying human rules to the universe, man has become rigid in his thinking, and has lost more knowledge than he has gained over the centuries, believe me."

"You're saying that we are more backward now than we used to be?"

"In some respects, yes."

"And you're saying that a few thousand years ago, people knew how to change other people into animals?"

"Yes. Modern man holds himself apart from the animals, but in truth we are not that far from the beasts, you know."

"Then you are Lord Azhur."

He nodded.

"What were you doing here at the hotel?"

"I assume I was here as the panther, following Mustofa's man."

"Well, if you are Lord Azhur, you are also the man in the story you told me about, the one with the commander of the Egyptian army and the priestess Senefret."

"Yes. But you must tell no one."

She couldn't believe it. She was sitting on a bed talking with a man who had been mummified alive three thousand years ago, a man who had been searching for the woman he loved for centuries. Preposterous! Unbelievable. When she tried to pull her hand away, however, he clasped it firmly and drew it to his chest.

"I know you find my tale hard to believe, Karissa. But you must realize that I am telling you the truth."

"Why should I believe you?" she retorted. "How could you appear as a real man to me now if you'd been mummified alive?"

"I have been partially freed of my curse," he replied gently.

"How?"

"By you. When you came to the sphinx and shouted 'no,' you released me from my tomb, but not from the curse of being a panther."

"How could I do that?"

"I am not certain. I think it had something to do with the particular resonance of your voice and the single word you spoke."

"You mean I set up some sort of vibration in the sphinx?"

"Perhaps. I also believe you are somehow connected to my past, though in what capacity I am not sure."

"But if you are the panther, why couldn't you find the sphinx yourself? You saw where it was after it collapsed."

"I have no memory of the time I spend as a panther."

"You don't know what you do when you're the cat?"

"No."

"You are a killer."

"I have heard that and read accounts of it, but I have no memory of it."

Karissa stared at him, wondering what it would be

like to lead the life allotted to Asheris in which he lost every night to the ruthless nature of a big cat.

"That is why I tried to locate you for so many years, Karissa. I believe that you are the key to finding Senefret and ending this accursed life of mine."

The mention of Senefret brought back her heartache in full force. She looked down to hide the hurt in her eyes from him.

"You should have told me the truth right from the start," she remarked. It required great effort to keep her voice from cracking in anguish.

"I felt that you would not have understood. You would have been afraid of me." He kissed the tips of her fingers. "But you are not afraid of me now, are you?"

She shook her head, knowing things would be simpler he wouldn't treat her with such warmth and kindness. It broke her heart to think that he had pledged his love to someone else.

"But it wasn't fair of you to lead me on."

"Lead you on?"

"Yes." She glanced up at him, knowing her gaze was full of recrimination. "You led me to believe you cared for me when all along you saw Senefret every time you looked at me."

"That is not true."

"Then why did you give me her dresses to wear, her jewelry to put around my neck?"

"Because when I look at you, Karissa, you are everything I remember from the days I was a whole man. The modern world falls away when I am with you. I can forget the centuries of loneliness when you are in my arms. There is something about you that calls to me, deep inside in a place that has no voice—no words to explain—only feelings that cry out to be heard. Yes, you remind me of Senefret, but that is only the barest beginning of what I see in you."

"I don't believe you!" She jerked her hand away and rose to her feet. She realized she was crying. His words had moved her but she still couldn't trust him. Karissa swiped at her wet cheeks. "You are obsessed with her!"

"I search for her out of love and honor, Karissa. I must assure Senefret a proper journey to her afterlife. I could have done much more for her had I gone back to Thebes in time. I might have saved her life. But I chased after my own glory. And I soon discovered that glory was meaningless, empty, nothing!" He sighed bitterly. "I had to learn my lesson about the importance of love by losing the only woman I had ever cared for."

"And you still love her, don't you?"

"Yes, I love her—the memory of her. When you truly love someone, it is forever."

"I see." Karissa reached for her cotton pants and pulled them on, stuffing the khaki shirt in the waistband. She felt as if she would shatter into a thousand pieces of despair if he said anything else about his priestess. The sooner she got him out of the hotel and into a cab, the sooner she could get him out of her life and begin the long battle to forget him.

He stepped up behind her. "Why must you be upset?" he asked.

"I'm not upset. I'm simply in a hurry. We don't want anyone coming up here and asking questions, do we?"

"No."

"So hang on and I'll get you something to wear."

Asheris regarded her for a long moment as if he wanted to say more, but then seemed to think better of it. He reached for the bourbon. Karissa hurried to the door that connected her room with Josh's and slid back the dead bolt. She turned the knob, hoping that Josh hadn't bolted the door from his side. He hadn't. The latch clicked open and she swept into the room.

Asheris was taller and more slender than Josh, but Josh's clothes would do in a pinch. She grabbed a pair of jeans, sandals, and a shirt out of his messy suitcase and returned to the room.

"Here," she said, handing them to Asheris, "I'll tell Josh that we borrowed these."

"I do not think you understand all that I have said," he put in.

"Oh, I understand." She brushed back her hair in a brisk gesture, trying to affect a casual air. "I respect you for keeping your vows, I really do. But from now on, just leave me out of your obsessions, okay?"

He frowned slightly and then sighed, as if he had abandoned the effort to explain himself to her. Then he untied the robe. It fell to the floor before Karissa could turn around. Didn't he care that she would see him naked?

She headed for the door while he pulled on the clothes. "Hurry, Asheris. Josh is bound to return any minute." She turned to see if he were dressed.

"I am ready." He looked up.

For a moment Karissa gazed at him dressed in Josh's blue and white striped shirt tucked into a pair of blue jeans. Asheris' lean frame lent the clothes a neatly tailored look, completely different than the way Josh appeared in them. Asheris was the type of man who would look well-groomed in anything, but she knew it had more to do with the carriage of the man inside the clothing than the clothing itself.

They took the elevator to the lobby. On the way down, Asheris sank against the back of the car and closed his eyes.

"Are you all right?" Karissa asked, watching the color fade from his face.

"I feel light-headed," he replied.

"You lost a lot of blood out there in the garden," she said. "Here, put your arm around me. I'll help you keep to your feet until you get to the cab."

Asheris seemed grateful to drape his arm around her shoulders. "If I use you as a support, will not people think there is something amiss?" he asked.

"No. They'll probably think we're just crazy about each other."

"And are we not, Karissa?" he asked quietly, looking down at her with his smoldering golden eyes. "Do you not understand what it is I feel for you?"

She shook her head slowly, mesmerized by the heat in his eyes.

"You are as part of me," he said. "Your eyes speak to my heart."

Before she could say anything, he bent down to kiss her, his breath faintly laced with bourbon. His lips and his words drove a shaft deep into the very core of her and pierced through the armor she had been wearing as protection against his charm and kindness. In the face of his confession, her armor fell away, leaving her emotions more raw than ever. She reached up to touch his cheek as her heart surged in her chest and the elevator dipped to a stop. Only the sound of the elevator doors sliding open kept her from turning in his arms and revealing how she felt about him.

She was yanked back to reality by the sound of a familiar voice.

"Karissa! What in the world"—

Karissa pulled away from Asheris' mouth to see Josh standing in the lobby with a stunned look on his face. She straightened and Asheris let his arm slide away.

Josh stared at them, from one to the other, as Karissa and Asheris stepped out of the elevator.

"Karissa?" he asked, his voice cracking. "What's going

on? What's Asher doing here?"

"Mr. Asher has a discovery to show me," she said. "We're going to the desert for a couple of hours."

"But—what about our flight?"

"I don't know, Josh."

"But"— Josh moved to the side as Karissa brushed past him. "Wait a minute, he's wearing my clothes!"

"I'll bring them back, Josh."

"You'll bring them back?" Josh exclaimed. "What in the hell is going on?"

Karissa saw a few hotel patrons and the desk clerk turn their heads and look at them. "Please, Josh, keep your voice down."

"Okay, but"— Josh sputtered as he followed them toward the front door of the lobby. "But Karissa, you can't go like this. We're flying home together in a few hours. And I came all this way just for you!"

"I know, and I appreciate it, Josh, but I can't go back right now."

"What about the PBS interview?"

"I'll be there in time."

"But I thought you and I"— he broke off and glanced at Asheris and then back to her. "I always thought we— aw, the heck with it!"

He came to a complete stop at the door of the hotel, as if the truth had suddenly dawned on him. Karissa glanced at him and could hardly bear to look at the crestfallen expression on his face.

"It would be best if you went back to Baltimore," she said gently. "Really, Josh."

"Karissa is safe with me," Asheris put in kindly. "Though you cannot see it now, Mr. Lambert."

"I can't believe it, Karissa. You've always given the cold shoulder to every man you've ever met. Why not this guy? What's so darn special about him?"

"I'll explain when I get back," Karissa said, pushing open the door. "But right now we've got to run. Good-bye, Josh."

"See you in Baltimore," he replied in a resigned tone.

Relieved that Josh had accepted the situation, she followed Asheris through the doorway and out to the sidewalk where a taxi waited at the curb.

By the time they tended to Asheris' wound, ate a light meal, and drove out to the site of the sphinx, the afternoon sun was already well on its way toward the horizon and the desert was an inferno. Karissa drove the Land Rover to spare Asheris the pain of shifting, and by the time they arrived at their desert destination, his high coloring had returned and he appeared to have more energy. Karissa was relieved that he was recovering so swiftly from his loss of blood. By the time they reached the rock formation, he claimed to feel much better, except for the soreness in his shoulder.

They got out of the truck and Asheris led her to the site where laborers had cleared away an impressive amount of sand to reveal a jumble of pink granite blocks. In the pile was a dark hole as tall as a man. Karissa shaded her eyes and peered in the direction of the opening.

"A passageway," Asheris remarked. "Come, I will show you."

They hurried toward the twenty or so men who were streaming in and out of the passage carrying buckets of sand and dumping them a few yards away. A single man in long flowing robes and turban stood near the entry with a rifle cradled in his arms. When he caught sight of Asheris, he strode up to them.

"Mr. Asher," he greeted with a huge grin and then flashed an interested glance at Karissa. "We have found something!"

"What, Jamal?"

"A sealed room! We have been waiting for hours for you to come and see!"

"I was detained." Asheris took Karissa's elbow. "Let us have a look."

"We cannot show you now."

"Why not?"

"It is too late." Jamal glanced around fearfully. "You know that the men will not stay here after sundown because of Lord Azhur."

"I told you not to worry about Lord Azhur. He is only a character in a legend."

"The men will not agree to stay. No matter what you pay them, it will not be done."

Karissa glanced at Asheris, wondering what he would do. Already the men had stopped working and were piling their tools in a rusting, battered old lorry while others climbed in the back.

He squeezed Karissa's elbow. "We'll find the room ourselves. Is there a lantern in the sphinx?"

"Assuredly. Five of them, sir. Keep to the corridor and go to the right. You will find the sealed room. No problem."

"Thank you." Asheris frowned. "Has there been any trouble with Mustofa or his men?"

"No, Mr. Asher. They do not see us working on this side of the dune. We are discreet, as you have instructed."

"Good. Then I will see you tomorrow."

"Tomorrow then, sir, at dawn as you wish." Jamal gave a quick bow and then hurried toward the truck, which was already idling. The men motioned for Jamal to hurry.

"Come," Asheris said. "Let's see what we can find."

Karissa surveyed the jumble of blocks, remembering in vivid detail the way the sphinx had collapsed upon itself many years ago. "Is it safe?"

"Once we get in the corridor, we will be out of

danger. The temple was solidly built. Only the booby-traps collapsed. You will see."

Asheris led her forward.

By the time they turned right into the long corridor, Asheris' heart was thudding in his chest, not from the effort of walking, but from anticipation. After centuries of separation and grief, he might be meters away from Senefret. He held the lantern aloft and grimaced from the pain that shot through his left shoulder.

"There's the sealed doorway," he said, almost in a whisper.

Karissa clutched his upper arm and drew close to him. Even though he realized she was frightened, he loved the way she clung to him in the dark, as if she depended upon him to keep her safe. He would give his life to protect her and wished she would believe his feelings for her were genuine.

"What do the seals say?" she asked, releasing his arm to reach out and touch the ancient plaster of the arid subterranean chamber. The walls were preserved so well they still looked freshly-painted.

Asheris stepped forward and craned his neck to see the hieroglyphs stamped in the plaster. His heart skipped a beat as he glimpsed the familiar group of pictures surrounded by an oval line that made up the cartouche, or symbol, of Senefret's name.

"It is her name. She is here!" he said. The raspy sound of his voice echoed in the darkness. "This is Senefret's tomb!"

Karissa squeezed his arm, happy to share his excitement.

Then Asheris noticed the way the plaster was roughly applied and the crooked placement of some of the seals. He bent down and inspected the wall.

"What's the matter?" Karissa asked, noticing his disquiet.

"This door has been sealed twice, Karissa. Someone entered the tomb after the burial and sealed it up again." He touched a crooked seal. "The second seal was done in haste."

"Do you think grave robbers might have plundered the tomb already?"

"Thieves would not take the time to reseal the chamber." He put the lantern on the dusty floor. "Give me the crowbar and I will get started."

Feverishly, he chipped away each seal until a rectangular line showed the entrance to the tomb. All the while he worked he wondered why someone had gone into the tomb after the burial. What would he find? Most of all he worried that someone might have burned Senefret's mummified body, thus eliminating the possibility of an afterlife for her. He couldn't bear the thought.

Like a madman he hacked away at the blocks, pulverizing the old plaster and limestone. He had to know. He had to find her. With every stroke he prayed to the gods that he would discover Senefret's mummy unmolested. He didn't care about the treasures with which she might have been buried. His only concern was to find her body.

After what seemed like hours, he loosened a block enough to push it into the chamber. The air of the room drifted past them, still fragrant with myrrh and cedar. Karissa stood near him, holding the lantern up to help him see his progress. Shortly afterward he knocked another block free. After that there was a quick succession of loose blocks, which afforded a opening big enough to crawl through on hands and knees. He dropped to all fours. His shoulder burned and throbbed from the exertion, but he refused to give in to the pain.

"Come!" he exclaimed, too excited to remember

proper English. "The lantern to me, please!"

Karissa relinquished the light and crawled after him into the chamber.

Once in the chamber, Asheris rose to his feet and grabbed her elbow to help her stand. They both took in the sight of the tomb as they stood hand in hand in a pool of light.

In the center of the small room stood a stone sarcophagus covered with hieroglyphics, on the top of which was a small cedar box. Asheris stared at the sarcophagus, stuck dumb with emotion. Here lay the once love of his life. All that remained of her.

He had known death on the battlefield. He had known the death of his own parents from fever. But none of those passings had affected him as much as the sight of Senefret's grave.

"Where are all her things?" Karissa asked. "Her furniture, her belongings?"

Asheris blinked away his grief and looked around at the bare floor, strewn with dried flower blossoms and wreaths.

"She died in disgrace. Perhaps the priestesses forbid her to be buried with anything that might help her in the afterlife."

"Could grave robbers have taken everything?"

Asheris considered the question and then shook his head. "No. See? The flowers have remained undisturbed except for that single path from the sarcophagus to the door. As you can see, no one has walked anywhere else in the chamber."

"So what's in the little box?"

"We shall see," Asheris replied, stepping toward the sarcophagus. "And then we will find out if Senefret is here with us."

He picked up the cedar box just as running footsteps

echoed in the corridor outside. Karissa grabbed his arm in alarm. Asheris reached for the crowbar and thrust the box into her hand just as a gun and a man's arm appeared in the opening of the tomb.

Chapter 9

"I WILL KILL WHOEVER MOVES FIRST," barked a voice in the darkness. Hoping no one could see her, Karissa slipped the cedar box into her shirt. Asheris held the crowbar in the air, ready to strike, although they both knew that it would be little defense against a gun.

The armed man motioned for someone to crawl into the chamber. Two other men scuttled forward on hands and knees. Asheris made a move to accost them, but the man with the gun shouted, "I will shoot Miss Spencer if you so much as strike one of my men."

Karissa recognized the voice of Mustofa.

With an exasperated sigh, Asheris stepped back to protect Karissa, while Mustofa crawled into the chamber and got to his feet. The lantern threw shadows on his gaunt face, accentuating the hollows of his cheeks and his cold deep-set eyes. He smiled.

"This tomb seems rather barren," Mustofa continued, sweeping the air with his hand. "But I am sure there are others, are there not?"

"The others should not be disturbed, Mustofa," Asheris warned. "There is a reason this place is called the Valley of the Damned."

"A ruse, surely," Mustofa sneered. "To deter those of us who seek the treasure buried here."

"It is no ruse."

"Then what are you doing here?"

"It is a matter which involves personal honor, something I do not expect you to understand."

Mustofa narrowed his eyes. For a moment he studied Asheris and then his regard landed on Karissa. She kept her expression as blank as possible, all the while praying he wouldn't notice the box in her shirt. His sneer pulled his mouth to one side.

"Tie them up, Rashad," he ordered. "Ali, get the lid off this coffin."

A short squat man strode forward, slipping a coil of rope off his shoulder.

"No tricks, Asher," warned Mustofa. "Or Miss Spencer will be punished. Do you understand?"

"I understand."

"Then put down the crowbar," Mustofa said.

Asheris dropped the tool. The sound of metal stiking stone enchoed through the old temple. Rashad kicked the tool across the room, well out of range. Then Rashad stepped behind them and ruthlessly pulled Karissa's arms behind her. The cedar box dug into the tender flesh of her belly but she made no sound. He lashed the rough rope around her wrists and pushed her down on the floor where he tied her ankles as well. He did the same to Asheris.

Meanwhile Mustofa and Ali had managed to slide away the heavy stone lid of the outer sarcophagus and lean it against the wall. Mustofa stepped closer to see inside of the coffin. He picked up the lantern and held it near his head.

Karissa watched him, knowing from her father's lessons that Mustofa was probably looking at a wooden sarcophagus. Many nobles and kings were buried within three sarcophagi—stone, wood and lastly solid gold. She found herself holding her breath as the other men gaped at the contents of the coffin.

"Let us get the other lid off and we will see if this is worth our trouble." Mustofa held the lantern high as his man pried off the wooden lid of the second coffin. Once he got it loose, he heaved it over the side as if it had no value, even though it was covered with intricate paintings and inlaid with semiprecious stones. She knew what they were interested in—the gold layer.

She glanced at Mustofa as he looked upon the treasure of the inner sarcophagus and his eyes lit up with delight and greed.

"Ah, look at that beauty!" he exclaimed. "We are rich!"

Karissa exchanged a look of frustration with Asheris. He yanked at the ropes that bound him, but couldn't pull free.

Mustofa looked down at him. "You might as well accept your fate, Mr. Asher. You are not going anywhere. I cannot allow you to get in my way, not when a fortune is to be found here."

"Do not disturb the evil ones buried here, Mustofa!" Asheris warned. "You will unleash those better left entombed."

"Superstition and lies, Asher. I do not believe you for a moment! You want it all for your precious museums!"

Asheris scowled and glared at the flower-strewn floor of the tomb. There was no use arguing with a greedy man like Mustofa.

"Rashad," Mustofa ordered. "You will remain outside the tomb to make sure Mr. Asher and Miss Spencer stay where they are. Ali, you come with me. We must go back to Luxor for crates and weapons before Asher's men return in the morning."

"We will be back at dawn, Asher," Mustofa commented, stuffing his pistol in his belt. "Sleep well."

Then with a dry laugh, Mustofa took the lantern and

left them tied up in complete darkness. The gloom was so intense that Karissa couldn't see her feet in front of her. A sheen of sweat broke out on the surface of her skin. She was deep in the earth near the ruins of the haunted sphinx, very close to the place her own father had been crushed beneath a stone. How could she survive the coming hours without going crazy with fear? Would she perish in the same place as her father, but with no one knowing what had happened to her?

"Asheris?" she called through the blackness. Her voice quavered. She scooted closer to him but stopped in alarm when she heard the low growl of a panther.

"Asheris?" she called again. Had he transformed in the darkness and freed himself of the rope? She couldn't see a thing!

She heard a low growl vibrate the darkness.

Then something soft and velvety brushed her cheek. His tail? Karissa held herself stiff, wondering what the panther would do to her. She felt a warm shoulder rub gently against hers and then the cat stretched out along the side of her leg. In the stillness of the tomb, she heard the quiet thrum of his purr and felt the rise and fall of his powerful rib cage against her knee. For a long while she held her breath, not daring to move, until she realized the panther was simply standing guard over her. Gradually her tense muscles relaxed and she resigned herself to spending the night in the bowels of the earth with her strange otherworldly companion.

Hours later she awakened to the sound of a man's terrified scream. Karissa jerked to attention, unable to tell what time of day it was or what was happening. All was still completely black and she knew only that the cat was no longer lying beside her. Desperately she peered into the blackness, trying to make out something—anything—in the gloom. She heard a slow dragging sound go past the doorway of the tomb. And then all was quiet again. She struggled against her bonds to sit up, grimacing in pain at the cramps in her hips and shoulders, and waited in the oppressive silence for Lord Azhur to return.

After what seemed like hours, she saw a light pass by the tomb entrance and then the light came through the opening in the bricks. Karissa watched anxiously, and was relieved to see Asheris duck into the chamber. He glanced at her and slid the lantern toward her.

"Are you all right?" he asked.

"Yes." She tried to focus on his face, because he was completely naked again and it was a shock to see him unclothed. "What about the guard, Rashad?"

"He's dead."

She didn't ask anything more about Rashad's death. She didn't want to know.

Asheris stepped behind her and knelt down to untie her bonds. When he was finished, he pressed a quick kiss just below her left ear. "We must hurry," he said. "Dawn has come and Mustofa and his men will be back any moment."

Karissa slowly got up and rolled her shoulders as Asheris slipped into his clothes. She minced over on stiff legs to the sarcophagus and looked into the stone coffin. Inside was the golden inner coffin, still as luminous as the day Senefret had been interred. The funerary mask showed a lovely face with large eyes and a sensitive mouth. If the mask bore a likeness to the young priestess, she must have been very beautiful. No wonder Asheris had fallen in love with her.

Asheris came up behind her. "Help me lift the lid," he said, striding to the foot of the coffin.

Karissa reached down and felt with her fingertips for the lip of the cover. After a few minutes of prying and swearing, they managed to free the top. Though the cover was a thin shell, it was astoundingly heavy, having been fashioned from pure gold.

"It's too heavy!" Karissa gasped.

"Slide it your way then," Asheris said, straining with the effort of supporting most of the weight. Karissa staggered back a few steps, just enough to tilt the golden lid against the edge of the thick wall of the outer stone sarcophagus.

"Good," Asheris panted, carefully lowering his end. "I can reach inside. That is all that matters."

He stooped and grabbed the lantern, bending closer for a better look. Karissa moved to his elbow and peered in. She could see a linen-wrapped figure. A sweet musky smell rose up from the mummy. Dried flowers littered the body and the inside of the coffin.

For a moment Asheris stood there, simply staring down at the mummy, as if caught in his dreams. Gently Karissa touched his elbow.

"Is it Senefret?" she asked.

"It is her face on the coffin."

"She was very beautiful."

"Yes." He turned and held out the lantern. "Take the lantern and turn the wooden lid flat on the floor. We will use it to carry Senefret out of her tomb."

Karissa hurried to do his bidding and didn't question his directions, for she knew it would be impossible for them to drag the golden coffin out of the chamber, no matter how precious it was to Senefret's afterlife.

Reverently, Asheris lifted the mummy out of the half open coffin and carried it to the wooden lid. Gently he deposited the wrapped bundle onto the lid and then looked up.

"We will slide the lid out to the hallway. Then we can pick it up. It should not be too heavy."

"Okay." Karissa wiped her palms on her cotton pants.

The notion of walking around in the dark with a dead person's body made her break into a sweat all over again. "What will we do if Mustofa comes before we get out of the sphinx?"

"We will try to find a place of concealment along the way. Give the lantern to me and I will hang it on my arm."

She held the light out to him and then squatted down to push the lid along the floor. The small cedar box scraped against her ribs. In all the excitement, she had forgotten about it. Still, it would have to wait until they were out of danger.

The scraping sound of wood against limestone echoed through the corridor and made Karissa even more nervous. She was certain that someone or something would hear the racket. Hours seemed to pass before they hoisted the lid into the air and carried it down the darkened hall. Karissa took up the rear because it was easier walking forward than the way Asheris was walking backward. The only drawback to the rear position was the feeling that her back was vulnerable to the unholy inhabitants of the Valley of the Damned. Her heart thudded in her chest, making her light-headed and short of breath, and she kept her eyes and thoughts focused on the faint patch of light she could barely discern in the distance.

Just as they passed through the jumbled blocks of the demolished sphinx, Asheris lurched to a stop.

"What?" Karissa whispered.

"I heard an engine," he replied. "Someone is coming!"

Asheris glanced around quickly to locate a place to hide. Then he propped the edge of the coffin lid on one knee and used his right hand to turn off the lantern. She felt a tug on the wood as he guided her around a pile of blocks and into a closet-sized opening. Karissa scraped her shoulder on a piece of granite but stifled the cry that formed in her throat.

They watched in heart-stopping dread as Mustofa and his men tramped through the ruins carrying shovels, picks, and crates, ready to plunder as much as they could before Asher's crew arrived for the day. Then they'd most likely kill Jamal and his men or run them off. As soon as the others had turned the corner toward Senefret's tomb, Asheris moved out of the little hiding spot and pulled her toward the opening in the sphinx. They practically trotted, and Karissa worried with every step that the mummy would bounce off its unseemly bier.

The cold light of morning nearly blinded her. Her eyes watered and she sneezed as they stumbled onto the sand. Walking up the slope of the dune became a strenuous exercise as the sand gave way with each step they took. Karissa glanced over her shoulder, praying that Mustofa's men would not come after them. She couldn't remember feeling as desperate in her entire life.

Just as they reached the Land Rover, Karissa heard a metallic click deep in the earth, and then a resounding thud. Even from a distance the noise was quite loud. Memories from the past came rushing back in a hot flood as she heard the horrible and far-too-familiar sound of a giant block of stone sliding down a track.

She whipped around to say something, but Asheris held up his hand to stop her, his head cocked as he listened intently.

Then from deep inside the sphinx came a sound like the collision of two locomotives. Blocks of granite rolled out of the sand and bounced down to the bottom of the dune. The entrance to the sphinx disappeared in a shower of granite and sand. Someone screamed and the cry pierced through the thunder of the cave-in and then was gone. As if to answer the dead man, a sharp wind came whistling across the dune, blasting sand into Karissa's face, and blinding her to the murderous landscape below. She hunched away from the biting wind. "The sphinx is falling apart!" she cried.

"We must hurry! The whole area might give way."

Asheris threw open the back doors of the Land Rover and motioned for her to jump in. Then he hoisted the lid and the mummy into the back of the vehicle, slammed the doors, and ran around to the driver's side. Karissa knelt in the cargo hold to secure the mummy and then pulled the cedar box out of her shirt and put it on the floor beside Senefret's body. When she was sure the mummy wouldn't budge, she climbed over the back seat to the front just as Asheris pulled away from the rock formation and headed for the road.

Karissa fell into the passenger seat and looked back to see the dune sliding into a huge pit. Blocks of granite rolled into the pit, bouncing end over end as if sucked into a whirlpool of sand. Soon the wind became so fierce and full of sand that she couldn't see beyond the rock formation.

Pale and stricken, she turned to Asheris. "What do you think happened?" she asked, brushing the gritty hair out of her eyes.

"Mustofa must have tried carrying the golden sarcophagus out of the tomb. And his greed outweighed his caution."

"He set off a booby-trap."

"Very likely."

"Why didn't we set it off?"

"Some traps are fashioned to spring when a certain weight passes across a portion of the floor. We took nothing but the body of a woman—feather light after her long sleep."

"Do you think they're all dead?"

"Yes."

Karissa regarded Asheris' sharp profile and the sad turn to his sensual mouth. He had found his long-lost love and was about to give her over to the afterlife. He had nearly completed his task. So why wasn't he relieved that his work was almost done? He seemed more troubled than ever.

"What's wrong, Asheris?" she asked.

He reached over and placed his hand on her thigh. "I must think for a while, my sweet." Then he slid his hand away and glanced at her, but the usual warmth in his eyes was gone. In its place was a weariness and concern she had never seen before. She longed to ease his trouble, but realized she might help him most by honoring his request for silence. She sat back and closed her eyes, bone weary herself.

Six hours later, Karissa stood in a private guest cabin aboard the freighter Victoria, in quarters Asheris had booked for a trip down the Nile. Outside a windstorm raged, as if the gale had followed Senefret's body from the tomb to the river.

Karissa rubbed her arms and thought about Asheris while the ship rocked beneath her. He had gone below to make sure Senefret's crate was stowed securely. He was due back any moment. She wondered what she should say to Asheris in regard to her feelings for him. She couldn't imagine going back to Baltimore without telling him how much she cared for him. And yet if she did disclose her feelings, what good could come of it? She and Asheris were soon to return to their usual lives. Revealing her feelings would only complicate a smooth re-entry. And yet she longed for him to open his soul to her as he had once compelled her to open to him.

Asheris had spent the morning procuring a coffin and

a crate for the transport of Senefret's body, and making arrangements for this ship to take them down the Nile to a suitable burial site with which he was acquainted. He had convinced Karissa that it would be safer for her to accompany him and then be escorted to the airport the next day. Mustofa might have miraculously survived the cave-in and decided to come after them to keep them quiet about the treasure trove in the Valley of the Damned.

Karissa had agreed to his plan. If she flew out by tomorrow, she could still make the PBS interview, although once she got to Baltimore, she would hardly have time to take a breath before the film crew arrived at her studio. But she knew she didn't want to leave Asheris until the last moment. She might never see him again and every minute between now and tomorrow morning would be precious, even though Asheris had lapsed into a contemplative mood that shut her out and worried her.

She heard the key in the lock and slowly turned to face him.

He came in, glanced at her and smiled, and then carefully shut the door.

"Is everything all right?" she asked.

"Yes." He ran both hands through his hair. "Now we can relax for a few hours."

He let his arms fall to his sides and walked to the couch where he sank down and stretched his arms along the back of the cushions. He was dressed in tan cotton pants and a tan and white striped shirt with the sleeves folded up on his forearms. Yet when she looked at him, all she could see was his naked torso and the light dusting of black hair on his chest. She blinked away the vision and turned her gaze to his face. He was studying her.

"How is your shoulder?" she asked.

"It will heal in time."

"Time." She sighed and sat in a chair next to the

couch. "Everything has to do with time, doesn't it? I feel like a slave to it, especially now."

"I have been thinking about time all day," he said, "and how fickle it can be."

"And why is that?"

"Because of you."

She flushed with the pleasure at hearing him echo her own thoughts. "Because my time in Egypt is almost gone?"

"It is more complicated than that."

Karissa looked down at her hands. Why did she think he was going to talk about Senefret again? If he mentioned her once more, she'd have to leave the room because she wouldn't be able to hold back her tears. She longed to be the woman foremost in his heart and mind—in fact, the only woman in his life. And when he spoke of loving Senefret, he unknowingly caused her pain.

Then she felt him reach out for her hand. Asheris's rich voice rumbled softly. "In all the years I spent searching for a lost part of my life, I felt adrift. I believed I felt adrift because I was separated from Senefret."

That damned Senefret.

Karissa felt a lump forming in her throat and tried to pull away, but he wouldn't release her. She jumped to her feet.

"Let me go," she said, pulling her hand from his. "I can't bear to talk of Senefret!"

"Wait, Karissa." He stood up and took her shoulders. "You must hear me out this one last time."

She swallowed her anguish and stood there, loving the weight of his hands on her shoulders. He looked down and his dark lashes swept his cheeks. "You are not aware of all the feelings I possess. Senefret is with me now, on her way to her rightful resting place. I should spend the day praying for her reunited soul, her akh. And yet," He paused and raised his glance to look at her. "At the same time, the hours with you, Karissa, are quickly coming to an end."

Was he saying that he might choose a real woman over an ancient memory wrapped in gauze?

"I have been struggling with this for days," he added. "My head keeps reminding me of my duty to Senefret, but my heart is telling me to consider something entirely different."

"And what is that?" she asked, praying he would say the words she longed to hear, that he loved her and that she was more important to him than anything or anyone. "What is your heart saying?"

"That I should spend these hours with you."

She touched his cheek. "What would be so wrong with that?"

"It would show disrespect for Senefret. And unfairness to you. I do not even know where my own heart lies, Karissa, and yet I wish for you to give yourself to me."

"And if I give myself freely? No strings attached?"

"Still it would be unfair. I am not a whole man, Karissa, neither in heart nor in body, as you well know. I can offer only a part of myself."

"Then I will accept whatever you give me," she replied.

The pressure of his hands increased. "How can that be enough for you?"

"Because you will be more special to me than any other man."

"How can you be sure?"

"Because"— She stroked his temple and pushed her fingertips into his lustrous black hair. —"because I love you, Asheris." The words she thought would be difficult to say came out with surprising ease and warmth born of the truth in her heart. "Even if you don't love me in return, it still won't change the way I feel. I have fallen in love with you, and I can't deny it."

He stared at her, a strange light in his eyes, as if her words had paralyzed him. Then she raised up on tiptoe and pressed her lips against his. The instant their mouths met, she felt a melting sensation, a surrender in her body as well as in his. With a low moan, Asheris' hands slid down to her elbows as he bent to the kiss, and her hands slid up the front of his shirt and around his neck. The fragrance of his shampoo, his clean shirt, and his faint scent of coriander filled her senses as his tongue slipped into her mouth. She closed her eyes tightly, embracing him with all her heart as his hands moved up and down her back and into her hair. For a long lingering moment the only sound in the cabin was the rush of their breathing and the brush of his palms on her blouse.

How could his heart not be in his caress, his kiss? No one could be as passionate as Asheris without possessing deep feelings to fire his embraces. He simply couldn't recognize that he loved her just as fiercely.

"Asheris," she whispered, her skin tingling as he kissed her neck. Her body was crying out for his touch and for the feel of his naked skin against hers. She reached for the buttons of his crisp shirt.

"If we start this, I will not wish to stop," he said, his voice husky. "It is not my desire to hold back."

"No one is asking you to hold back."

She looked into his face and saw Asheris' mouth slanting upward in his dazzling slow smile.

Chapter 10

KARISSA PULLED HIS SHIRT OUT OF HIS PANTS and caressed his torso as a faint growl rolled up his throat. She slipped the shirt off his shoulders and down his arms. It fell on the floor behind him. Then she pressed a kiss in the center of his chest and hugged him, filling her soul with the glory of his warm skin against her cheek and the pounding of his heart in her ear. This was what she wanted more than anything in the world—to make love with Asheris, to hold him in her arms, to cherish him.

He eased her back, unbuttoned her blouse, and drew if off. He kissed her and unhooked the fastener of her bra. This, too, he peeled off to release her breasts. She looked up to see his face was flushed.

"You are beautiful," he whispered in awe, and he kissed her between her breasts, just as she had done to him.

Her nipples hardened with desire. She closed her eyes and sighed with pleasure as his golden hands swept down from her shoulders and the pads of his hands passed over the firm peaks of her breasts.

"Asheris!" she gasped.

As if to torment her, he captured her left breast in his hand and surrounded her right nipple with his mouth. He laved her, lightly at first, until she plunged her hands into his hair to draw him closer. She wanted him to consume her breast, to take her into him as she wanted to take him into her body. Soon he was pulling on her nipple, half sucking and half biting, and she arched back to allow him more room, while short cries of pleasure burst from her lips.

Then Asheris tipped her into his arms, sweeping her feet off the ground. As he carried her to the bedroom, she clung to him and rolled her head onto his hot bare chest, highly aware of the way her hips brushed across the front of his trousers with every step he took.

He laid her down on the coverlet and she sank back against the pillows. Asheris stood there gazing at her as he unbuckled his belt. She returned his regard and reached for the button on her waistband, but he stopped her so he could be the one to unfasten it. Then he unzipped her pants and slowly dragged them off. Next came her underclothes and she was naked.

With a few quick movements, he stripped. His manhood jutted out, swollen and huge and she felt a powerful stirring inside at the sight of him. When he knelt on the bed and straddled her, she reached out and stroked him, anxious to touch his hardened silken flesh.

"Ah!" he said, gritting his teeth.

"You are beautiful, too," she gasped, cupping the rest of his sensitive flesh.

"You are the beautiful one," he declared, kissing her. He lowered his torso until his chest grazed her nipples and his shaft brushed her belly. He moved upward slightly, just enough to create an erotic friction between them. She moaned in his mouth.

He eased her legs open and moved in between them, never once freeing her mouth. Her hands swept over his back and down his arms as she arched upward. With each brush of his body, she felt a throb of aching need blossoming deep within her. Nothing had prepared her for the hunger she felt for this man. When she rose up, he moved his hips forward, and his shaft came up against her. They both let out a ragged sigh.

Then as if they were molded to fit perfectly together, he found her entrance in a single stroke. Karissa gasped in ecstasy as he eased into her. She clasped the backs of his arms and sank into the coverlet, surrendering to him. He pushed farther inside her, filling her with his hard bluntness, and she smiled with joy at the sensation of taking him in. She had never wanted a man more, never wanted to be filled like this, never felt such profound rightness in lying beneath a man and accepting him. And she had never ever had this urge to grin.

Asheris kissed her smile. "You like this, yes?" he asked.

"Oh, yes!"

"It is beyond imagining."

"Yes!" She ran her hands down his back as he plunged deeper and deeper inside her until he pulled back with exquisite control.

"Please, Asheris," she whispered. "Don't stop."

"You want all of me, then?"

She knew exactly what he meant. He wanted to pour himself into her but didn't know if she would accept him. The truth was, she longed for his seed to flood into her. It was a startling realization and due to the glorious knowledge that she loved Asheris as she had never loved anyone.

Karissa took his face in her hands and looked him in the eyes. "Yes, I want you," she said, "all of you."

Her words sent him into a frenzy. He plunged into her, rocking her until her breasts were bouncing between them and his skin was wet with sweat, and she was grabbing his buttocks and writhing beneath him, chanting his name over and over again, and then his seed was bursting out in a glorious rush, filling her, and she was wrapped around his body and wrapped around his manhood, squeezing him until he was spent and trembling and collapsing upon her. She lay there rigid beneath him, grabbing the bedspread on either side as her body was racked by wave after wave of orgasm, pressing down on him, pushing him out.

Almost as soon as she sank back, breathless and shuddering, Asheris felt himself growing hard again. He had never recovered so quickly with a woman in his life. Giving her a few moments to catch her breath, Asheris kissed her breasts, her neck, and then her parted lips. Her eyes opened halfway as she regarded him with a sultry, sated expression that sent shafts of joy through him and made him surge anew inside her.

Her eyes fluttered open. For a long moment she gazed deeply into his eyes, a half-smile on her lips. He could feel a similar smile on his own.

"And how would you do this if you were a panther?" she asked, raising one eyebrow as if teasing him. Her question inflamed him, for he lately he had fantasized about that very thing.

He paused for a moment, weighing the possibility that he might alarm her with the truth. But somehow he knew that Karissa would not be afraid of anything he did with her. He slipped out of her and grabbed her wrists.

He saw the look of surprise in her eyes as he twisted her onto her stomach. With a few more nudges, he urged her onto her knees and elbows. Then he took her, his chest riding her back, his hands clutching her breasts, his body slamming against her sweet pale rump, his every thrust rocking her forward. She sank her forehead into the pillow and grabbed the edges of the pillowcase. He could see her knuckles growing white as he found his rhythm. This time he seemed to last forever, even through her cries of release.

Then what began as a climax for him transformed into a state of oblivion, into a timeless coming, of a shattering shimmering joining that went on and on and on. He heard his own voice uttering a growling noise and then he closed his teeth upon the flesh at the base of her beautiful neck as he let himself go inside her in a flood. He emptied himself completely, exquisitely, and utterly.

For a moment they hung there together unmoving, as if neither of them could believe what had just passed between them. Then Asheris let out a long sigh and raised his head. Slowly Karissa melted onto the coverlet and he melted with her, both of them slick with sweat and his seed. He kissed her hot cheek, stroked her outstretched arms, and then eased his body away. She moved her arm to allow him room and Asheris lay down beside her, his leg across her calves, while both of them struggled to catch their breath.

As the wind rocked the ship, Asheris relaxed and spread his hand across her flank. He liked the way his hand looked on her, possessing her like that. His manhood had burst twice inside her, and the experience had been phenomenal. But as he lay there, he felt his heart bursting with love for her, and the feeling was indescribable. He loved this woman. He loved her beyond anything he had ever known. And he longed to reveal his feelings. But how fair would it be if he declared his love knowing full well that he might never be able to give his heart completely.

He hadn't known until this moment that he could not settle for less. He wanted everything with Karissa. Giving parts of himself would never be enough, not for him and not for her. It would have to be all or nothing, even if it meant never making love with her again. Anything less would be too frustrating, too painful.

Desperate with anguish and despair, he gathered

Karissa into his arms and embraced her tightly. Unknowingly the priestesses of Sekhmet had reached across centuries to damn him again, for their curse was ruining his chance for love once more. What had he done to deserve such unhappiness? How could he bear it?

Suddenly the ship lurched so hard that they were flung off the bed. Asheris scrambled to his feet and reached for Karissa. He pulled her to her feet.

"What happened?" she cried.

"Perhaps we hit something." Asheris released her and stepped to the porthole between the bed and the door to the bathroom. He looked out at the whitecaps in the river, whipped up by the severe wind. "I believe we have run aground."

She scampered up behind him and wrapped her arms around his torso. Before he could reach up to touch her, he heard the captain of the vessel make an announcement over the intercom.

"All passengers and crew, report immediately to the upper deck. I repeat, report immediately to the upper deck."

Then the announcement was repeated in a variety of other languages.

The ship gave out a loud metallic yawn and listed again, and this time remained at an angle so severe that Asheris found it hard to keep his footing. He clutched Karissa's arm to keep her from falling. Her eyes were wide with fright.

"Asheris!" she cried. "Is the ship sinking?"

"It is probably just taking on water. Hurry and dress," he said, briefly kissing her on the lips. "You've got to get up to the lifeboats."

"What about you?" she asked, reaching for her underwear.

"I must go below and retrieve the crate."

"No, Asheris!" She grabbed at him, but he slipped past her and snatched up his pile of clothing.

"It's too dangerous," she cried. "You could be killed!"

"I must go. Hurry, now, Karissa!"

He yanked on his pants and left her calling at him to come back.

Asheris retraced his steps of a few hours ago, only this time the path was made much more difficult by the listing ship. By the time he reached the lower deck, he had to wade through shin deep water in places. That meant the hold was probably submerged. He pulled open the door that led to the companionway into the hold. Fortunately the door was on the high side of the listing ship, which allowed him a view of the watery expanse of the hold. Most of the freight the ship carried was too heavy to float. But a few barrels and crates bobbed on the surface in the dark. Asheris narrowed his eyes, searching in the gloom for one particular wooden box. He spotted it about fifteen meters away, near a cluster of barrels.

Without a second thought, Asheris ran down the stairs and plunged into the cold water, praying the ship wouldn't roll before he could get to the crate. He feared being entombed in the watery depths of the Nile and wondered vaguely what would happen to the spirit panther should it be trapped underwater as well.

A few minutes later he grabbed the rope handle of Senefret's crate and turned to tow it back to the stairs. The ship screamed again, louder this time, as iron and steel twisted under the weight of the huge vessel. The hold tilted and the water covered up the last of the small portholes near the ceiling. Asheris pushed himself to swim harder, faster, but the weight of the wooden box dragged behind him. He thought of Karissa and pressed on.

At last he felt the railing of the stairs and pulled himself up toward the angled door. He found the submerged stairs and used them for leverage as he hoisted the crate up the flooded companionway. The doorway proved a tight fit for the crate, but he managed to wedge it through. He slid the crate up the corridor toward the next door, pushed it through and then struggled up the next set of stairs, walking half on the wall and half on the stairs. The water dripping from his hair soon turned to sweat, both from the effort of dragging the box and the pressing need to get off the ship before it sank in the storm.

Finally he got to the upper deck, only to find the crew still struggling with the lifeboats. Due to the angle of the deck, they had lost many of the boats, and the passengers and crew were panicking all around him, running back and forth from the suspended useless lifeboats to the railing. The ship shuddered beneath his bare feet and lurched sideways. Asheris grabbed hold of the brass rail near the door and watched in horror as most of the other passengers careened across the deck and plunged screaming into the choppy waters of the Nile. In the deepening dusk, Asheris saw crocodiles slide down the far bank and slip into the river. Frantic, he glanced around. Where was Karissa in the melee? He couldn't see her anywhere.

"Karissa!" he yelled into the gale. He wiped his hair from his forehead and called again as dread curled in the pit of his stomach. Had she fallen into the river with the rest of them? "Karissa!"

Swearing, he let go of the crate and stumbled to the rail. The crate slipped across the deck, hit the railing, and bounced end over end, sailing through the air and hitting the water with a smack. Asheris saw it disappear and then bob to the surface a few meters away. Luckily it hadn't hit anyone. The surface of the river was churning with flailing terrified people and floating debris. Behind them he could see the nearly indistinguishable bumps of the crocodiles as they swam closer.

Then he saw Karissa. She was vainly trying to reach a barrel, but was continually thrown back by the waves in the water. Though she was fighting to stay alive, from all appearances, Karissa didn't know how to swim. Soon she would tire and the crocodiles would take her under.

Asheris looked back at the crate, which was quietly floating down river. He must make a choice and make it immediately. Either Karissa would die in the river or he would lose Senefret's body forever. He hardly took a moment to consider, for he knew where his heart truly belonged. Though he might never be a whole man, he knew without a doubt that he loved Karissa Spencer and would give up his own life, his own hopes and dreams and even Senefret's afterlife, to save her.

Bracing himself against the raging wind, he climbed onto the railing and jumped off.

He hit the surface of the water with a smack and went under. Up through the cold black water he swam, praying he would not be too late. He broke the surface with a gasp and looked around as water streamed into his eyes and a wave struck him in the face. Off to his right he glimpsed Karissa, just as she was sinking beneath the waves.

"No!" he yelled. He lunged forward and grabbed a handful of her hair as she disappeared in the current. With desperate hands, he cupped her chin and took off for the shore with swift sure strokes, knowing within minutes the crocodiles would be upon them. Already he heard the terrified cries of the less fortunate as they were snatched by the reptiles.

He prayed to the gods that he would make it to the shore in time, not only to escape the crocodiles, but also to outrun the setting sun. Once he transformed into the panther, he would be of no help to Karissa in the water. She was limp in his grip, and he wondered if she might already be dead. Distraught, he forced his arms and legs far beyond their limits, until his muscles screamed in agony. Still he pressed onward, concentrating on the dim lights of the shoreline and telling himself that he was nearly there.

Nearly there. Nearly there. Nearly there.

At last he felt the temperature of the water becoming warmer, and then the smell of mud and reeds filled his nostrils. His free hand struck sand. He had made it! Asheris dragged himself to his feet, clutched Karissa under her arms and hauled her out of the water. His knees were buckling even before he made it all the way to the warm beach. Gasping for breath, he eased Karissa onto her stomach and then collapsed on the strip of land beside her.

After he recovered somewhat, he looked around, thankful that no crocodiles lounged on this small piece of sand. Then he checked Karissa to make certain she was breathing and comfortable. A pang of happiness washed over him. He had saved Karissa, He looked toward the river as the pang grew bittersweet. Perhaps Senefret would one day understand the choice he'd had to make. Asheris reached out and lightly caressed Karissa's hair as he turned back to gaze at her delicate profile. He knew he would never tire of filling his eyes with her.

But there was nothing else he could do for her. His energy was completely drained. All he could do was pull her into his arms and wrap himself around her drenched body. He was tired beyond endurance. He couldn't walk another step. Perhaps a rescue crew would find them. Asheris lay his head on his arm. Then all went black as he lost consciousness.

He slept through the rest of the storm, the rest of the night, and didn't wake up until sunrise, when the sound of barking dogs startled him awake. Asheris jerked up, grimacing in pain at the stiffness in his muscles. He glanced at the sky, which was blue and clear, with no signs of the storm of the previous night. Then he glanced down at Karissa, still lying in the sand beside him, her cloud of black hair tangled around her shoulders.

Then he suddenly realized he was still dressed in his pants. He never returned from his forays as a panther with clothes on. In fact, he had learned to remove his clothing at dusk, so that he wouldn't ruin or lose any of his apparel during the transformations. Why hadn't he lost the trousers last night? Perplexed, Asheris glanced around at the sand. He couldn't see a single panther track. There was no evidence whatsoever that he had been a panther during the night. In fact, he had awakened still wrapped around Karissa in the exact position he had assumed before falling asleep. What could it mean?

A shudder rippled down Asheris' back as a startling possibility dawned on him. And yet, he found it impossible believe the truth staring him in the face. He had remained a man the entire night. But how could that have occurred? The only way the curse could be lifted was by the hand of a woman who truly loved him. But he had always assumed his destiny was linked to Senefret and a love that would remain forever out of reach.

He stared at Karissa. Yesterday afternoon she had said that she loved him, but he hadn't connected her confession to the curse. Could it really be true? Was he no longer cursed? Could he be a whole man at last, free of his wandering nights as a panther? Osiris, let it be so!

Just then the reeds above him parted and a dog's head poked through the blades. It yapped and growled, waking Karissa. An instant later, Jamal's face appeared directly above them.

"Mr. Asher!" he exclaimed with a huge grin. "Praise Allah! We have found you!"

Just after noon, Karissa stood at the side of the Land Rover while a manservant put a small bag containing her scant wardrobe and toiletries in the back. Then she walked into the house to see if Asheris had finished his telephone conversation. She wanted to say good-bye to him in the garden and not at the airport, where they would be in full view of strangers.

She said her good-byes to Eisha and then turned as Asheris walked up, dressed in white. He looked radiantly handsome.

"You really are going?" he said in greeting, talking her hands in his tan ones. "I can't change your mind?"

"I wish I could. But, all the arrangements have been made. I can't turn my back on my duty. Surely you understand that, Asheris."

"Yes." He smiled sadly. "I understand. But that does not mean that I like your decision." He pulled her closer and she nestled against him, feeling as she had felt from the very first that their bodies had been molded to fit together as one. He gazed down at her and smiled, which was highly infectious. She knew she was grinning back, unable to control the joy she felt in his arms. He had sacrificed a great deal to save her life, and his sacrifice meant the world to her.

"I'll come back," she promised. "As soon as I can."

"Tomorrow?" he urged, kissing her with longing and passion. She smiled beneath the kiss and he rose from her mouth. "How can I endure the hours until you are back in my arms?"

"I promise it won't be long."

"Good. Because you are part of me, Karissa."

She gazed up at him. It was true. A strong bond bound them together, unspoken, unbroken, undeniable. Only one thing marred the joy of the moment. Though

Asher had saved her life and given up Senefret's crate, he still had not admitted that he loved her.

She touched his cheek. "Asheris, why don't you just come with me?"

"I would, but for the call I just received."

"And?"

"It seems a fisherman found my crate."

"Oh." Karissa felt a twinge of disquiet that she instantly pushed aside. If Asheris could countenance her leaving for the PBS interview, she could countenance his efforts to give Senefret a proper burial. She tried to smile. "You'll phone me, won't you, once you find out what's in that little cedar box?"

"Of course. I will call you every day, just to hear your voice."

He kissed her again, embracing her until the manservant appeared and discreetly suggested that they leave for the airport.

"Just a moment," Asheris said, stepping back but keeping her hand in his. "There is something I want to do while you are still here."

"Yes?" Karissa glanced up at him in surprise.

"I have been thinking about personal freedom very much lately."

"Yes?" She still didn't comprehend what he was getting at.

Asheris walked to the nearest birdcage and lifted the latch on the door. "At one time I thought these birds were beautiful and fascinating to watch. But now I see them only as pitiful hostages."

Karissa's heart swelled anew with love for Asheris as she looked at the falcons sitting on the perch. She knew very well why he had been fascinated with birds. He was part cat in his soul. The only thing she didn't understand was why his fascination for birds should suddenly change.

"I thought I was protecting them," he continued, "when all the time I have been keeping them from living their natural lives."

"Safety isn't what makes life worth living," she replied. "I've learned that lesson well enough."

He glanced down at her. "That's why I thought you might like to see the birds set free before you go."

"I would," Karissa said, as tears came to her eyes. Asheris had set her free of her past, of her guilt. And she would always love him for it.

Asheris opened door after door and the birds took wing, soaring over the garden like angels spiraling to the sun. One of the falcons rose up above their heads and circled the garden, crying out a haunting call of scree scree.

Karissa shaded her eyes and watched the birds as Asheris stood behind her and wrapped his arms around her.

"They will come back to my garden," he said softly into her hair, "of their own free will. I am certain of it."

She nodded and rested her head against his chest, reveling in his wonderful combination of strength and sensitivity. Just like the birds, she would return to Asheris, too, back to his garden and the man she had come to love with all her heart.

Chapter 11

Baltimore, Maryland

KARISSA HEARD A PRYING SOUND IN THE BACK of the gallery and put aside her wine glass. She was quite certain she was the only person remaining after the film crew had left. Even Josh had waved good-bye and had gone to have a drink with one of the blond make-up artists.

"Who's there?" Karissa called, tiredly rising up from the chair where she had been interviewed. The filming had taken two days and she was exhausted. But her spirits were dragging more than her body, for Asheris had not called her once since she had flown back to Baltimore. Something had happened to him or he had decided to forget her. Either possibility was devastating.

She walked toward the rear of the room. "Who's there?" she called again.

No one answered.

She peered into the darkness, wishing she would have turned on the lights. And then she saw them—two golden eyes gazing at her from out of the gloom. Her voice caught in her throat and her heart began to pound furiously.

"Ebony," a low voice rumbled near the back door. "If you sculpt a cat out of ebony, you will find satisfaction."

She couldn't believe her eyes or her ears.

"Asheris?" she whispered.

He stepped out from behind a wooden crate and held out his arms. He was dressed in his long black coat and gloves, and she knew she never seen a more beautiful sight in her entire life. With a cry of joy she vaulted into his embrace.

After a long hug and an even longer kiss, Asheris pulled away from her mouth. "Look what I have brought for you," he said, pushing aside the lid of the crate.

Karissa glanced at the contents of the box. In the shadows, she could see nothing but a dark lump. "What is it?"

"Ebony," he declared proudly. "For your next and best sculpture."

"How can you be so sure? I haven't been successful yet in capturing the spirit of the panther."

"Ah, but this time you will."

"Why do you say that?"

Asheris held her close. "Because the panther spirit is no longer trapped within me. It is free to be captured by your hands and brought to life in the wood I have brought you."

"Asheris!" Karissa pulled back. "What are you saying? You are no longer under the curse?"

"No. Your love freed me, Karissa." He smiled, his teeth flashing in the darkness. "I am a new man!"

"But why didn't you say so before? Before I left Egypt?"

"I was not certain then. I had to see if the night belonged to the panther or to me. And I was reluctant to mention it to you in case my hopes were too high. Then when I found out, I longed to tell you myself in person, not on the telephone."

His silence of the last two days was instantly forgiven. She grinned and hugged him tightly, wondering what it could mean for the two of them. Was he whole now, whole enough to give himself completely to her? Or did part of him still belong to Senefret?

"There is more, Karissa," he said, stroking her hair.

"Yes?"

"I barely know how to begin." He laughed and looked down at her, and his face was full of joy. She had never heard him laugh before and the sound nearly brought tears to her eyes.

"Come and sit down," she urged, pulling him by the hand to the interview set. She sat down upon the upholstered chair, but he remained on his feet and paced back and forth in front of her.

"Well?" Karissa asked, dying of curiosity.

He glanced at her and smiled again. Then he pulled off his gloves and stuffed them into the pockets of his overcoat.

"Do you recall that small cedar box?" he inquired.

"Of course."

He reached into the inner pocket of his coat and drew out a folded paper. "Inside the box was this letter to me. From Senefret."

"What?" Karissa thought she hadn't heard him correctly.

"Yes. Senefret was the one who had broken into the tomb, left the box, and then resealed the entrance."

"Senefret?"

Asheris nodded, his eyes alight.

"But I thought it was her tomb, her mummy!"

Asheris nodded again. "So did everyone. But in fact, the mummy was the body of a young priestess who had died of a wasting disease at the same time Senefret was to be executed. She was entombed in place of Senefret."

"Why?"

"To fool the pharaoh. For you see, Senefret escaped the Temple of Sekhmet, leaving the priestesses with no one to punish, no one to offer as sacrifice to my half-brother."

"Senefret escaped?"

Asheris grinned. "Senefret was resourceful. She left the box there, hoping someday I would return to Thebes, perhaps break into her tomb, and find the letter she had written to me."

"So what ever happened to her?"

"She fled to the outer provinces."

His eyes gleamed and he sat down next to Karissa. "How I wish I had known all of this. I have spent an eternity grieving for Senefret, when all the time she was never in the Valley of the Damned at all!"

Karissa stared at him in shock. Then she reached out a trembling hand. "May I see the letter?" she asked.

"It is a copy," he said, giving it to her. "And translated in English so that you can read it."

His thoughtfulness never ceased to amaze her. She scanned the text which explained most of what he already told her. At the bottom of the page, however, were words that tugged at her heart.

I know of no other way to contact you, my heart, for to be seen with you would mean certain death for both of us, and I could never put your life in danger. I only hope that someday you will come to know that I live for you, if not in this lifetime, perhaps through my daughter, and her daughter after her, for a love such as ours was meant to endure.

Karissa looked up from the letter to find Asheris studying her intently. She frowned. "How do you know this is genuine?" she asked. "How do you know it wasn't a cruel joke and that the mummy really was Senefret?"

"There was one way to find out," Asher replied grimly. "Senefret was cursed by the priestesses of Sekhmet and marked with a special brand on her neck. When I unwrapped the mummy, I found no such mark. Had it been there, it should have been evident, even after thousands of years."

A chill coursed through Karissa. "What kind of mark was it, exactly?"

"A red spot in the shape of a cat, to identify that she was condemned by the Temple of Sekhmet."

Karissa was so shocked, she dropped the letter. It fluttered to the floor but she took no notice.

"Karissa, what is wrong?" Asheris stood up.

"I have such a mark," Karissa whispered, slowly rising to her feet. "So did my grandmother Menmet and her mother before her."

"A mark in the shape of a cat?"

"Yes."

"Where?"

"Here." Karissa pulled back her hair into a pony tail and lifted it off her neck, while she turned her back to Asheris. "See there at the base of my hairline?"

He stepped closer. "I do not believe it!" he exclaimed.

"I've been told it's a family birthmark."

She felt Asheris' warm touch on her neck as he outlined the shape of the cat with his index finger. Then he slowly turned her around and regarded her, his eyes dark and probing.

"You never mentioned your mark."

"There was no reason to." She stared up at him, realizing the impact this had on both of them. Could she belong to the same family as Senefret? Could she be genetically linked to the beautiful priestess who had captured Asheris' heart? Could she possibly be the very same essence of woman as the Senefret of long ago?

"Oh, God, Asheris!" she gasped. "Could it be that"—

"Yes!" he exclaimed, squeezing the tops of her arms. "You are of her lineage! That explains everything!—the way I was drawn to you, the way you spoke to my heart, the way I've been in love with you from the very first."

"You're in love with me?"

"Yes, but I could never tell you. How could I? I was not whole. I was half-panther, half-man, and half-devoted to a woman I thought long dead." He laughed and squeezed her again, "But she is in you as surely as you are standing here!"

"You love me!"

"I love you as surely as the sun rises in the east!" He embraced her, crushing her in joy. "Ah, Karissa, I love you boundlessly, hopelessly, eternally!"

She felt her heart blossoming with happiness, the likes of which she had never known. In that moment she knew why she had the mark, why the land of Nile had always called to her, and why this man had become part of her heart in so many ways in such a short time. Her blood was the blood of the priestess, flowing through eternity toward Lord Azhur as the Nile has flowed to the sea since time began.

"Then I come from an ancient line," she murmured near his ear. "I'd like to explore that heritage."

"The only way to do that is to come back to Egypt," he replied. "And employ the services of an expert."

"And who might that be?" she teased.

"Though I dislike braggarts," he said, "I must admit that I am the best."

"Yes, you are." She hugged him fiercely.

"And if you can be persuaded to travel with me again, I have two tickets for luxury accommodations on the Cairo Queen leaving New York in four days."

"Another ship?" she asked, cocking her eyebrow.

"I rather enjoyed our voyage before we hit the

sandbar." Asheris kissed the tip of her nose. "And I thought you might like a longer trip this time."

"As long as you don't have any crates with you."

"No more crates, my love," he replied. "I am finished with the past now. All I want is the future and you in it."

"A little bit of here and now wouldn't be so bad either," she said, pulling him down to her mouth.

"Mmmm," he mumbled, drawing her against his body.

"Are you sure you are no longer a panther," she asked, kissing his cheek. "Not even a tiny bit?"

"What do you have in mind?"

She whispered her request in his ear.

He growled.

THE LORD OF THE NILE was an exploratory journey into the Egyptian world of LORD AZHUR. Karissa and Asher's story continues in a full-length novel enttitled THE LOST GODDESS.

Author's Note

During the research for this story, I turned up some fascinating facts about ancient and modern Egypt, including a new theory regarding construction techniques of the pyramids and the mystery surrounding the sphinx. Not even experts are certain as to the purpose of the sphinx. Some scientists even claim that the sphinx is much older than we think! Not being able to leave such mysteries lie, I decided to write another book about the land of the Nile in which I explore the enigma of the sphinx while uncovering the startling secret of the Spencer family in The Lost Goddess.

Find out more at http://www.patriciasimpson.com/books.asp

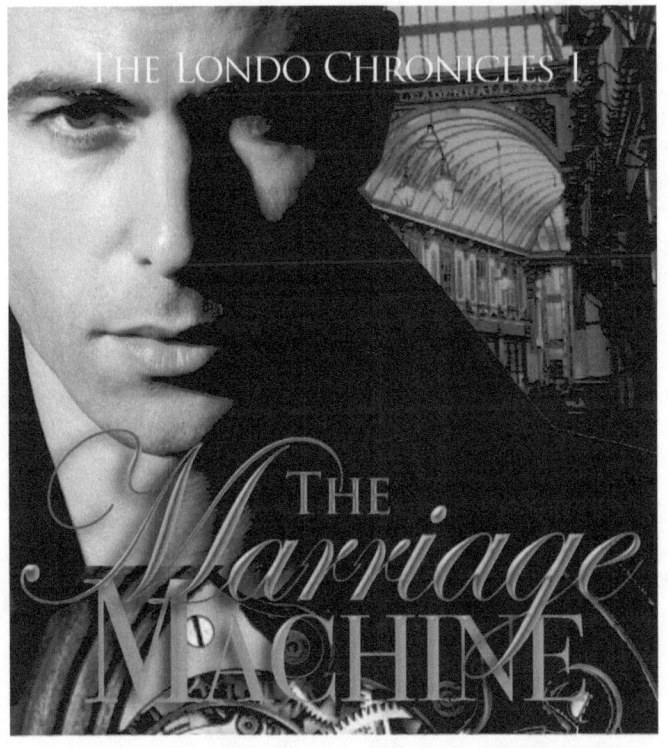

Electricity and love are banned in this
dystopian steampunk novella set in
a foggy future London.

Chapter 1

ELSPETH SHUTTERHOUSE PEDALED FIERCELY down the rain-slick alley, dodging puddles and potholes in the dark as she searched the lane for landmarks. It was difficult locating an address in the rain, and dangerous to be out in the dark alone. But the alley route was part of the instructions she'd been given an hour ago. *Cycle to 17 Charing Cross, don't let anyone see you, and don't stop, eat or sleep until the repair job has been finished.*

As she sped through the rain, the silver envelope she'd received earlier that day and stuffed in her chest pocket jabbed the top of her arm. She ignored the stab just as she planned to ignore the social obligation the envelope held.

Black door, brick archway, freight delivery door. She had arrived at her destination.

Elspeth jumped off her cycle, stashed it behind a stack of crates, locked it to a pipe, and splashed to the door she had been told to use.

She knocked and then chafed her frozen hands together. Her leather jacket and leggings had kept her warm during the ride through Londo City, but her hands were like icicles.

Light oozed through the crack under the door as someone approached with a lantern. Elspeth swung her heavy backpack off one shoulder and down her arm, just as the door opened. A tiny man with a bald head peered up at her through lenses set in a pair of brass goggles. He reminded her of a lizard she'd seen in her great aunt's ancient and totally forbidden *Encyclopedia Britannica* text, *Volume G-H,* entry *Galapagos Islands*.

The man lifted the lantern to get a better view.

"SteamWizards," Elspeth announced, pulling out her badge to display her credentials. "Citizen Shutterhouse."

"Right this way," the man swung open the door and motioned her in. His leather robe failed to conceal his thickening middle. Economic sanctions would be coming his way if he didn't do something about his physical condition.

Overindulgence today starves the infant on its way.

Elspeth shut off the dogma. She had always scoffed at the indoctrination of her childhood and did her best to live under the radar of the Overseers, but sometimes the slogans seeped into her psyche anyway.

She followed the man down a shadowed hallway, hoping she would be given a glass of ale after her ride, but the man made no such offering and ushered her through a door on the right. He reached for a control on the wall and turned up the gas lamps. Light bathed the huge bay beneath the house, illuminating the lines of a monstrous juggernaut of metalwork and gears, topped off by a fantastic filigree of wrought iron vines surrounding a sculpture of two gilt swans set beak to beak.

Elspeth stopped in her tracks, thunderstruck.

"It's the Marriage Machine!" she gasped.

She rarely ever gasped.

The bald head rotated her way, and the goggles found her face. "Never mind what it is. Can you fix it?"

Of course she could fix it. Elspeth could fix anything. That's why she had been singled out for the job. She might be young, but she had a special knack when it came to mechanical objects. Her father had noticed her aptitude early on and had taught her as much as he could before his untimely death.

She edged closer. "What's going on with it?" she asked, as she surveyed the complicated mass of wheels and belts.

"We have no idea. It won't start up. We've sent word to the manufacturer, but apparently the owners of the patent are the only ones who know how to fix the machine. They hail from the Outer Islands. It's a long journey. And with the holiday the cyclones always start, you know. So it's hard to predict when someone will actually get here. That's why I called the SteamWizards."

Elspeth had quit listening to his chatter at the first mention of the term "owners."

"A Ramsay?" Elspeth stared at the small man. "Is coming here?"

"You know of them?"

She nodded. Of course she knew of them. In a household of mechanics, you either loved or hated the plutocratic Ramsay family. She hated them. To her way of thinking, the Ramsays were responsible for the numbing and dumbing down of the entire female population of Londo City—and had made a profit on it in the bargain.

She studied the machine in which the "lucky" women exchanged marriage vows with preselected strangers and were never the same again. The Marriage Machine was usually displayed as a wedding bower, with its inner passage draped in velvet and fringe, its outer workings concealed with silk ferns and orchids, and its dark influence invisible to all who ventured inside.

Elspeth had always wondered how the Marriage Machine worked. And now she was about to find out. She could actually discover what made the Marriage Machine tick.

And then she could destroy it.

Talk about perfect timing.

Elspeth placed her backpack on the floor, and the tools clanked as they settled upon the wooden planks of the stage where the machine had been installed. Then she straightened and placed her fists on her hips. "I'll need to see the schematics," she said, sure that the Ramsays guarded the secret of their machine from all but their inner circle, but hoping she might get her hands on a diagram if she bullied her way forward.

"I don't have any," the bald man said. "The machine's been operating for nearly two hundred years. My predecessors didn't keep the documentation."

"Parts list?"

"Nothing." The man shrugged. "It's never had a problem until now. It's got a lifetime guarantee."

"Whose lifetime would that be?" Elspeth walked around the chassis of the machine, sizing it up, looking for leaking valves and broken lines. It took about five minutes to see that a hole had been poked in a slider valve supply line. She could repair such a problem with her eyes closed.

"I have ten weddings lined up for tomorrow and twenty more on Friday. I can't tell you what a travesty this is. It's the holiday season. I could lose my job."

Elspeth frowned and shook her head. "I don't know, citizen—"

"Davies. It's Citizen Davies."

"I don't see anything wrong right off the bat, Davies," she lied as she reached for a lever topped with a black onyx ball. "Is this how it's turned on?"

"Yes."

Elspeth yanked the brass arm downward. She heard a burst of air, a wheeze, and then nothing.

"See?" Davies motioned toward the machine. "That's all it does."

Elspeth crossed her arms over her chest as her future closed around her like a dark tunnel. She had decided long ago that she would rebel against the preordained future if she ever received a silver envelope. Well, she had received the dreaded envelope just that morning. But this Marriage Machine development had increased the implications of her personal rebellion a hundredfold. She had more than just *her* future in her hands now. She held the future of all the women of Londo City.

If she decommissioned the Marriage Machine, her career would be ruined. She would be ostracized from society, and would probably be sentenced to life in the work camps. But the authorities would have to catch her first. And whatever freedom she knew on the run, even if was only a handful of days, would be worth it. This was her seminal moment.

But finding the key to a complete system breakdown would take some time.

"I need to perform a series of diagnostics." She reached inside her pack for an apparatus she had made for herself, a portable light she could hold in her hand, with a powerful beam produced by a magnesium ribbon. It was only a prototype, held together with a clumsy set of clamps and topped by a crude lens, but it was perfect for small dark spaces. That's where she usually worked.

"What is that thing?" Davies asked, peering around her elbow.

"Something I'm developing. I call it a hand-torch." She switched it on. "Now if you don't mind, Citizen Davies, I prefer to work alone."

"Of course." Davies backed away. "Summon me if you need me. I won't be able to sleep anyway. The PneumoSpeak is by the door."

As soon as the man disappeared, Elspeth ducked into the chamber of the Marriage Machine to begin her search for the heart and soul of the beast.

The block clock tooted out twelve blasts muffled by fog just as Elspeth found the heart of the Marriage Machine. She had labored six hours disassembling countless housings and gears, all arranged in neat rows behind her in the order in which she had unfastened them. By midnight, she was exhausted, and had begun to wonder if sabotage was even possible. But at the last stroke of midnight, the beam of her hand-torch found the innermost secret of the machine, and all fatigue vanished.

"Helloo!" Elspeth whispered, awestruck.

Suspended at eye level in a frame of brass was the largest ruby Elspeth had ever seen. In fact it was the *only* ruby she had ever seen. Respectable citizens didn't wear jewelry or colored fabric or anything that could be considered superfluous adornment. In these hard times, there were more important things to concern oneself with—like merely surviving.

She traced the gem with the tip of one finger as she studied the surrounding machine works. The jewel was at least six inches in diameter and glowed with an otherworldly luminescence. Light must be refracted through the gem's faceted depths, passed through the human body, and was somehow able to affect a person's reproductive system and mental outlook. She felt for the heavy nuts that held the frame in place on the backside of the jewel. She estimated it would take her a good half hour to free the ruby from the intricate frame, and would probably ruin her knuckles. She reached for a wrench.

It was during the shredding of her knuckles that she came up with an even better plan than destroying the Marriage Machine.

A door slammed and awakened Elspeth. She jerked to

a sitting position, banged her head on a pipe and gawked at her surrounds—completely disoriented. She had fallen asleep in the bowels of the Marriage Machine. Elspeth rubbed her skull as she heard Davies talking to someone in the room outside.

"A repair person has been working around the clock," Davies sputtered. "We're doing everything we can."

Elspeth struggled to her feet, ignoring her aching muscles and sore back. She was sure there was a pattern of rivets stamped into her butt. Trying to gather her wits, she pulled out the pocket watch she wore around her neck and squinted at it. Good heavens, it was nine o'clock in the morning. She couldn't remember falling asleep or finishing the job for that matter. But a quick glance around the chamber told her that every gear and every nut and bolt had been returned to its place. No one would ever suspect what she had done during the night. As the two men talked outside the machine, she replaced the walnut panels and headed for the door of the bower.

Elspeth picked up her backpack just as the door of the Marriage Machine was flung open with a clang.

"And what have we here?" a voice boomed.

Elspeth stared at the man staring back at her. She had never seen such a creature. He had to be over six feet tall. No man in Londo City was over five and a half feet. He wore a long leather traveling coat with rain flaps at the collar that failed to disguise his massive shoulders. But even more shocking was his hair. It was black. As black as tar. She'd never seen black hair before. Everyone in the LC had the same mousy brown hair—a product attributed to centuries of inbreeding.

Elspeth threw back her shoulders. "Citizen Shutterhouse, SteamWizards."

"Sleeping on the job, were you?" the man demanded. His blue eyes raked her up and down.

The man's ingratitude infuriated her. He had to be one of the Ramsays.

"A girl needs her beauty sleep." She jumped out of the Marriage Machine and aimed to land on his right foot, but he stepped aside just in time to escape injury. She shot a glance at him, amazed that such a large man could possess quick reflexes.

"She's all fixed, Citizen Davies," Elspeth announced, hoping the giant would back off once he knew his family's precious machine was functioning—at least to the casual observer. But instead of smiling in relief, he glanced at the injured supply line she had fixed, as if doubting her claim.

"That's wonderful news!" Citizen Davies exclaimed, clapping his hands. "Oh, you've made my day. Remarkable work, Shutterhouse. Remarkable!"

"Have you tried it?" the tall man broke off his stare. "Have you powered it up?"

"Not yet," Elspeth retorted. "But I'm certain it will work."

Davies skittered to the start lever and pulled it downward. The Marriage Machine sputtered, shimmied, and then chugged to a start. Davies' goggles turned her way. He beamed. "Glorious!" he cried. "I am the happiest man on earth."

"And I'm the thirstiest, Davies," the tall man retorted. "I've been traveling all night. Spare me a whiskey, would you? And Shutterhouse as well."

"Indeed!" Davies trotted to the door. "I have a single malt I've been saving for a special occasion. I'll only be a minute."

"I don't drink on the job," Elspeth slung her backpack over her left shoulder. "And I really must be getting back to work." She turned toward the door.

"Not before you tell me what you've been doing here

all night."

Elspeth paused and looked over her shoulder.

"*Citizen*," he drawled.

His tone and his dark regard made her heart race with alarm. But she'd never let him see it. She planted a fist on her hip. "And why should I tell you? I have no idea who you are."

"I'm Ramsay." He inclined his head stiffly. "Captain Mark Ramsay. 1 assume you are acquainted with the name."

"Not with yours particularly."

"With my family's then."

"I'm not *dead*."

His eyes narrowed. "But you might wind up in that condition, if you don't tell me what you were doing here all night."

She frowned. He had some nerve, threatening her. She raised her chin and sent him the most withering glare she could muster. "Is that the thanks I get for fixing your damn machine? Bloody hell!" She stormed toward the door, but he caught her arm, surprising her again with his speed. His large hand easily encircled her bicep.

"A respectable citizen doesn't swear." He warned. "I could report you."

"And I could report you!" she shot back. "For manhandling a female. Let go of me!"

"Not until you tell me what you've been up to." His face loomed inches away from hers. He had amazingly white teeth. She could see his nostrils flare. His nose was large and sharp, and unnervingly provocative when in such close proximity to hers.

"What part of fixing don't you understand?" she retorted, shaken by her reaction to him.

He squeezed her arm. "It couldn't have taken twelve hours to repair what was wrong with that machine."

"And how would you know?"

"Just a lucky guess."

"I was tired. I fixed the Marriage Machine and decided to take a nap while I could."

"You're lying."

"That makes two of us." She struggled to break free. "Now let me go, or I'll call out."

His grip relaxed as his wide mouth curled up at one corner, almost as if he were struggling to hide a smile. The smirk only infuriated her more. She wrenched her arm out of his grasp and brushed all traces of him off her leather sleeve.

His blue eyes flashed down at her. She'd never seen blue eyes before either. Everyone in the city had brown eyes. Fascinated, she stole a second look, unused to color of any description in her foggy, monochromatic world. She imagined the sky had once been the color of his eyes. But she had only heard about such a sky in the tales of her great aunt.

Then she noticed his eyes darkening to a deeper color, as if the sky were melting into the warmest and most cerulean of oceans. He must have noticed her studying his face.

Elspeth flushed. She was gawking at a Ramsay, and daydreaming of a wonderland of color. What in the Name of Wanda was the matter with her?

Ramsay gave a short laugh, as if he'd registered her mental lapse. "Since when did the power company start sending girls out to do their work?"

"I'm not a girl."

"Really?" He cocked a brow. "Then what are you, pray tell?"

"An ace mechanic who happens to be a woman."

His cool glance surveyed her figure a second time, but his expression remained impassive, unreadable, as if he took no pleasure from the view.

Elspeth was only too aware that she hadn't been blessed with feminine contours. Her aunt often chided her to eat more and work less, and maybe then her breasts and hips would have a chance to develop. But she'd never taken the advice. There were too many projects to work on through the night after her long hours at the power company, and too many diagrams to draw. Moreover, she hadn't cared about the size of her breasts until she'd been sized up by Ramsay just now and obviously found lacking. If she had possessed ponderous breasts like her cousin Amelie, she would have unfastened her jacket and flaunted her attributes in Mark Ramsay's face. She would bet his nostrils would flare then.

Unfortunately, her breasts were not of the flaunting variety.

"A woman?" He snorted. "You look barely old enough to wear a corset."

"I'm twenty-five, I'll have you know. And was top of my class."

"In what—Advanced Impertinence?"

"I'm not being impertinent!"

"You stare. You don't mind your tongue."

"It is my right to speak my mind." She raked him up and down as thoroughly as he had surveyed her. "Just because you were born into the *esteemed* Ramsay family, and have every luxury at your disposal, doesn't give you any more rights than me, *citizen*."

"If you believe that," he sneered. "Then you are woefully naive."

Her flush deepened.

Again, their glances locked, and this time his eyes flared with challenge. But before either one of them could say anything more, Citizen Davies whisked through the door with three glasses on a tray.

"*Days of cake and cream should be far and few between,*" he said, smiling. "But I believe this is one of those days. I do believe it is."

Elspeth suspected that he had enjoyed more than his share of such days.

Davies picked up a glass of whiskey and held it out to her. "Citizen Shutterhouse?"

"Thank you, but I must be going." At the door, she turned to look over her shoulder, sure that Captain Ramsay would be watching her departure with a triumphant sneer on his handsome face. Instead, he was sipping his drink and staring at the Marriage Machine, deep in thought.

Chapter 2

AFTER PUTTING IN A FULL DAY AT WORK, Elspeth arrived home just after six that evening. The single lamp in the center of the square cast an eerie glow in the fog but failed to reach her aunt's doorstep. Exhausted, Elspeth pushed open the foyer door, pulled off her boots and stowed her backpack in the corner. All she wanted was a bowl of soup and her bed. But just as she reached for the door to the parlor, someone opened it and flooded her with light.

"Happy birthday!" two voices called in unison. Her aunt and cousin clapped, delighted with themselves for having caught her by surprise.

Elspeth had completely forgotten about her birthday. Technically, it had occurred yesterday, December 18th, but she'd been too busy fixing the Marriage Machine to celebrate.

"We were so worried you'd have to work overtime again," her aunt pulled her toward the settee table where a small white cake sat on a platter. "And that the cake would go bad."

"You could have eaten it without me," Elspeth said. But she was glad they hadn't. Her mouth watered at the sight of the uncommon treat.

"Never," her aunt retorted. "It's your twenty-fifth birthday, Elspeth. A very special birthday for a woman. We'd never have eaten the cake without you. Now sit down and relax for once."

"Thank you, Aunt Fi." Elspeth had to admit that sitting down felt like the best birthday present of all. "It's been quite a couple of days." She sank down onto the worn cushions of the sofa.

"But you did manage to fix the problem, dear?" her aunt asked, even though she never quite grasped what Elspeth did for a living. Aunt Fi handed her a piece of cake on a chipped plate.

"I certainly did." Elspeth answered.

"That's good to hear. But as I have said before, you should speak to your boss. He makes you work too hard."

"It can't be helped, Aunt Fi. It's the nature of my job. Londo City would collapse without the SteamWizards."

"Never mind your dreary old job, El." Amelie sat down with her baby on her knee. Her ponderous breasts had increased geometrically since the birth of her child, and they docked on either side of Benjamin's shoulders like twin dirigibles. "What I am dying to know is if you got one."

"One what?" Elspeth savored a soft bite of cake. Sugar was so scarce, she couldn't remember the last time she'd had anything sweet.

"An envelope. *The* envelope."

Elspeth reached into her blouse, pulled out the now-tattered envelope and tossed it on the table.

"I knew it!" Amelie grinned. "I knew you'd be chosen."

Aunt Fi was more perceptive. She sat down across from Elspeth, her slice of cake all but forgotten. "But you aren't pleased, Elspeth. What's wrong?"

"Everything! I fail to see what's so wonderful about being forced to marry a complete stranger and never having another independent thought for the rest of your life."

"It's not what you think," Amelie kissed the downy head of her child. "In fact it's changed my life in ways I never imagined."

It had changed Amelie all right. Amelie used to write and draw in her spare time. But a few minutes in the Marriage Machine had dried up her cousin's creative juices. She hadn't written a line since her marriage.

Nothing could be done about it now, so there was no use mentioning the fact to Amelie. Instead, Elspeth gave her a smile. "It's fine for women like you, Amelie. You were meant to be a wife and a mother. But we all know that I would be miserable in that kind of life."

"Maybe you wouldn't," her aunt reached over and patted her wrist. "It's what a woman was born to do, Elspeth—bear children and raise the next generation. It's important work. And not everyone gets the opportunity. It's quite an honor, you know. You shouldn't take it lightly."

"What's your date?" Amelie asked.

"I have no idea." Elspeth put down her plate. She'd lost her appetite for cake and for celebrating. "I haven't opened it yet."

"You haven't opened your envelope?" Amelie swooped down and grabbed it. "I can't believe you, El, I really can't."

Elspeth sighed. "Why would I want to know the date of my last day of freedom?"

"Oh, El! You have to grow up some day." Amelie shook her head as she ripped the silver paper and drew out a card. Her face went white. "Oh, my!"

"What?" Aunt Fi blurted, a piece of cake balanced precariously on her fork.

Even Elspeth's curiosity was piqued. She glanced at her cousin.

"You've got a holiday date." Amelie looked back down at the engraved card. "December 25th in fact. C-Day. Oh, my word, Elspeth!" She fluttered a plump hand in front of her face, as if she were overheating with the news.

Elspeth stared at her cousin, completely baffled by Amelie's excitement. She knew all there was to know about pistons and valves, but she was completely ignorant when it came to the social aspects of life. She had no idea why a C-Day wedding was significant. "And that means?"

"Only the loftiest citizens are married on C-Day. The date is in such demand and so auspicious for a good marriage that only the upper crust is married then. Your groom must be an Overseer agent or at least a commissioner." Amelie's eyes gleamed. "You are so lucky! You won't have to work the rest of your life—I'll bet on it!"

Not working sounded like a prison sentence. Elspeth jumped to her feet. "Too bad you're going to lose that wager. I'm not going through with the ceremony."

"What?" her aunt sat back in her chair, appalled.

"I am warning you, Aunt Fi, I'm not going to go through with it."

"But you can't refuse. It's unheard of." Aunt Fi fluttered her hand in front of her face just as her daughter was doing.

"I'm going to be the first woman to say no."

"El!" Amelie gasped. "You can't do such a thing."

"I mean no disrespect to either of you or the lives you lead. In fact, I will never be able to repay the kindness you showed me by taking me in after Father died."

"We couldn't have done any less," Aunt Fi replied.

"But that machine does something to a woman's mind."

"Don't be ridiculous. It allows a woman to conceive." Amelie hugged her son. "I wouldn't have Benjamin without the Marriage Machine. And I can't imagine not having him."

"Well I can't imagine marrying a stranger. And I won't have some man thinking he can tell me how to live my life."

Amelie paled and looked away.

Elspeth wouldn't let her turn away as she had done so many times since her marriage. She stepped directly in front of her cousin. "I am referring to your job, Amelie. You loved that job. You loved working at the newspaper. Tell me you didn't."

"My child is more important than any job."

"And who decided that?" Elspeth demanded. She planted her fists on her hips and leaned down to confront Amelie face-to-face. "You or Edward?"

"We both did," Amelie stammered. "At least, I'm pretty sure we discussed it." Her voice trailed off.

"Don't remember?" Elspeth chided.

"Not exactly, but—"

"That's just my point!" Elspeth crossed her arms over her chest. "The machine does that to a woman. I bet you hardly argued your case with Edward—if at all."

"Elspeth, please," her aunt put in. "Let her be. It's for the best having her home with the baby. And it's your birthday. Let's just get along for once, shall we?"

Elspeth sighed and plopped back down on the couch.

Aunt Fi patted her hand again. "Please, Elspeth, don't do anything rash. Please think this through, dear."

"I have thought of little else for the past year, Aunt Fi. Believe me."

"What will you do?" Amelie had gone very pale.

Elspeth shrugged. "I'm not sure yet. But there's one thing I know I *won't* be doing and that is showing up at," she grabbed the card and glanced at the silver script. "Boswellian Bower on December 25 at 4 o'clock."

"You'll be ruined," Aunt Fi put in.

"They might even send you away," Amelie added. "What if you had to work in the coal mines in Norsea for the rest of your life? We would never see you again."

"It would be better than spreading my legs for some weasel who thinks he *owns* me for the rest of my life."

"Elspeth, really!"

"Sorry, Aunt Fi. But that's how I see it. Thanks for the cake." Elspeth hurried from the parlor and ran up the narrow stairs to her tiny bedchamber under the roof. She had to get away from people who would never understand her. And that might possibly be the entire population of Londo City.

Solitude was not to be hers, however. Before Elspeth could strip off her work clothes, she heard a loud banging at the front door and insistent voices down below. Elspeth froze.

"Elspeth?" Her aunt called from the bottom of the stairs. She could hear alarm in her aunt's voice.

Panic streaked through Elspeth. She had planned to run away a few days before the ceremony and lose herself in the Outskirts. But they had come for her sooner than she had anticipated, and there was no way to escape from her bedroom—certainly not from the tiny first story window behind her. She had no choice but to face whomever it was in the parlor. Swallowing hard, Elspeth trudged down the steps.

Two officers of the law stood in the parlor with lamplight glinting off the metal buttons of their uniforms and the handles of their enforcement clubs. As she gained the last stair, they turned in her direction.

"Elspeth Shutterhouse?" The taller one barked.

"Yes?"

"You are under arrest."

"What?" Aunt Fi's hands flew to her cheeks in shock.

Elspeth couldn't believe it, either. How could anyone have discovered what she had done in so short a time?

"On what charge?" she demanded.

The officer's handlebar mustache curled close to his nose as he shot her a look of disdain. "You have been accused by an upstanding citizen of committing a crime."

"What kind of crime?"

"Theft and transport of unlawful goods."

"What are you talking about?" Elspeth feigned cool ignorance while she burned like a brand on the inside. There was only one person in the world that could have possibly turned her in to the authorities: that bastard Ramsay.

"Don't make it worse for yourself, citizen, by feigning ignorance." The officer looped a restraining cord around her wrists. "You were seen burying stolen property in broad daylight."

"You must be mistaken," Aunt Fi cried. "Elspeth would never steal."

"You can't take her!" Amelie put in. "It's her birthday!"

"I suggest you hire an advocate, madame." The officer glared at Aunt Fi. "That is, if you haven't spent your entire fortune on *cake*." He yanked Elspeth toward the door.

"Elspeth!" Aunt Fi cried. Tears burst from her eyes as she lunged for her niece. But the officers wouldn't allow the women to hug each other good-bye. Elspeth took a good long look at her family, knowing she might never see them again. Remorse washed over her. She had expected to pay a price for her rash actions, but it had never occurred to her to consider how her decision might devastate her aunt.

That was the worst of it—watching her beloved Aunt Fi fall to the floor in a dead faint, and not being able to help her. While Amelie blubbered and Benjamin wailed, the officers jostled Elspeth out of the house, shoved her into the back of their chugger wagon, and took her to the station a mile away.

Elspeth spent another night huddled on a hard surface, this time on a bench in a detention cell. She was too worried about the future to sleep, and jumped to her feet the moment she spotted a warden walking her way down the dark corridor. She had no idea how long she'd been held. Her father's pocket watch had been taken from her, and there were no windows in the cellblock to allow her to gauge the passage of time.

The warden didn't even look at her as he turned a key in the lock and pulled at the barred door. It opened with a screech. He motioned for her to exit.

"Where am I going?" she demanded. Her legs were stiff and her head throbbed from lack of sleep, but she ignored the pain.

"To collect your belongings." He swung the door shut. "And after that, I don't much care."

She studied his florid face and bushy sideburns. "I'm getting back my things?"

"You're being released, citizen. Charges have been dropped."

"What?"

"I'd quit asking questions if I were you."

She was being released? Elspeth could hardly believe her luck. Suspicious, she followed the warden to a small chamber where a woman pushed a wire basket toward her. There she found her watch, her tablet, and her mother's ring. She shoved them back to their rightful places, worried all the while that someone would shout out that there had been a mistake, and that she should be returned to her cell.

Luckily, no such call was made. Minutes later, she burst out of the detention compound and into the bleak morning light. Cold air hit her like a wall. With the cold front had come a strange clarity in the atmosphere. She could see details three blocks ahead of her. And was that the moon in the distance? For a moment, Elspeth paused to gawk at the muddy-looking orb hanging over the rooftops. She had never seen the moon.

But Elspeth couldn't waste any time staring at the scenery. She hugged her arms and hurried toward her aunt's house, hoping she could get there before she froze to death. The WeatherWizards had predicted snow by the end of the week. But it hadn't snowed for over a hundred years, so she suspected the promised miracle would not occur this week either.

She prayed the weather would return to its normal foggy blandness. Cold like this would complicate the life of someone who might have to sleep on the streets for a few nights. And that would be her. She planned to say good-bye to her aunt, pack a bag, and leave Londo City before the police showed up again, as she knew they would.

A block from Aunt Fi's, she noticed a Flying Horse turn a corner and head her way, its vapor cloud billowing around it in the frigid air. Fearful of who might be in the vehicle, Elspeth increased her pace to just under a run.

The vehicle whisked up beside her. She kept walking and looked straight ahead, even though she had never seen a Flying Horse up close. She could see it was designed to look like a horse from a carousel, fashioned of polished black wood and chrome. She would love to study it more thoroughly—especially the motor, but getting home and away was her priority. One block more, and she would be back at Aunt Fi's.

The driver must have read her thoughts, for the vehicle swerved abruptly to hover over the walkway and block her path. She dashed to the left. The vehicle countered the movement, turning with ease on its cushion of air. She cursed at the new technology that allowed such agility. No doubt the agents of the Overseers would be driving such vehicles soon, and there would be no chance of escape for people like her—on land or in the air.

A window opened. "Shutterhouse!" a voice called. "Get in."

Get in? The driver must think she was an idiot. She dashed around the floating car.

"I got you out of jail," the deep voice boomed. "Spare me a moment."

Elspeth recognized that voice. She skidded to a halt and glared over her shoulder. Captain Mark Ramsay had climbed out of his vehicle and was peering through the vapor cloud at her, his blue eyes and black hair unmistakable even in the fog.

"Get in!" he ordered. "It's freezing out here."

"Not on your life, Ramsay!"

"I can have you re-arrested."

She shuddered.

"I know about the ruby," he added. "I had you followed."

"So you *were* the one who turned me in. I knew it!"

"No, I was the one who got you out. Some loyal citizen turned you in."

She frowned. It didn't matter who had turned her in to the authorities. It only mattered that she had failed. The risk she had taken to disable the Marriage Machine had all been for nothing. No doubt Ramsay *could* have her arrested for the crime. Unlike the rest of the citizens in Londo City, the Ramsays could go where they liked and do what they wished, a privilege they enjoyed for having saved civilization from extinction hundreds of years ago. She was forced to hear Mark Ramsay out or face the consequences.

He raised a black eyebrow and opened the passenger door.

Chin in the air, Elspeth slipped onto the seat of the Flying Horse while Ramsay gently closed the door beside her. She put her elbow on the tufted armrest and tried not to gape at the knobs and gauges that surrounded the steering arc of the Flying Horse. Ramsay settled into the driver's seat and glanced down at her.

"Your jaw has dropped," he commented with a droll smile.

Elspeth snapped shut her mouth and flushed.

"So you like my new toy?" he queried.

"It's okay. But I don't have all day. This better be quick."

"I have a job for you."

It was her turn to stare at him. "A job?"

He nodded as he guided his craft into the street.

"I'm taking you somewhere we can talk in private, and you can freshen up. Don't panic."

He drove southward, toward the river, and didn't say another word. Elspeth couldn't help but marvel at the smoothness of the ride and Ramsay's mastery of the vehicle. She felt as if she were zipping along on a cloud—a nice warm cloud with a glove-soft interior.

They whizzed through the streets as the city awakened. Lamps turned on in apartments. A newspaper boy trotted by with his bag. Men hurried to their factory jobs while street vendors opened the shutters of their stalls.

As Elspeth's frozen extremities warmed, she became more aware of the man who sat beside her—and far too close for her liking. But for a small gear housing, his left thigh would be touching hers. His thigh was long and muscular, his knee twice the size of her own. She shifted her leg to the side to avoid him as much as possible. Then she became aware of his large hands and long fingers, which seemed perfectly suited to working the controls of the craft.

As their bodies heated the air in the Flying Horse, she noticed how wonderful he smelled—as if he had bathed but moments before and had dusted himself with a refreshing powder laced with lime. He smelled so good that she had a wild compulsion to bury her face in the small of his neck and suck in a deep breath of him. The collar of his shirt, bleached to a blazing white, grazed the sharp line of his prominent jaw. His skin was smooth and tan and shaved to perfection. She almost reached out to touch him, to make sure he was real.

Shaken by her reaction to him, Elspeth glanced at his sharp profile. The first time she'd seen him, she had pegged him as conventionally handsome. But upon closer inspection, she realized that there might be more to Mark Ramsay than good looks and intoxicating cologne. There was something in his blue eyes—mental agility perhaps. Or cunning. She wasn't sure which.

He must have felt her staring at him. He shot her a questioning glance that made her flush all over again.

When he quirked his wide mouth like that, and flashed his white teeth at the side, her head flooded with a vision of her pressing kisses on his undeniably masculine lips. She had never seen such perfect teeth. Most people she knew had crooked discolored teeth from the lack of health care and proper diet.

"Yes?" he purred.

"Nothing."

Elspeth shook herself back to reality. What was she thinking? Mark Ramsay smelled heavenly. She hadn't bathed for three days. He was practically a nobleman in their socialist society. She was an impoverished mechanic. Worse, she was this man's prisoner. The sooner she got away from him, the better.

Captain Ramsay transported her to a redbrick townhouse tucked away on a quiet street that overlooked one of the few greenbelts left in the city. After the Modification Program undertaken centuries ago, when all buildings containing toxic material and electrical components were razed, only those structures built before 1880 were allowed to remain standing. So now, across from the townhouse, was a greenbelt where Scotland Yard, the once revered police unit, had operated. That police force was long gone, leaving the park as its tongue-in-cheek namesake. Scotland Yard ran all the way from this block to the Thames, and only the very rich lived along its border.

Ramsay parked the Flying Horse in a space beneath the house, and motioned for her to follow him up the stone stairs that led to an interior door.

"I can procure a chaperone if you like," he said, holding open the door for her. "My neighbor is always keen to make pocket change."

"I don't need a chaperone."

"Do you not?"

"I will never undergo a premarital inspection. So no."

He nodded, as if he took it for granted that a woman like her would never be selected for marriage. His reaction insulted her, and she was about to retort that she'd received a coveted silver envelope—thank you very much. But good sense muffled the words before she uttered them. Besides, it was considered impolite to discuss a person's upcoming nuptials with a stranger. Not everyone was "lucky" enough to be selected. A lot of people got passed over.

Elspeth swept into the townhouse. She expected to enter a lavish interior of velvet drapery and lush woven carpets. Instead the décor was comprised of simple black wood furniture, white upholstery, and gray walls—a plain but not unpleasant arrangement. A single painting hung over the ancient unused fireplace. Elspeth looked up at the portrait of a man in an old-fashioned suit and was struck by his blazing blue eyes framed by prominent dark brows and black hair. He wore a critical, penetrating expression that bore down upon her.

"My great-grandfather," Ramsay commented behind her. His cologne settled over her in a seductive cloud. "Alexander Ramsay."

"I see a resemblance."

"That's what they tell me."

"He looks as if he was a stern man."

"Times were dire when he sat for that portrait. Everyone was stern." He touched her elbow. "Come. Bathe yourself, eat, and then we will talk."

Elspeth pulled back. "What's there to talk about? And why me?"

"I need someone who knows their way around that machine." His lip curled. "Don't take it personally."

"I don't intend to." She glanced back at the stern visage of Alexander Ramsay.

The sight of Mark's relative reminded her of her own family. "Is there a way to get a message to my aunt?" she asked. "To let her know that I am all right, and where I'm at?"

"I will take care of it."

She had to trust him to do as she asked. She was powerless to do anything else. Like he had said, he could have her re-arrested in an instant. She decided not to argue with his agenda either. A bath and a decent meal would restore her. After she'd eaten, she would escape.

Elspeth followed Ramsay up a grand staircase to the

first floor. He ushered her into a chilly bedchamber that was larger than her aunt's entire house. Before she could tell him that she could manage on her own, he started a bath and then fetched a small box from a closet. She watched, curious, as he wound a key in the back and set the box near the tub. It whirred, issuing a wave of hot air.

"Whatever is that?" Elspeth gasped, ambling closer and holding out her cold hands.

"Something I've been working on." He watched her bask in the glow of the small heater. "It's damnable cold in these windowless Londo houses."

"These windowless houses saved us from the radiation cloud."

But thoughts of the past dissipated as she studied the box he'd produced. Surely, she was looking at the future.

Fascinated, she glanced up at him. "How can it be so small and yet create so much heat?"

"It's based on the same technology as the Flying Horse."

"Bacteria biofuel?"

"Yes, but in a more compressed form." He walked to the tub. "In small cartridges. It costs next to nothing to run."

Elspeth stared at the contraption. "You developed this?" she murmured.

"Surprised?"

She was. Mr. Big was becoming an even bigger enigma the more she got to know him. "Have you passed this by the Energy Board?"

"It's still in the testing stage." He shut off the water. "Besides, do you really think they'd ever let such a cheap source of heat hit the market?"

"What do you mean?"

"It's my theory," he handed her a towel, "that the

Overseers maintain their hold over Londo City by keeping the citizens cold and hungry. When a man's hungry, he thinks of nothing but his next meal."

Elspeth nearly dropped the towel. "You could be sent to the camps for saying that."

"Don't tell me you haven't thought the very same thing."

She met his serious gaze. For a long moment, all she could hear was the whir of the little heating unit and the thud of her heart as she stared up into his clear and—what she was beginning to suspect were—highly-intelligent eyes.

For a moment she thought of sharing her disdain of the Overseers and their reactionary ways. She wanted to. But blabbing about her rebellious political views was far too dangerous, especially with a Ramsay.

"Am I not right, Shutterhouse?" he prodded.

He was obviously fishing for information, probably to use against her in the future. That's what the privileged few did to keep their distance from the rabble of Londo City. They took what they liked, when they liked, and then turned their backs on their inferiors with no repercussions whatsoever, as long as they didn't violate the Edicts of Conduct set forth by the Overseers. But not many edicts pertained to the protection of the rabble, so in effect, the tiny plutocracy of Londo had free rein.

Elspeth was sure the Overseers saw the citizens of Londo as an expendable commodity, much like a herd of cattle. Their low opinion of common man infuriated her. Sure, there were many people who plodded through their lives and had no ambition beyond getting to the next day. But there were plenty of young people like herself who yearned for a better life and a say in how the city was run. There had to be a better way for people and more freedom of choice. She wasn't a cow. She wasn't part of a herd, and she wasn't going to be poked and prodded until she did what the Overseers wanted, especially when it came to her future.

There had been a time when the Overseers were needed. They had been angels of mercy, a handful of men who possessed great wisdom and resources. They had saved the human race from extinction after a nuclear accident—the Grave Mistake—had sparked a planetary war. Entire countries had been wiped out in the vicious battles that had followed the accident, and it was surmised that most of the people who survived the initial bombings died in the endless nuclear winter that followed.

But no one really knew how many humans had survived. No one in the Anglo Territories had heard from the rest of the world in over five hundred years.

After the war and ensuing chaos, a military state was needed and a socialist government required just to survive. As a safeguard against future disasters, the Overseers decreed that anything considered a threat to peace should be demolished. Entire neighborhoods were razed. All manufactured components and technological developments built after the year 1880 were destroyed. The use of electricity was outlawed. Only natural power— steam power—was allowed. Anything else was considered dangerous, with too great a potential for repeating the events that had almost destroyed the earth.

The lesson learned from the Grave Mistake was that human beings could not master the technology they developed. So the Overseers set the clock back to the machinery and mores of the 1880s, and there the Anglo Territories remained.

So far, their plan had worked. In fact, in the last ten years, the birth rate had actually begun to climb. Food was not rationed quite so strictly. The weather was beginning to change. And that's why Elspeth was determined to make a stand. A new day was dawning. It was time someone convinced the Overseers to take a step back.

The trouble was, the Overseers were unapproachable, and for all intents and purposes, invisible. They lived in a well-guarded compound that had once been known as Buckingham Palace and were never seen coming or going. It was impossible to get an audience with an Overseer as well. There were numerous administrative levels to get through just to lodge a simple complaint or request. No one had ever made it all the way to the top.

Elspeth frowned.

"What I think won't change the world," she finally replied. "And might only get me in trouble."

"Not with me."

"And why should I trust you?"

"I'm beginning to suspect we might have many similarities."

For a moment, she glanced back up to his face. He gazed down at her, his navy eyes dark with smoldering intensity. The way he looked at her made her feel as if his every thought was focused on her reply and that he might actually be interested in her views. In that moment, she felt more power over a man than she had known in all her twenty-five years. But such power was fleeting. If he could turn on his charm like that, he could turn it off just as quickly. His interest in her was probably just an act.

"Sorry, I keep my thoughts to myself," she quipped, "And I work alone." She headed for the bath before he could say anything more.

Still, his charm had wormed its way through her defenses, enough to set her heart banging against her ribs. Then and there she made a vow that she would never again let her guard down when in the man's company.

Chapter 3

"Shutterhouse." Elspeth became aware of a presence.

"Elspeth."

Someone nudged her right shoulder.

She sighed, too groggy to open her eyes and respond to the person summoning her. To avoid further attempts to rouse her, she turned over on her back. A cool rush of air washed over her, startling her.

"Good heavens!" a man exclaimed.

Then it hit her. She felt a chill because she had just rolled out of the huge towel she had been draped in. And she was stark naked beneath it.

Startled, Elspeth blinked to complete consciousness and was appalled to discover Mark Ramsay staring down at her, his eyes wide. For an instant, they were both immobilized by shock. The next instant, each of them plunged into action.

Elspeth scrambled to a sitting position and struggled to conceal her nakedness with her hands and the strands of her recently shampooed hair.

Ramsay laughed out loud and turned his back.

Elspeth fumbled for the towel. Her hands shook from being awakened so abruptly. She could feel a blush flooding her face, and wasn't sure what made her more upset—the fact that he'd seen her naked or the fact that he was laughing at her. "You shouldn't sneak up on people like that!" she cried.

"Sneak?" he retorted over his shoulder. "I've been calling for you for five minutes."

"Five minutes?" She yanked the ends of the towel around her torso.

"At least five. I thought you might be dead. I had to come in. For your own good." He turned around to face her. "And you were dead all right. Dead to the world."

Elspeth glanced around the room. Apparently she had taken a bath, gone to the bed to dress, sat down on the comforter and had fallen asleep still wrapped in the large towel. "It's no wonder. I haven't had a decent night's sleep for days."

"Obviously." He reached out his hand. "But come."

She glanced at his fingers, and before she thought twice, she raised her hand to meet his. His flesh was warm, as if a roaring furnace fired his body. A melting sensation washed over her as he drew her to her feet. Then he lifted her hand closer and frowned.

"Your knuckles," he commented. "What happened?"

"Nuts." She snatched away her hand, appalled yet again that he had noticed her ugly fingers. "In hard to reach places."

"I see." He seemed to find the explanation amusing.

"Comes with the job."

"Ah." His grin widened.

"I fail to see what's so funny."

"Forgive me, Shutterhouse. I am accustomed to the humor of my men. I read the wrong meaning behind your words." He bowed his head slightly, more to hide a chuckle than to show remorse. "But you have one more task ahead of you. And then you may sleep as long as you wish."

"What task is that?"

"I'll tell you over dinner."

"Dinner?" Her stomach rumbled in protest. Her knees felt weak. She didn't think she could wait that long to eat.

"Yes, dinner." He released her hand and reached for a shirt draped over the end of the bed. "Put this on and come down. The food's growing cold."

Elspeth glanced around the room again, searching for a clock this time.

"Shutterhouse?"

She turned back to look at him again. His blue eyes danced as he gazed down at her. "It's six o'clock. You slept the entire day."

Elspeth sat down in the chair Ramsay pulled out for her at the dining table. She hadn't eaten supper with a man since her father died. And she'd never eaten supper while dressed in a man's shirt. But the unusual external trappings of dinner paled when she looked down at her plate.

"Are those peaches?" she whispered, shooting him a glance.

He nodded. "I brought some supplies with me from the island. I know they're canned, but I thought you might like them all the same."

She couldn't believe her eyes. "There are peaches on the island?"

"Sometimes. If the weather is just right." He laughed again. He had an easy laugh. When a person didn't have to struggle for every penny, for every loaf of bread, life was probably something to laugh about. She looked up at him.

"Go ahead, Shutterhouse. Try one."

"I've never tasted a peach."

"I guarantee you will like it." He smiled. Again, his white teeth gleamed, lighting up his face.

Elspeth picked up her fork and sliced through the soft flesh of the peach. She admired the deep orange crescent tinged with crimson as she raised the fruit to her lips. Then she placed the slice on her tongue, closed her eyes, and sat back.

"Well?"

She chewed slowly, savoring every succulent morsel of the delicate fruit.

"Shutterhouse?"

Elspeth raised her hand, silencing him until she swallowed. Then she smiled and opened her eyes as pleasure washed over her. Finally, she sighed and looked at him. He was watching her, his lips slightly parted.

"That must be what an orgasm is like," she murmured.

He choked and reached for his ale. "Pardon?"

"An orgasm."

"What do you know of orgasms?"

She wanted to blurt out "plenty." But then she would have to tell him where she had learned about orgasms: under *Hormones, Female, Encyclopedia Britannica*, Vol. G-H. If anyone found out she possessed forbidden literature, she would be in even bigger trouble.

Elspeth shrugged. "I've heard about them."

"Well, there's no such thing."

She looked up, not believing his claim.

"Not for respectable citizens." Ramsay finished his ale in a gulp. "You know that as well as I do."

Elspeth recalled one of the verses that had been pounded into her as an adolescent.

Communion between a man and wife has but one purpose: to create life.

"Maybe it's just respectable *men* who don't have orgasms," she mused, cutting into the chicken breast he had arranged on her plate. "And women just pretend not to have them. So no one is the wiser."

"And what do you think an orgasm is?"

"A series of muscle contractions."

"Like a cramp?" He put down his empty glass.

"But one that produces euphoria." Elspeth sighed and looked across the room toward the front all. "I'd like to experience euphoria someday."

She looked back at Ramsay to find him studying the side of her face. As soon as she noticed his stare, he broke it off and grabbed his knife and fork.

"And you consider the act of eating peaches similar to the orgasm?"

"For me it is." She lifted another slice to her lips. "Perhaps for you, a pampered scion of the Ramsay family, peaches have lost their cachet."

"You think I'm pampered?"

"Really, Ramsay." She shook her head as she scooped up a spoonful of the creamiest potatoes she had ever eaten. "You live like a king compared to the rest of us."

His eyebrows rose. "I beg to differ."

"This house, the Flying Horse, this food…"

"All my great-grandfather's. And only when I am in town."

"And at the Outer Islands?"

"There I mostly live out-of-doors." He set his jaw and leveled his sapphire gaze upon her. "Come now, Shutterhouse. Do I look like a man who spends his days lounging about the house, sipping tea?"

She couldn't help but run a glance over his massive shoulders and powerful torso. "Actually no," she replied. "But what *do* you do?"

"I'm a soldier, mostly." His gaze shifted, as if his consciousness had switched to another time and place. "There are a lot of wild things out there—both man and beast, all wanting what we possess here in Londo. My men and I patrol the border islands, to keep the rest of you citizens safe."

She opened her mouth to protest that she found it hard to believe a Ramsay would put himself in danger for the rest of society. But a second glance at his firm mouth and large hands, and her harsh opinion of his family died on her lips. In fact, for the first time she noticed scars on the backs of his hands and just under his chin. A person didn't get scars like his from teacups and scones.

"I'm the second son," he added. "My family clings to the old ways."

"And that is?"

"The first son inherits. The second son enters the military. In my case a private army."

"Do you have a lot of siblings?"

"Just the one. Thomas." He refilled her glass. "And you?"

"None. My mother died young."

"I'm sorry to hear it."

She glanced at him in surprise. The sincerity in his voice warmed her.

"Don't be," Elspeth replied. "I didn't know my mother. And my father and great aunt more than made up for her loss. I had a wonderful childhood."

He smiled in his engaging way and leaned back. "And I take it, a somewhat unconventional one?"

She nodded. "I was taught as if I was neither girl nor boy. I was allowed to investigate whatever interested me."

"Even mechanics."

"Especially mechanics. My father was the best mechanic in Londo City. A genius. He made me what I am today."

"Well he certainly did *some* job."

Elspeth shot him a stare. "What do you mean?"

"It's a compliment, Shutterhouse." He grinned and

leveled his gaze on her. When he directed his attention to her like that, she felt as if she were swimming in warm butter. She tried to adhere to her vow of keeping up her guard but was finding it impossible.

"I have to confess," he murmured. "I've never met anyone quite like you."

Elspeth gaze locked with his. For a moment she took Ramsay's words at face value. For a moment, she let herself enjoy the marvelous feeling of talking to Mark Ramsay without the censure of her aunt or cousin to hold her back. She sensed a fellow independent spirit in the man. In fact Ramsay was the first person she'd talked so freely with since her father had died. She couldn't believe how wrong she had been about the man—and perhaps his entire clan. She hoped what she felt was real, and prayed that he wasn't deceiving her. The more she got to know the man, the more she ached to lower her guard completely.

But her great aunt—a spinster who had never entered the Marriage Machine—had not raised a fool. Elspeth would think twice—even three times—before trusting a man.

Shaken by her reaction to Mark, Elspeth reached for her ale. She knew it was best if she turned to the conversation to a less personal topic. "So I take it you will eventually tell me why you snatched me off the street?"

He smiled. "I have a proposal for you."

"And that is?"

"First, let me tell you about my great-grandfather."

"The one in the painting."

"Yes. Perhaps the most famous custodian of the Marriage Machine."

"Oh." Elspeth couldn't hide her look of disdain.

"Don't dismiss it so out of hand, Shutterhouse. It's the machine that saved mankind from extinction."

"You don't think we would have survived?" Elspeth countered. "Without mechanical intervention?"

"That will always be an unknown." Ramsay sobered. "But it did serve one purpose to be sure."

"The taming of females?" Elspeth put in, her voice harsh.

"To survive, Shutterhouse." He held up his hand to cut off her protests. "To survive, the human race had to return to a more conventional way of life. Someone had to work and someone had to raise the children to be decent human beings with strong values. To really take the time. I know it sounds prehistoric, but women and men had to learn to work together for the greater good. And *stick* together."

"Funny how women were the ones to be altered."

"Females simply proved to be more sensitive to the machine. I'm sure my ancestors did not plan such an outcome."

"My cousin has never been the same since she stepped into that machine. Or two of my older friends. They do whatever their husbands ask."

"But are they unhappy?"

Elspeth thought of Amelie bouncing her son on her knee and laughing.

"Are they, Shutterhouse?"

"No, but as my father used to say, 'No brains, no headache.'"

"To ensure the survival of the human race, men and women have to marry. That's a fact, Elspeth. Would you rather be trapped in an unhappy marriage and be miserable for the rest of your life, or have your sharp edges worn off a little so you don't even know what you were missing?"

"You can ask me a question like that with a straight face?" Indignant, Elspeth jumped to her feet.

He jumped to his. "What other choice is there?"

"Not to be trapped at all!" She threw her napkin on the table.

"You don't wish to be married? To have children?"

She planted a fist on her hip and threw his own words back at him. "Ramsay, do I look like a woman who lounges around the house, sipping tea?"

She glared at him, and for a moment she thought he might strike her. But in the next instant he threw back his head and laughed.

"I don't find it amusing!" she exclaimed.

"I do." He held his shaking torso as if trying to hold back the laughter rumbling through his muscular frame.

"And if you have brought me here, thinking I'm going to put that ruby back, you are sadly mistaken." She turned and dashed for the door.

Ramsay's laughter broke off as he pivoted to stop her. He grabbed her arm and yanked her to a halt. "That is precisely what you are going to do," he retorted, all humor dropped from his tone. His eyes flashed at her, cool as ice.

"Never!"

"I will return you to jail and make sure you are sentenced to life."

"You wouldn't!"

"I would." He glared down at her, his color high. She could imagine that glare made his men quake in their boots. But she refused to back down.

She glared back at him. "Tell me you would personally choose to marry a woman like that."

"A woman like what?"

"One whose edges have been smoothed by that machine."

"How do you know I haven't?"

"You don't seem the type."

His eyes changed, almost imperceptibly. But Elspeth noticed the way his pupils widened, darkening his eyes to navy.

"Listen, Shutterhouse," he growled. "I don't care if you plant a bomb in that machine. But not until after my great-grandfather passes away."

"He's still alive?" She sensed that she had begun to reach some sense in Ramsay and quit pulling from his grip.

"Yes, but barely. He's 101 years old. And he's damnably proud of that machine. For good reason."

Elspeth was uncharacteristically lost for words.

"He vowed to stay in this realm until he saw one last marriage ceremony. He wants to go to the beyond knowing the Ramsay name will live on through my brother."

"Your brother Thomas is getting married?"

"On C-Day."

A chill raced down Elspeth's spine.

"And as you know, the machine guarantees conception."

Elspeth thought back to her cousin's prediction—that she had been chosen to marry someone of the upper echelon of society. What if she were destined to wed a Ramsey? The chill spread through her, doubling her resolve to avoid her date with the Marriage Machine.

"My job is to see the ceremony goes off without a hitch." Ramsay quirked one of his dry smiles. "Or *with*, as the case may be."

He released her arm, and she backed away, her thoughts swirling.

"Why can't you just keep the ruby out of the equation?" she sputtered. "It's so well concealed within the casing of the machine. No one would ever know it was missing."

"My great-grandfather might."

"How?" she shrugged. "He's 101 years old."

"And he knows every inch of that machine." Ramsay sighed. "As a matter of fact, he's called for an inspection of the Marriage Machine. He'll be here first thing tomorrow morning to conduct the inspection personally. If he finds one bolt out of place—one loose screw—I don't know what it will do to him."

Elspeth stared at Ramsay.

"I love my great-grandfather, Elspeth. And there is nothing on this earth that I wouldn't do for him. Nothing."

"So how do I fit into this grand scheme of yours?"

"You and I are breaking into Boswellian Bower tonight. And you are going to replace the ruby."

"But it will take hours to get to the heart of the machine."

"You've done it before." Ramsay pulled out his pocket watch and glanced down at it. "I estimate that you could complete the job in five."

"You have no idea how complicated that machine is."

"Perhaps. But you will have me to assist you."

Elspeth gave him a scathing glance. She could imagine Ramsay with a gun. She could imagine him in a fistfight or brawl. But she could not imagine him with a screwdriver.

"I'm not completely unfamiliar with machines," he added.

She would give him that. He'd built the simple heater. There was hope.

"And if I can't do it?"

"There is no such thing as can't." He shot back.

"What do I get if I actually succeed?"

It was his turn to scald her with a glance. "Isn't your freedom enough?"

"No."

Ramsay tilted his head. "What then?"

"I want safe passage to the Outer Islands."

"You don't know what you're saying."

"I want to leave Londo City. I don't belong here."

"You don't want to go to the Outer Islands." He scowled. "It's no place for a woman."

"You live there."

He crossed his arms. "I'm not a woman. Or at least I wasn't the last time I checked."

"Your family lives there."

"In a compound." He swept the air with an impatient wave of his hand.

"Promise me safe passage, Ramsay."

"Very well!" He sighed. "Replace the ruby without complication, and you shall be transported north." He stuffed his watch into the pocket of his vest. "Now hurry up, Shutterhouse, and dress. We leave in ten minutes."

Chapter 4

ELSPETH WAS SURPRISED AT HOW COLD IT WAS when she jumped out of the Flying Horse and grabbed the tools Ramsay had procured for the job. It was what she supposed a winter night might have been like in the old days—without the snow. The air was crisp, ice covered the puddles in the alley, and frost crawled up the windows. She could see Ramsay's breath when he told her to wait while he parked the vehicle around the corner and out of sight.

Wrapped in a long coat that belonged to a member of the Ramsay family, Elspeth waited for him to return. The coat was warm, so she wasn't cold, but she shuddered all the same. At ten o'clock on a December evening, the alley behind Boswellian Bower was dark and deserted. Even the rats had taken cover on this cold night. Elspeth glanced up at the sky and searched for the moon she had spotted earlier that morning. There it was again, like a big eye, watching her—even clearer this time. She wondered if the WeatherWizards were right—that the fog lying over Londo City would finally lift after its century-long stay.

Ramsay trotted up, his winter coat flapping around his shins, his boats gleaming in the moonlight, and the many buttons of his coat glinting as he ran. His shirt, knotted at the throat, glowed above his vest and lit up his eyes.

"Why must we break into the Bower?" she asked,

following him to the back door. "Why not just tell someone that the machine has to be repaired?"

"I can't take the chance that my great-grandfather might discover his beloved contraption has been tampered with. Davies thinks everything is fine. I want to keep it that way." He turned at the door and cupped his hands. "Come, Shutterhouse."

Elspeth glanced at his linked fingers. "What do you have in mind?"

"I'm going to hoist you up to that transom."

Elspeth glanced up to the arched window at the top of the door.

"I'll wager the transom is not locked. I'll lift you, you will open it, crawl through, jump down and then let me in the door."

"You've got to be joking."

"I am not." He nodded his head toward his hands. "Come. Step into my hand."

"You think I can get through that window and jump seven feet to the ground?"

"I'd do it myself if I thought you could lift me." He cocked one of his expressive black brows.

There was no argument to be made. She could no more lift the giant in front of her than she could fly to the now visible moon. She would do her best to sabotage the machine, but with Ramsay breathing down her neck, she probably wouldn't have a second chance to disable it. Her best recourse would be to look for an opportunity to escape—but only after she and Ramsay got off the street and out of sight. For now, she had to cooperate.

Elspeth deposited the satchel of tools on the pavement beside him, slipped out of her coat, and placed it on the bag. Then she lifted her foot. To steady herself, she was forced to plant her hand on Ramsay's shoulder. The man was a rock of muscle. With a grunt, she shifted her weight onto her foot and propelled herself forward as he raised her upward. She braced herself against the wooden door as he straightened his legs and lifted her past the top of the door. When he grabbed her knees and lifted her higher, she wobbled but caught herself by clutching the sill of the transom. Then she pushed the stained glass with her right palm. The transom moved inward.

"Is it unlocked?" His voice was muffled by her clothing.

"Yes."

"Can you get it open?"

As she struggled with the window, she felt him brace her feet on his shoulders. The cold soon took hold of her fingers, making her clumsy. But she managed to crack open the transom far enough to wiggle through. She looked down, worrying about how she was going to get through the window and position herself to jump without falling face first onto the floor below. But as her eyes grew accustomed to the darkness of the corridor, she had an idea.

"Hold my ankles," she instructed.

She felt Ramsay's big hands wrap around her boots.

Elspeth pushed through the opening and bent at the waist. Then, straining, she could just reach the inside handle of the door. As the blood raced to her head, and the transom sill cut into her midsection, she explored the latch with her nearly numb fingers. Then she found the locking mechanism. She shifted it open.

"Got it?" Ramsay asked.

"Try it."

Still holding one of her feet, Ramsay turned the latch and pushed the door, just enough to make sure it was unlocked. Then Elspeth wriggled out of the transom, crouched, and slid down Ramsay's back. When her feet hit the ground, he turned and clutched her elbows.

"Good work." He gave her a brief survey. "Are you all right?"

"I'm fine. Just cold."

She broke away to grab the coat and tools, and they slipped into Boswellian Bower.

Elspeth had been to a few weddings. Her acquaintances were slowly turning twenty-five, and the lucky ones received silver envelopes. Although Elspeth didn't consider marriage the right choice for her, nonetheless she attended the nuptials of her friends to show moral support. But those weddings had been conducted in a much more modest bower. From what she could see in the shadows, Boswellian Bower was appointed in understated grandeur.

She followed Ramsay down a corridor comprised of marble floors, embossed wallpaper, and ornate brass lamps. He seemed to know where he was going, and led her into a large room, much like an auditorium, with gilt and plush chairs, and a thick carpet that ran from the entry doors to the stage. Squatting on the platform behind velvet curtains and stage lamps, was the Marriage Machine.

"There she is," Ramsay remarked in a hushed tone beside her. "The Marriage Machine."

Elspeth's heart beat a bit faster. This was the place Fate waited for her. Here would begin the life the Overseers had calculated to suit her and her groom. She frowned and stuffed down her panic. *Not if she could help it.*

"Is there a watchman?" Elspeth asked.

"I am not sure." He motioned her toward the machine. "So try to be as quiet as possible."

"But surely, a watchman will see our light."

"Not if we keep the curtains well drawn." Ramsay strode to the side of the stage and worked the ropes until the curtains swished closed. Elspeth stepped into the now-silent bower and pushed back the curtains that lined the interior, knowing that she must remove the carved walnut panels before she reached any machine parts.

Ramsay lit the lamp they had brought, and set it down in the middle of the bower, just as Elspeth turned for the tools. They straightened at the same time, their noses inches apart. Ramsay gazed down at her, his firm mouth accentuated by the light below. She could see his chest rise and fall with each breath, and wanted to reach out and touch him just below the vee at the top of his vest, to feel what she was sure was the center of the furnace that fired him. He seemed as dazed by the moment as she was. But unlike her, he made a move.

He caught her hands and pressed them between his blazing palms.

"You're frozen," he remarked.

"I'll thaw," she stuttered.

"And much lighter than I imagined."

"My aunt says I'm scrawny."

"Scrawny?" His mouth slanted upward in the sardonic smile that was beginning to have a physical affect on her, especially when he stood so close to her. A flush blossomed deep inside her. "I wouldn't say scrawny. Lithe comes to mind."

"Lithe?" She wondered if she had heard him correctly. She had always thought of herself as skinny. Unfeminine. Boyish, even. The word "lithe" cast her figure in an entirely new light. She blushed and hoped he couldn't see her reaction in the darkness.

"Like a mink," he added.

"What's a mink?" She tried to pull away her hands, but he held fast.

"An animal I've seen in the north. They are as slender as you are. With a pelt as soft and sleek as your hair. Quick, smart, and damnably difficult to catch."

His comparison shocked her. No one had ever paid her a higher compliment. She pulled at his grip again.

"Shouldn't we be getting to work, Ramsay?"

He sighed. "You're right." He released her. "Just tell me what to do."

Elspeth would have liked to tell him to lean down and kiss her, to wrap those big warm hands around her and pull her into his fiery chest. But she was positive such a command would backfire, and the only one to suffer would be her.

"Give me uh," she pointed at the satchel. She had to give herself a mental shake, to get her mind back on the job. "Get me a slotted screwdriver." She walked to the nearest panel, knelt on the soft carpet, and held out her hand.

Hours ticked by. As Elspeth worked her way toward the heart of the Marriage Machine, she handed each machine part to Ramsay. He in turn, arranged each piece on a sheet behind him, in the order she gave it to him. They worked swiftly, efficiently, and never spoke a word, until Elspeth arrived at the ornate brass frame that formerly held the ruby.

"What were you going to do with the ruby anyway?" Ramsay asked, breaking the hours of silence.

She shrugged. "I hadn't decided. I just didn't want to store it at my Aunt Fi's house and get her in trouble. So I buried it."

"I see."

"I never could have sold it. A citizen with a stone like that?" she shook her head as she unfastened the large nuts behind the frame. "I would have been sent to the camps for sure."

"So you didn't think further than burying the jewel?"

Ramsay asked.

"No. I didn't think anyone would ever find out it had been taken."

"I see." Ramsay sighed and took a gear housing out of her hands. "You should never let your guard down, Elspeth. You should always assume that you are being watched."

"I know that," she replied. "Now."

After a half-hour, she lifted the front of the frame off and set it at her feet.

"Ready?" Ramsay asked behind her.

"If I must." She sighed. "This goes against everything I believe in."

"Do it for my great-grandfather."

"I don't give a fig for your great-grandfather."

"Then do it for me."

She pressed her lips together. There was no denying the regard she felt for Mark Ramsay was growing with every minute she spent in his company. But she could never let him know.

"For you?" she forced a laugh. "That's a real motivator, Ramsay."

He fell silent behind her, and she turned slightly to find his expression had changed from open to closed. Surprise and guilt washed over her. She had never guessed she possessed the power to hurt a man's feelings.

Without a retort for once, he pivoted and reached into the satchel for a bundle wrapped in wool. Elspeth watched him slip the ruby out of the cloth.

She could not deny the allure of the jewel, no matter how she felt about the Marriage Machine. Even in the low light of the lamp, the ruby glowed as if it had a heartbeat of its own. Ramsay pushed it toward her outstretched hands.

"Careful," he warned. "And no tricks. One slip, and

the jewel will shatter."

"I'll be careful." She took the jewel in both of her palms and lifted it toward the frame.

They didn't speak again until the Marriage Machine had been reassembled, cleaned, and polished to perfection.

As dawn crept over the frozen city, Elspeth and Ramsay whisked back in silence to the Ramsay townhouse. Elspeth kept her eyes on the road and her hands in her lap, and wished she had some of the ice outside to place upon her newly skinned knuckles. They parked under the house again, and Ramsay told her to follow him, but held a finger to his lips.

"My family is here," he warned. "They must have arrived for the wedding while we were gone."

She remained standing by the Flying Horse. "I should go."

"*Where* will you go?" He mounted the stairs. "You can't go to your aunt's. The police may have questions about the ruby that you would be better off not answering."

"You promised me safe passage to the north."

He rolled his eyes. "Not today."

"When, then?"

"You'll have to have a pass. I'll have to get one for you."

"How long will that take?"

"A day or two." He put his hand on the latch of the door. "Or you could wait and go back with my family. They would get you through the border without a problem."

"Would they agree to such a thing?"

"They would do whatever I asked."

"I see." She paused, wondering what it would be like to have such power and such loyalty as the Ramsay clan seemed to possess.

"So you must come inside. You have only to wait a few days, whatever you decide to do. And then you shall be a free woman."

She took a step toward him. "What will I do in the meantime?"

"Whatever you like." He opened the door to the main level. "What do you normally do in your free time?"

"Work."

He smiled down at her. "That you shall not do here."

"It's all I know."

"Well, you're going to have to change your spots, Shutterhouse, at least until after the wedding."

Chapter 5

ELSPETH PADDED AFTER RAMSAY as he strode into the house. She assumed he would take her up to the huge bedchamber on the first floor, but he turned left before mounting the grand staircase.

"Drink?" he asked. "I confess I need to transition before I can sleep."

"Thank you, I would like one."

He nodded and ushered her into what had once been the library off the main hall. The books had been confiscated long ago during the cleansing, leaving a bank of polished walnut shelves. Instead of books, the shelves displayed stuffed animals, trophies, and cut and polished stones.

Ramsay headed toward a cabinet at the end of the library as Elspeth wandered to the center of the large and unnecessary room, taking in yet another aspect of the wealth of the Ramsay family. But her survey was cut short by a sharp rap behind her.

She whirled around, shocked to see an ancient man in a wheelchair in the doorway. He looked like a skeleton dressed in a suit. His face was dotted with age spots, his ears were enormous in comparison to his waspish neck. But he still had an amazing head of white hair that floated in the air around his skull. This had to be Mark's beloved great-grandfather. Before Elspeth could utter a greeting, he rapped the floor again with his cane and glowered.

"Where the devil have you been?" he shouted. His wrinkled lips showed a surprising number of teeth in such an old human being.

"Out wenching," Mark replied. He strolled up beside Elspeth and offered her a glass of cut crystal. Then he leaned over and patted his great-grandfather on the shoulder. "Nothing to worry about, Gramps. Don't overtax yourself."

"Overtax? Overtax?" the old man's icy eyes blazed. "Your mother has been beside herself wondering where you are. I doubt she slept a wink. And who the devil is this?" He jabbed his cane at Elspeth.

She had to steel herself to keep from stepping backward.

"The wench I was wenching with."

Elspeth blushed scarlet. She was not accustomed to such confrontation or such language, especially with a member of the older generation. The ancient man's blue regard raced over her. He snorted in contempt.

"Don't look like the wenching sort."

"I'm not," Elspeth shot back, insulted by the old man's rude behavior—and the young man's as well. Had they lost their manners? No one had even introduced her.

"I'm Elspeth Shutterhouse, mechanic."

"You don't say," the old man retorted. He cocked one brow and glared at her hands. "And what brings a mechanic to my house at the ungodly hour of six a.m.?"

Elspeth noticed Mark taking a swig of his whisky, as if playing for time. Of course, he couldn't divulge what they'd been doing for the past ten hours. Maybe he was having trouble coming up with an alibi.

"Actually, your great-grandson came to my assistance."

"Oh?" the blue stare shifted to Ramsay. "In what

way?"

"He helped me escape from my indenture. I was apprenticed to a man who was very cruel to me. In fact he used me as a slave. I would never have got away, had it not been for Citizen Ramsay."

"Heroics? Mark?"

Mark nodded and took another drink.

"He found me on the road last night, running for my life. My master actually caught up with me, however, and dragged me back. It took Citizen Ramsay a good deal of time and trouble, but he freed me early this morning. And here I am."

The intense stare landed on her again. "And what does my great-grandson propose to do with you?"

"Shutterhouse would make a good addition to the compound."

"Or anywhere else on the Outer Islands," she put in, certain she would rather be free of the Ramsays if they were all as rude as this.

"She's a hard worker, Gramps. She's careful."

"And how do you know such things?"

"My boss told him." Elspeth clutched her drink, hoping the old man would believe her tall tale. "That's why he wanted me back so badly."

"How old are you, young lady?"

She threw back her shoulders. "Twenty-five. And I have a good fifty-five years of work in me, at least."

"Hmph." The bushy white brows lowered as the older Ramsay inspected her.

"I don't believe you're a wench, but I don't believe your story, either."

Elspeth paled, fearful that she might be thrown out on the street without a pass to the north.

"That coat you're wearing." He pointed the tip of the cane at the long wool garment Elspeth still had on. "People think I'm deaf, blind and doddering in the bargain. But I recognize my granddaughter's town coat when I see it."

"It was in the Flying Horse," Ramsay put in. "Elspeth was cold. Frozen to the bone in fact."

"A likely tale, boy."

"I told Shutterhouse she could have safe passage north," Mark put in. "We could use more citizens like her in the Outer Islands."

"And how do you expect that to occur?" the old man turned to stare up at his great-grandson. "Does she have papers?"

"No. But surely you can get her through."

"Why should I?"

"Because I made a promise to her."

Elspeth was highly conscious that Mark remained standing shoulder to shoulder with her, lending his support in the face of the older Ramsay's censure. Still, Elspeth found herself holding her breath.

Alexander Ramsay wrapped his gnarled fingers around the handle of his cane and scowled. "I don't know what you two have been up to. But it's high time you made your presence known to your mother, boy. Off with you."

Mark cupped Elspeth's elbow. "Shutterhouse?" He urged her toward the door.

"Not her," Ramsay barked. "She stays. Let her finish her drink."

Elspeth knew she was doomed.

Elspeth watched Mark leave the library. She sipped her drink, uncomfortable and worried. She could feel Alexander Ramsay staring at her.

"The truth, young lady." He squinted one of his eyes as he peered up at her. "I will have it. Now."

Something told Elspeth she would never leave this library and likely never leave Londo, unless she told the truth to the gentleman in the wheelchair—or at least a teeny, weenie version of the truth. She put her glass on a side table and slipped out of the luxurious wool coat.

"I work for the SteamWizards." She stepped closer so the old man could see her uniform.

Ramsay shot a glance at the badge above her right breast.

"I'm one of their top mechanics."

"You don't say."

His scrutiny brought back the dogma from her childhood.

Women are wrong if they think they are strong.

Elspeth held herself as straight as possible.

He sat back. "I could tell by your knuckles that you work with your hands."

She nodded. "I was called to make a repair, and that's how I met your great-grandson."

"So your apprenticeship story was claptrap."

"Yes."

"Why the lie?"

"Because Mark believes you are too fragile to handle the truth."

"The devil!" He stamped his cane on the ground. "What truth?"

"He thinks you would not survive the shock should you discover the Marriage Machine needed to be repaired."

Ramsay's jaw fell open, but that was the extent of any physical reaction on his part. He quickly recovered his composure. "Something went wrong with the machine?" he demanded.

"Technically, no." Elspeth took another step closer, warming to the crusty old man as she had warmed to his great-grandson. "It's my opinion that the machine had been tampered with."

"Tampered with?" Ramsay bellowed. "No one would

dare!"

"But I fixed it. It was a simple repair. Probably caused during transport."

"I'll have Davies' head!"

"Sir, it was a simple puncture. It could have happened to anyone. Anytime." She crossed her arms. "But the Marriage Machine is as good as new—unfortunately."

"What do you mean by that, young lady?"

"I mean no disrespect, Citizen Ramsay. Your family's invention may have saved the human race—"

"There is no doubt that it did."

"And again, no disrespect." She paused, hoping her words would not over excite the man and cause him to have a heart attack. But she didn't think he was as frail as Mark had led her to believe. She sensed in him an indomitable physical being and an even more indomitable spirit—much like she hoped someone would see in her someday.

She raised her chin. "I believe the Marriage Machine has seen its day."

"What?" he sputtered. "You have no idea what you are talking about." Spittle flew from his wrinkled lips "What's your name again?"

"It's Shutterhouse, sir."

"Shutterhouse, before *my* great-grandfather invented that machine, we were lucky to have a handful of births a year in Londo City. The damned radiation cloud had made everyone sterile."

"I am aware of that. But that was long ago. The world is changing."

"People's reproductive organs were malfunctioning."

"I know. My great aunt told me all about it."

"You stand here today, Shutterhouse, because of the Marriage Machine. Without the machine, your own mother would never have realized the full bloom of womanhood."

"But as I have said, times are changing." Elspeth pressed forward, wanting to be heard for once by someone who might be able to make a change, even though she suspected her philosophy would not only ostracize her from Londo society but from the Ramsay clan as well. "Women's bodies are changing, citizen. But no one has the courage to speak out."

The wrinkles on his brow deepened. "What do you mean, women's bodies are changing?"

"Young women are reaching menarche on their own, without mechanical assistance. We are overcoming what the Grave Mistake did to us."

For a moment the old man gawked at her, as if he couldn't make sense of her words. Then he fought back his shocked expression.

"You're speaking nonsense." Ramsay shook his cane in the air. "Whoever heard of such a thing?"

"My cousin began bleeding at the age of twenty. My best friend at nineteen. And I myself have menstruated since I was twenty-two. But no one will come forward. They are too afraid of being labeled as freaks. They *want* to be selected for the Marriage Machine."

"And you don't?" he stared at her.

"No. Not when there are such side effects."

"Couldn't be helped." He cackled to himself. "And who wouldn't want a woman that's always happy to see you—is never upset by anything?"

"Weren't dogs bred for that?" Elspeth retorted, her voice cold. "And look what happened to them."

Ramsay stared up at her from under his bushy white brows.

"I doubt *your* wife was a drone," Elspeth remarked. "I bet she wasn't a little brown mouse from Londo City, dumbed down and silly."

Ramsay's watery eyes slanted away. For a moment he gazed at the wall of blank shelves as if looking back to earlier days, to the days the library had been full of books and perhaps a beautiful young woman who had loved him and at the same time challenged him. For a moment, he lapsed deep into thought.

"I'm tired," he snapped, without looking back at her. His shoulders seemed to have disappeared beneath the shell of his suit. "All this talk is wearisome."

"I'm sorry, but the truth is hard to take," she said. "And change is even harder."

He glanced at her, and their eyes locked. For a moment she thought she had gotten through to him, and that he was going to say something. But then he broke off the stare and rapped his cane on the floor.

"Mark!" he shouted. "Mark!" He scowled at her, as if he'd come to a decision. "I don't know where you belong, young lady," he exclaimed. "In a detention center or an insane asylum."

Elspeth sucked in a breath, damning her faulty judgment in having said too much to the wrong person.

"But I can assure you, Shutterhouse, that you will not leave this house until the Overseers have been notified."

"Please do not betray me," she begged.

He frowned, pursing his lips over his prominent teeth as he regarded her with his watery but sharp regard. "I have no choice. It was high-handed know-it-alls like you who caused all the trouble in the first place. It appears that you have learned nothing from history."

She had, but not from the history the Overseers had fed them.

Elspeth swallowed and glanced around the room. She was trapped for certain if she didn't take a move before Mark returned.

She dashed around the old man in his wheelchair.

"Where are you going, young lady?" Ramsay shouted. "Come back here!"

Elspeth sprinted down the hall, ran past the stairs and yanked open the front door of the townhouse. She fled across the street to Scotland Yard and plunged into a grove of yews, just as the first flakes of snow began to fall.

Chapter 6

ELSPETH SAT ON THE HARD BENCH OF HER CELL, a piece of paper in her hand, and her stomach churning with anger. After being pursued through Londo City like a dog, she had been captured two days later and thrown into the detention center near her aunt's house. Wet, cold, and exhausted, she had been dragged into the same cell as before. They hadn't given her dry clothing or shoes and had left her to suffer the cold and to reflect on her transgressions. Hours later, an agent of the Overseers had delivered their decision.

The document in her hand ordered her—on the pain of death—to attend her wedding ceremony. She would be transported there by two guards, who would make sure she did not run away. Her aunt would be allowed to bring her a dress for the occasion, but that is all the contact she would have with her family until after the ceremony. They deemed the marriage punishment enough for her rebellious behavior—and they were right. Tying her to a man was the worst prison sentence she could imagine.

Elspeth's dinner sat untouched on a tray on the small table near the wall. She had no appetite, both for the food and for the day to come. She would be married at Boswellian Bower tomorrow afternoon at 4:00.

She sat there, tired, angry and frustrated, and barely took notice when two people approached her cell. If more agents had come to preach to her, she would cover her ears, curl up against the wall, and refuse to recognize their presence.

"Shutterhouse," a familiar voice called.

Shivering, Elspeth raised her head, shocked to see Mark Ramsay approach the other side of the bars. Words fled. She couldn't even utter a greeting. He was dressed in his usual black traveling coat, unbuttoned now, and displaying black and white eveningwear, set off by a white cravat tied at his throat. His family must be celebrating his brother's wedding by going out for the evening—a rare occasion for anyone these days. He must have come to mock her or upbraid her for disturbing his great-grandfather. Why else the thunder in his expression?

"Why hasn't this woman been given dry clothes?" Ramsay bellowed, glaring down at the guard.

"It was what the warden ordered."

"Get her clean things at once!" Ramsay pointed at the corridor behind him. "A blanket as well. And make it quick."

"I can't leave you here alone with her."

"You've searched me. I pose no threat. I'm only here to speak to her. Now off with you, before I report such inhumane treatment to the detention commissioner."

The guard scurried away as Elspeth rose, grateful for Mark's intercession but surprised to see him all the same.

"Good Lloyd," he grasped the bars and stared down at her. "Look what you've got yourself into, Shutterhouse."

"The worst is yet to come."

"You should have let me handle it."

"Why?" she retorted. "You have only one thought, to protect that infernal Marriage Machine."

"You should never have told my great-grandfather the truth."

"Someone needed to." She clutched the bars.

"Someone has to speak out. If your great-grandfather is the custodian of that machine, maybe the Overseers will listen to him."

"It doesn't necessarily work that way." Mark wrapped his warm fingers around her cold ones. She tried to snatch her hands away, but he held her fast.

"How does it work then?" she retorted. She had nothing more to lose. She might as well speak her mind. "Who *does* have the ear of the bloody all-powerful Overseers?"

"No one." His voice held no reproach. Only gentleness. She had to force herself not to break down in tears. "Unfortunately."

He stared down at her and did not chide her for being a fool, as everyone else had. She paused, suddenly wondering why he had actually visited, if not to berate her.

"Why didn't you tell me you had received a silver envelope?" he asked.

"You know the rules—no talk of envelopes outside the family."

"So you follow some rules and not others?"

She glared at him, still trying to get away, but fighting an entirely different battle on an internal level. Though it made no sense, she was glad to see Mark Ramsay. His outrage at her predicament had warmed her on the inside, just as his hands were warming her frozen fingers. His looming bulk was a bastion of strength between her and a world that had spun out of control. But worse, when he touched her and looked down at her with concern darkening his unusual eyes, her heart pattered in erratic leaps of elation.

Her breath caught in her throat. He seemed to notice, and for a moment he stared down at her lips. She thought he was going to kiss her. She ached to be kissed by him. She had never felt such a compulsion in her life. As she stood there, her hands surrounded by his big paws, she realized that she felt closer to Mark Ramsay than she had to anyone in her entire life.

But with the revelation came a bittersweet irony. This was one man she might be able to live with and not chafe at the bindings of matrimony—even without the Marriage Machine. But Mark was not destined to be part of her future.

"I'm told you are to be married tomorrow in fact," he continued.

"It hasn't escaped my notice," she replied. "Or anyone else's, it seems."

"A damnable situation." His voice rumbled with repressed emotion, and she glanced up at him, shocked. His grip tightened.

"Elspeth, it can make little difference if I speak my mind, but I—" He studied her face, and then seemed to think better of what he was about to say. He let his words fall to nothing and sighed.

"Why the sudden holding back?" She studied his face, wondering at his odd behavior. "You've been frank with me up until now. What are you hiding?"

"Some things are better left unspoken." He clamped his jaw tightly. She could see a muscle work on the left side of his face. "Forgive me. I forget myself."

"Mark," she jiggled her hands under his, trying to make her point, and trying to rattle him to his senses. "I'm to be married tomorrow. I'll never be the same. I'll never desire the things that I want so badly today. I'll be just a shadow of myself. Tell me what's on your mind."

He looked down and shook his head.

"It's *not* for the best," she continued earnestly. "Getting married in that machine. Maybe at one time it was. But it's no longer right or necessary that a woman lose herself for the greater good." She pressed her face to the bars until her nose nearly touched the cravat at his throat. "Please, Mark, can't you get me out of here? Just let me run?"

"You can't live outside society, El."

"I could!"

"It will be just another prison sentence. It's not the solution."

Elspeth leaned her forehead against the cold bars and fought back tears.

Ramsay's coat rustled as he stepped closer. "Perhaps it *will* be best if the fire in you is doused, El. You could burn for the rest of your days, if life is not what you want it to be—if you aren't with the right man."

"I would rather burn than bow."

"Don't say that." He glanced sharply at her. "Don't do anything drastic, Elspeth. Don't make a martyr of yourself."

"Better a martyr than a matron."

"You might get part of what you desire in life. But not everything. That's the way life is." He squeezed her hands. "Promise me you won't try to escape. That you won't do anything rash."

"Why?" she asked, puzzled by his cryptic words.

A door slammed behind him. She could hear the clump, clump of the guard as he walked toward her cell.

"Listen to me." Ramsay reached through the bars and cupped her cheek with one of his callused hands. "Don't fight this, Elspeth. You cannot win like this. Trust me."

"Trust you?" she repeated, accustomed to using sarcasm when speaking to him. She began to retort that she trusted no one, least of all him. But the words died on her lips. She did trust Mark Ramsay. Deep in her heart, she trusted him implicitly.

His eyes locked with hers, and for a long moment, she experienced a communion with him that she had never shared with another human being. The gaze was much deeper than a kiss and far more intimate.

"Citizen Ramsay," the guard barked. "Please step aside."

"Don't despair," Mark urged, his voice raspy. His thumb caressed her cheek as he drew his hand away and stepped back. "Don't fight it."

"Visitation hours are over," the guard said, pulling out his key. "You've had all the time you're going to get, citizen."

"Very well, I'm going," Ramsay growled. He glanced over the head of the guard. "I shall see you tomorrow, Shutterhouse, at the bower. Try to rest."

Elspeth tried not to despair. She did her best to keep her fighting spirit alive. Even so, by two in the afternoon on the day of her wedding, she felt as if she were headed for the guillotine. They had allowed her to keep her pocket watch this time, and she had monitored the minutes as they raced past noon. Soon she could no longer put off the inevitable. She had to get ready for the ceremony. They were coming for her at three.

Although Elspeth didn't care what she might look like at the bower, she didn't want to embarrass her aunt and cousin by showing up in her SteamWizards uniform with her hair wrapped in its workaday bun. Her relatives would never hear the end of it.

The guard had given her a basin of cold water and a cloth with which to wash herself, a coarse towel, and a brush for her hair. Aunt Fi had delivered her gown and slippers, but had been prohibited from visiting her. Her aunt had probably never imagined she would spend the wedding day apart from her niece, and was most likely weeping inconsolably. Elspeth felt like weeping too, but she would never let a single teardrop fall. The Overseers would love to see her cry, and she would never give them the pleasure.

Elspeth lathered her grease-stained hands, careful not to brush her tender knuckles. As she scrubbed her nails, she thought of the hours she had worked with Mark Ramsay, and the silent camaraderie they had shared. She thought of him standing beside her while his great-grandfather quizzed them and never once betraying her. She had known plenty of men as colleagues, but she had never allowed a male to get close enough to truly get to know her. Only Mark Ramsay had been privy to her thoughts and schemes. It was such a waste to lose that closeness.

Still, she'd only known him a matter of days. It wasn't as if a huge portion of her life were going to fall away—even though it felt like it today.

She decided to stop tormenting herself with thoughts of Mark Ramsay and concentrate on her toilette. Hiding her nakedness as best she could, Elspeth bathed portions of herself at a time. She wished she had been given a razor to shave her legs and underarms. She didn't know much about what went on after a marriage ceremony, but she had heard that most women shaved their entire bodies in preparation for the wedding night. Her spouse would be forced to deal with her natural body. Too bad for him.

The thought that the man might have to suffer a little in return cheered her a bit. But she still felt the looming guillotine blade poised above her maidenhood. She knew most women would laugh at her for feeling such desperation, especially since she was to be married on the holiday and to a man that was probably in a lofty position. Who knows, she could even be marrying Mark Ramsay's brother, Thomas. But that thought plunged her even deeper into despair. How would she ever endure a life married to one brother while she longed for the company of the other? Perhaps the Marriage Machine would wipe her memory clean of her feelings for Mark. She could only hope it would.

The future is for times ahead, not for the present hours' dread.

Elspeth smiled grimly as she splashed cold water over her face.

Finally, a shred of dogma that proved useful. Or maybe it was the harbinger of her downward spiral. Dogma was starting to make sense.

After she finished washing herself, she dragged on her underclothes and dropped her only good dress over her shoulders. She felt her spirits sink as the black silk settled around her ankles. It was really going to happen. She was going to step inside the Marriage Machine. She was going to become some man's wife.

At three, the guards came for her. They took her elbows and guided her down the dark corridor to the wagon just outside the back door of the detention center. She tried to get a glimpse of the outdoors, but they forced her head down and shackled her in the windowless cab in back. One of the guards sat across from her, tapping his enforcement stick on his knees and glaring at her, as if he expected her to lunge forward and attack him. He didn't say a single word to her on the ride to Boswellian Bower.

Because she was a criminal, she was ushered into a side door of the building and dragged through the dark to the left wing of the stage. When her eyes adjusted to the gloom, she discovered that she stood with four other young ladies, all dressed in long gowns. One had gloves on. One had pulled her hair back with simple combs. Another wore a small gold bracelet around her wrist. One had even stained her lips and cheeks with cosmetics. Such luxuries were allowed once in a lifetime. Only Elspeth stood unadorned, with her ash-colored hair hanging to her waist.

"Happy C-Day," the gloved young woman whispered

to her.

"And to you," Elspeth replied. "What is going on?"

"The last group just finished. We're next."

"Is there any kind of order?"

"There was a number on your card. Didn't you notice?"

Elspeth had only looked at the address and time of day. "I confess I didn't."

"Well, I'm number twenty," the girl said, peering past the curtain into the crowd. "And I'm on pins and needles. Someone said the Ramsay family is here."

"I believe they are." Elspeth strained to look over the other woman's shoulder. The auditorium was dark. All she could see was a room full of white faces in a sea of black staring up at the stage. "I've heard Thomas Ramsay is to be married today."

"One of us may be marrying a Ramsay?" whispered the young lady with the combs. She crowded in to look. Even in the dim light, Elspeth could see her eyes sparkling with eagerness. "Where are they? I've never seen any of the Ramsays."

Elspeth scanned the crowd, and caught sight of a wheelchair rolled against the left wall of the auditorium. Surely the Ramsay family would have the best seats. She surveyed the front row until she spotted ancient Alexander Ramsay. Sitting beside him was a tall black-haired woman with a regal air about her. That had to be Mark's mother. And there he was, just getting up from his seat in the center of the first row. Mark Ramsay was attired in a crisp black suit with tails and slender trousers. The tight-fitting cut of the jacket accentuated his wide shoulders and slender waist. His great-grandfather was issuing some kind of command—probably to order Mark to make sure all went well behind the scenes.

A chill washed over Elspeth. She had better get

behind the scenes herself and quick. Her escape window was closing with every passing minute. She swallowed and glanced at the guard. He stood between the Marriage Machine and the far wall. The other guard stood directly behind her, within arm's reach. To escape, she would either have to run into full view of the crowd or push the guard behind her out of the way. Manhandling the guard seemed an unlikely choice.

Sweat broke out at her hairline as Citizen Davies, the master of ceremonies, padded across to the ladies and softly called out a number. The woman with the bracelet sucked in her breath and flashed a smile at her comrades before she swept out on stage. Applause heralded her appearance as a young man joined her from the other side. Citizen Davies ushered them up the step and through the door of the machine. Their vows were spoken privately inside the bower as a string quartet played for the crowd and the ruby worked its magic.

Elspeth's heart pounded so hard, she thought it might burst from her chest. Time was running out. Soon, she would have to make her choice to stay or escape. There really was no choice. Even though Mark Ramsay had told her not to do anything rash, she had to run.

After the couple had spoken their vows, they were taken to the edge of the stage and announced as man and wife. They shared a brief kiss while everyone cheered. Then together, they walked down the steps to the waiting arms of their newly conjoined families. Davies turned to his podium and looked down at his roster. He walked to the gentlemen in the wings and then approached the women. Elspeth could hear the floorboards creak with each step he took.

"Number 16," he called.

"That's me," the woman with the painted lips squealed. She minced into the light, blinking and touching her hair.

Elspeth moved forward to the edge of the curtain and tried to calculate the steps it would take to dash across the stage and get to the exit sign on the other side. Surely no more guards were stationed where the men stood in the shadows. She gathered up her skirts in her sweating hands.

But then she saw him.

Mark Ramsay walked onto the stage, holding out his hand to the woman with the painted lips. The instant Elspeth spotted him, all thoughts of running vanished from her mind. All she could see was handsome Mark Ramsay's fingers entwining with the young lady in front of him. He was going to marry the painted woman. In a matter of minutes, those red lips were going to press into the wide, masculine mouth she wanted for herself.

It was that moment that Elspeth realized a bone-shattering truth. She had fallen in love with Mark Ramsay.

"No!" Elspeth groaned, waylaid by anguish. The wads of fabric slipped from her hands. She could not believe how her heart was breaking at the prospect of Mark being joined to someone else. How could he have kept his upcoming nuptials a secret like this? He had been scheduled for marriage on the same day as she, and he had never mentioned it. Perhaps that was what he had begun to tell her yesterday at the detention center. Perhaps he had wanted to warn her, but had guessed the news might cause her distress.

"No!" she breathed again, bringing her injured knuckles to her lips. "Mark, no!"

The tears she had vowed not to spill welled in her eyes. Mark's tall figure, so commanding in his dark suit, wavered before her as he turned for the steps of the Marriage Machine. In moments he would belong to someone else for the rest of his life. She had thought her own marriage would be the worst thing imaginable. But it paled to nothingness in comparison to what she felt about Mark Ramsay's.

The door closed behind the couple.

"Wait!" Elspeth cried. She dashed headlong onto the stage, her arms wide, her head reeling. "Stop the ceremony! Stop it. You have to stop it!"

"Citizen!" Davies turned toward her, his face contorted with shock.

She grabbed the handle of the Marriage Machine door and rattled it. "Mark!" she cried.

"Contain that woman at once!" a voice yelled from the audience.

"Young lady." The master of ceremonies grabbed her arm. Wildly, she turned to face him. "Oh, it's you, Shutterhouse."

"Stop this ceremony, Davies," she exclaimed. "You have to stop it."

The crowd jumped to its feet.

"Come away," he urged. "Before you cause a scene."

"No!" Elspeth shrieked. Something had cracked inside her. She had lost control. The sight of Mark Ramsay touching another woman had completely undone her.

She yanked open the door of the Marriage Machine.

"Contain that citizen!" someone shouted. From the sides of the stage, the guards came running, their clubs held high. For a moment, she thought they were going to beat her into submission. They grabbed her and pulled her back from the bower. Men surged onto the stage, jostling her to the side. Women were gasping and chattering as Elspeth was dragged to the wings of the stage where the grooms had awaited their brides. People pressed all around her. She couldn't breathe. She couldn't think. All she knew was she had to get away.

Then she heard a familiar voice bellow. "Gramps!" Someone rushed by her and vaulted off the stage.

Elspeth wiped her eyes and peered at the crowd as she saw Mark kneel down in front of his great-grandfather. All Elspeth could glimpse through the melee was the old man's hands hanging over the sides of his chair, as if he had collapsed.

"Someone call a doctor!" a woman shrieked.

Elspeth felt the blood drain from her face.

In that moment, she saw the events of her life turning back on her in a black wave. Seemingly compatible marriages had never killed anyone. But her refusal to comply with the rules had possibly killed old Alexander Ramsay, and most likely alienated Mark from her forever.

Chapter 7

"LET ME GO!" ELSPETH COMMANDED, yanking at the hands that held her. "I promise I won't run. I need to go to the Ramsays."

"You're not going anywhere, citizen," snapped the guard at her right.

She writhed. The guard's grip burned her wrist. She could see the crowd milling around Alexander Ramsay. She pulled. The guard held fast. She gave a quick yank, but only strained her own joints. Desperate, Elspeth bent down and bit the soft flesh at the guard's elbow while at the same time she stomped on the top of his foot with the heel of her shoe. With a yelp of pain, he released her. She lunged toward the steps that led to the crowd below.

"Elspeth!" she heard a woman cry from the back of the room. She recognized the voice of her aunt. But she couldn't take the time to worry about Aunt Fi or her cousin Amelie.

Elspeth pushed through the throng to find Mark patting the face of his great-grandfather, and his mother fanning the old man with her program.

"Grandfather," the regal woman called. "Can you hear me? Grandfather!"

The old man slumped in his chair, his head lolling to the side, his eyes closed, and his complexion a frightening shade of gray. His respiration was so shallow, Elspeth couldn't tell if he was even breathing.

"Gramps!" Mark urged, his voice quaking. He smoothed back the older man's hair at his temple. "Gramps!"

Elspeth's heart caught in her throat. "Sir!" she cried. "Wake up! Please, I won't cause any more trouble. I promise."

Mark glanced back at her, his eyes dark and damning.

"I'm sorry," Elspeth exclaimed. "I'm truly sorry, Mark."

Without a word, Mark turned back to his great-grandfather. In that moment, Elspeth's heart broke all the way in two.

She didn't care what happened to her now. She didn't care whom she had to marry. She would do anything to make reparation for what she had just done to Mark and his family.

Elspeth edged closer, near enough to touch the old man's hand. "I know I've been headstrong, sir. I know I've wanted to have my way. But I just couldn't bear to see your great-grandson getting married." Elspeth didn't care that everyone heard. She was beyond caring about her reputation. All she could hope was that Alexander Ramsay might hear her and return to consciousness. "I just cracked. I'm so sorry, sir."

Elspeth felt stares brand her from every corner of the auditorium, but the shameful glances washed over her unheeded. She thought she saw Alexander's left eyelid flutter.

Elspeth squeezed his gnarled fingers. "If I have to get in that machine of yours, I will. I'll do anything it takes. Just come back to Mark. Please come back."

The eyelid fluttered again.

"Gramps!" Mark exclaimed, patting the old man's

cheek. "Gramps!"

Alexander's watery blue eyes opened. He blinked and struggled to find Elspeth's face. She leaned closer.

"Shutterhouse," he wheezed.

"Yes, it's me."

"You damnable interfering chit."

She blanched. "I won't interfere anymore, Mr. Ramsay. The wedding can continue. I promise I'll keep quiet. I swear I won't make any more trouble."

He raised an arthritic hand and wiggled a finger. She bent close to his mouth.

"Love him?" Alexander whispered into her ear.

She rose up and gave a slight nod.

The old man squinted one eye and stared up at her, panting.

Mark took her arm, unaware of what had just been said between the old man and Elspeth. "That's enough, Elspeth. You're disturbing him." He helped his great-grandfather straighten in the chair.

She rose to her feet, encouraged that Alexander had returned to his senses, but struck numb by Mark's cold gruffness. She backed away, which prompted the crowd to step back as well.

"Someone, please get my grandfather a glass of water," Mark called out.

"Make that a sherry," the old man gasped. "My heart is fluttering like a damn girl's."

A young man went running for the drink as Mark and his family restored the old man in his chair. Slowly, the audience drifted back to their seats as Citizen Davies approached the Mark Ramsay.

"Shall we continue, Citizen Ramsay?" he asked, training his goggles on Mark's face.

"Yes." Mark sank into the chair next to his great-grandfather.

"Come, Citizen Shutterhouse," Davies said, holding out his hand.

Elspeth allowed herself to be led back up the stairs while a million questions swirled in her head. Why had Mark sat down with his family? Wasn't he next in line to be married? And would he ever look at her again? She stumbled to the side of the stage, worried and perplexed, but knowing she might not get any answers before the afternoon was done—if ever. She had promised to not make any more trouble. And she would keep that promise.

"Thanks so much!" the bride with the painted lips hissed as she walked by. "You've completely ruined the mood!"

"Sorry," Elspeth muttered. "But look at the bright side."

"What could possibly be bright about any of this? No one has ever had her marriage interrupted. No one!"

"Then you'll have *some* story to tell your little Ramsay brood, won't you—about the scandal that happened on your wedding day." She brushed past the woman. "That is, if you *can* remember."

"What do you mean—*can*?" The bride planted her hands on her generous hips. "I will never be able to forget this horrible bungle, no matter how hard I try. Never!"

"Sixteen, you're up again." Davies put in with a tremulous smile. He motioned for the woman to come back on stage.

She flounced off.

Only the woman with the gloves and Elspeth were left. The other bride stood to the side and stared at her as if she were infected with a contagious disease. Elspeth sighed and stepped backward into the shadows.

She had made a mess of everything, including her fledgling relationship with Mark Ramsay. She had almost killed his beloved great-grandfather. The least she could do was stand quietly by in the gloom and wait her turn. But one thing she couldn't watch was Mark Ramsay being married to another woman. She turned her back and concentrated on straightening her tousled hair. She yanked down her dress where the sash had been pulled crosswise by her struggle with the guard. Then she pinched her cheeks, knowing she probably looked as deathly pale as Alexander Ramsay.

While the quartet launched into a lively minuet, Elspeth felt the strain of the last week descend upon her. She couldn't remember the last time she had eaten. Had it been the peaches and chicken at the Ramsay townhouse? And when had she last slept? At the townhouse as well? Swirls of blackness swam before her eyes as she stood in the wings. Her knees wobbled and her ears began to ring.

A vague shape approached. Citizen Davies? She couldn't tell. Everything wore a fuzzy halo. She heard the number eighteen called. It echoed over and over again, as if she stood at the end of a long tunnel. Voices and music buzzed in her ears, all jumbled together in a nauseating cacophony. A gloved hand propelled her forward. She stumbled onto the stage. There, the bright footlights blinded her, and she tripped on the hem of her dress. She plunged forward, but someone caught her and steered her toward the stairs of the Marriage Machine. And that is all she remembered of her wedding day.

Elspeth woke up, her head on fire, and glanced around in surprise. She was on the couch in her Aunt Fi's house, with a blanket thrown over her and a pillow under her head. Her aunt sat nearby, calmly sewing a bib for her grandson. For a moment, she wondered if everything she'd just experienced in the last week had been nothing but a bad dream. But as she threw back the blanket, something glinted in the light, and she saw a golden band encircling a finger of her left hand.

It hadn't been a dream. She was a married woman. But if she was married, why was she still at her aunt's house?

"Oh, there you are, dear," her aunt exclaimed, smiling at her. "How are you feeling?"

"Okay." Elspeth struggled to sit up. "What happened?"

"You fainted. Hit your head." Aunt Fi set aside her sewing and stood up. "Really, Elspeth, that was some show you put on. People are still talking about it. I don't think I'll ever hear the end of it."

"I'm sorry, Aunt Fi."

"You were such an outspoken young lady." Her aunt touched her shoulder. "I always worried about you. Thank goodness that's all over now. You'll discover a great sense of peace with the calmness of marriage. I promise you."

"You're right, Aunt Fi. It was stupid. And nothing was gained from it." Elspeth threw her legs over the side of the couch. "Is Citizen Ramsay okay?"

"Do you mean the old man, Alexander?"

"Yes."

"Yes, he revived quite well after the glass of sherry. He seems surprisingly resilient for such an old man."

Relief swept over Elspeth. Then her heart twisted. "And Mark Ramsay? Did he seem happy? To be married, I mean?"

Aunt Fi shrugged. "It was hard to tell. He was quite upset with you. And then you fainted. And really, the ceremony kind of went to pieces after that."

"Great." Elspeth stood up. For a moment her senses reeled. "But I did get married."

"Yes." Aunt Fi took her arm to steady her. "Perhaps

you should sit down, Elspeth. You don't look well."

"But I do have a husband. I *am* married."

"Yes."

"Then why am I here?"

Aunt Fi glanced at the door and frowned. "Your husband said he would prefer that you stay with me until you came to your senses."

"Oh." That didn't seem normal to Elspeth, but she was glad for the breach of protocol. The last thing she wanted was to try to be nice to a stranger when all she could think about was Mark and Miss Lipstick together and how depressed that made her.

Depressed? Wait a minute. She should not be sad if she had spent the allotted time in the Marriage Machine. Something was not right.

"Are you *sure* I'm married?"

Aunt Fi nodded. "I saw it with my own eyes, dear."

"Who did I marry? Did you recognize him?"

"He asked that he remain anonymous until you come to your senses."

"I've *come* to my senses." Elspeth said. "I never *lost* my senses. That's what everybody doesn't understand." She ran her fingers through her tangled hair, careful not to touch the bump on her skull, and looked over at her aunt.

"How long have I been sleeping?"

"Since the wedding last night."

"Maybe they're still in town then."

"Who, dear?"

"The Ramsays." She headed for the stairs. "I have to go, Aunt Fi. Mark Ramsay promised to take me to the Outer Islands. And I'm going to hold him to his word—if they haven't left already."

"Do you think that's wise? You've had quite a bump on the head."

Elspeth nodded. "I have to, Aunt Fi. I can't be married to someone I don't love. It will never work. I won't be happy. And I will make my husband unhappy. I would rather live in the wilderness than face that kind of life. And I intend to go before your calmness of marriage descends upon me."

"But the Outer Islands, Elspeth?" Her aunt looked at her and sighed. "I will never see you!"

"Oh Aunt Fi." Elspeth wrapped her arms around her and hugged her tightly. "You will. The world is changing. I've ridden in a Flying Horse—did you know that? I bet one day, they'll be all over the city, and people will be able to travel again."

"In my time?" Her aunt drew back.

"Without a doubt." Elspeth kissed her on the cheek. "But for now, I must go."

"I understand, dear. But do be careful."

Elspeth nodded and hurried up to her tiny room, packed a bag, and slipped out of the house into a wonderland of snow.

Elspeth stopped in the middle of the square, and slowly turned around, thunderstruck. The ground was covered in white fluff three feet deep. The sky was clear of fog and blue—as blue as, as blue as Mark Ramsay's eyes. The air smelled fresh and clean and full of promise—almost as if the world had been born anew.

Elspeth gaped at her surroundings and sucked in a deep breath of the cool crisp air. The world was different. But by some quirk of Fate, she was still the same old Elspeth, with the same old fire and determination. She knew nothing inside her had changed. Though the thought puzzled her, she set off at a quick trot, her tools clanking in her backpack, her spirits high.

Chapter 8

THE MOMENT ELSPETH CAUGHT SIGHT of the townhouse by the greenbelt, her spirits plummeted. It was plain to see she would not have a private audience with Mark. The entire Ramsay family was leaving. Three small steam cars chugged at the side of the road as the family loaded their bags in the back. Alexander sat in his wheelchair at the end of the walkway of the house, waving his cane and obviously fully recovered from his lapse at Boswellian Bower. Mark's mother was opening the door of the car in front, ready for Alexander to be loaded into it. Someone else, probably Thomas, worked at the third vehicle, loading bags and equipment. Mark guided Madame Lipstick toward the second vehicle, holding her on his arm and taking great care that she didn't slip on the icy walk.

Steam puffed into the chilly air, obliterating their faces. Elspeth was glad. She didn't want to discover the truth, that Mark was now happily married and off to start a new life with his pretty bride.

She shouldered her backpack and walked forward. No time like the present to barge in on their postcard-perfect tableau.

"Excuse me," Elspeth called. "Mark?"

The new bride turned to look over her shoulder. "Oh, it's you," she drawled, staring down her nose at Elspeth. She was dressed in a long wool coat and carried a fur

muff, and already sported the aristocratic sneer she had
assumed the Ramsays would have possessed but hadn't
after all.

Mark paused and stared down at Elspeth. His eyes
were cold, bereft of friendliness. Elspeth couldn't blame
him for looking at her like that, after the trouble she had
caused. Someone touched her elbow. Elspeth turned,
to see the tip of Alexander's cane, and was glad for the
sudden diversion. Mark didn't look all that interested in
hearing what she had to say.

"Mr. Ramsay," Elspeth pivoted to survey him. "How
are you doing, sir?"

"Well enough, after all the excitement."

"Please accept my apologies."

"Hmph." He rolled his eyes. "People need excitement
every now and then. Keeps the blood high."

She stared at him, not sure she heard him correctly.

"They were talking of taking you away. Execution.
The fools! Someone had to do something."

"You faked that collapse?" she sputtered.

"It was the only thing that came to mind. Not the
most elegant idea, but effective."

"But I thought you were on *their* side."

"Mark did a thorough job of convincing me
otherwise. Kept me up half the night talking about recent
developments in the female constitution."

The regal woman with the raven-colored hair came
up behind the old man and grasped the handles of the
wheelchair.

"Elspeth, is it?"

"Yes."

"I'm Eleanor." She held out her hand.

"Pleased to meet you." Still trying to digest Alexander's
words, Elspeth shook the gloved hand of Ramsay's mother
and was struck by the serene strength in the woman's

face.

"Mark is busy at the moment, but he will be with you shortly. Why don't you wait for him in the third car?" She gestured toward the blue car in the back. "It's terribly cold out here."

The regal glance swept down her uniform and across her boots, as if seeing for herself that Elspeth really did work for the power company. Elspeth made a mental note to contact her boss. He would expect her to return to work after the holidays and her honeymoon, but she had to let him know that she would never return to the SteamWizards.

"Thank you. I will."

Elspeth scurried to the last car in the line, grateful to be away from staring eyes, while she struggled to compose the opening line she would use, once Mark appeared. She set her bag at her feet and closed the door, grateful even more for the warmth of the steam heater. She ran some phrases through her head. She didn't want to demand, and yet she didn't want to beg. She didn't want to lay blame at his feet for what had occurred at the bower, and yet she didn't want to take all the responsibility for it either. How would she ever come up with the right words? And what, precisely, did she want to say to the man? That she wished him well with his life? Of course she did.

But not with that woman.

Frustrated and disconsolate, Elspeth glared down at the floor.

Suddenly the door opened on the opposite side of the car, startling her out of her troubled thoughts.

"Shutterhouse?" a familiar voice called.

She glanced up, surprised when Mark bent to get into the car. He sank down into the driver's seat and put his hand on the gearshift. His cool unfriendliness had transformed into the charming demeanor she knew so well. Her heart did a little flip flop.

"So, you decided to join us?" he asked.

"You promised me safe passage."

"I did. But I didn't think you would be up to things so soon."

"I'm up to it."

"Are you?" He leveled his blue eyes on her and she looked back at him. His lime-scented cologne billowed out, enveloping her in an intoxicating cloud. Her prepared speech vanished, replaced by an ache deep inside that fanned out in an unbearable wave. "What changed your mind?"

"I never changed my mind about going to the Outer Islands."

"Oh, that. I see." A shadow passed through his eyes, making Elspeth suddenly suspect that they were speaking of separate things. He slammed the door. "It's damnable icy today. We'll have to watch our speed."

"Mark, I just want to say something. I need to say something."

He clenched his jaw and waited, studying her face.

"Mark," she began and then broke off, suddenly overcome by tears. They ran down her cheeks. "Why didn't you tell me you were getting married?" Angry with herself for just blurting out her feelings, she brushed away the tears with the sleeve of her jacket, scratching her cheek in the process. "Why did you make me find out like that?"

"I had no choice. At that time I didn't know if you were going to be my bride or not."

"What do you mean, *at that time?*"

He shook his head and turned the key to engage the motor. As the car rumbled from merely heating the air to full throttle, he paused and glanced over at her. "Shutterhouse, why didn't you trust me? I asked you to trust me. Why couldn't you do that one simple thing?"

"What good would have come from trusting you?"

"It could have made the ceremony a lot more enjoyable. I would have *liked* that."

"Oh, well." Elspeth swallowed the hard lump that had lodged in her throat. "I'm sorry I ruined your big day." She swallowed back a sob.

"Both our days, Elspeth."

"Sorry, I guess I'm not into the marriage thing as much as you." She clenched her teeth. "And as for that, why in the hell am I so unhappy? Wasn't that stupid machine supposed to make me *happy*?"

Mark's hard expression softened into a smile. But his smile only made her more upset. She crossed her arms and shut her eyes, struggling to control herself and doing a poor job of it.

"Shutterhouse, have you ever heard the expression, there are two ways to skin a cat?"

"Yes," she retorted, feeling cross and heartbroken at the same time. "And it sounds positively barbaric."

He pulled into the street, following the two cars ahead of him. Elspeth sat up straight, suddenly at attention.

"Where are we going?" she sputtered.

"To the Outer Islands."

"Your mother is driving?" Elspeth gasped. "She drives?"

"Of course. You can learn, too. Thomas is a great teacher. He's a lot more patient than I am."

Elspeth's thoughts raced. *Thomas*. She'd forgotten all about him. She glanced at her left hand, and the golden band winked at her, as if mocking her. So she had married Thomas after all. That was why no one in the Ramsay clan had been all that surprised to see her.

"But shouldn't you be in that car?" she pointed at the brown vehicle ahead of them, where Madame Lipstick languished. He'd probably kept her up most of the night.

"With Mariam?"

"Yes."

Mark shrugged. "I'll get to know Mariam soon enough. We've got years to get acquainted. And I wanted an extra car." He turned the corner, heading toward the boundary of the city. "But back to what I was saying."

"You mean about cats?"

"Yes. There are two ways to go about things. The hard way and the sensible way."

He glanced at her. She stared at the side of his handsome face, confounded at where the conversation was headed.

"You aren't following me."

"Not really."

"Okay, then," he said, obviously enjoying himself. "Do you know the official components of scientific inquiry?"

"Like hypothesis, method and results?"

"Exactly. And part of the scientific method is using something called a control."

Elspeth brightened. Mark didn't seem all that changed by the Marriage Machine, and she didn't feel any different either. He was married to someone else, but still carrying on a lively conversation with her. Perhaps she could bear such a life. She still wanted to kiss him and to feel his arms around her, but she might be able to live without those things if she tried hard enough. And if Thomas didn't begrudge her spending time with his brother.

His voice, full of amusement, interrupted her thoughts. "Shutterhouse, are you listening?"

"Yes," she replied. "A control?"

"A good experiment always has a trial group and a control group. But what if there can only be one group studied at a time because of equipment restrictions?"

She shrugged, still not sure what point he was trying

to make.

They headed into a curve, and the car ahead of them fishtailed and nearly skidded off the road. Mark swore and honked. The car tooted back at them.

Mark continued undaunted, as if the incident had never occurred. "What if the first data are gathered, then a single change is made, and the second group of data is gathered. Would it still be a valid experiment?"

"I would assume so."

"Do you think a scientist could be persuaded to believe the results of such an experiment?"

"Yes, but what are you getting at, Mark?"

"Even the Overseers?"

At her shocked stare, he looked over at her. "Even if it involved the Marriage Machine?"

"The Marriage Machine?" She gaped at him. "What are you saying?"

"I'm saying that you should have trusted me, Shutterhouse."

Elspeth stared at him—at his firm mouth, his sharp nose, and his lively, intelligent eyes—and suddenly the events of the past few days fell into place and all made sense.

"You *did* vandalize that machine, just as I first suspected!" she gasped. "You were the one that poked the hole in the supply line."

"I had it done," he replied. "So I could come in as a repairman—with no one the wiser."

"But I beat you to it."

"And stole the ruby, hoping no one would ever suspect the machine didn't actually work—at least not in the way it was intended to."

Elspeth nodded.

"Great minds think alike." Mark shifted into a lower gear as the vehicle cleared the final milepost of the city.

Elspeth would have liked to look out the window at a landscape she had never seen before, but she was too caught up in what Mark was saying to care where the car went. "That was the exact same thing I intended to do," he added. "I had begun to suspect the very same thing you did, that the human body had at last overcome the effects of radiation. And what better way to find out than change the machine before my own wedding."

"My Gottfried," Elspeth whispered.

"And that's where the cat skinning comes in. You can try to make your point by being a martyr and facing the wrath of the Overseers—and perhaps never change a thing. Or you can show the Overseers scientific proof that the machine is no longer needed. If the women from your group and the groups thereafter get pregnant after our holiday ceremony without the benefit of the real ruby in place, the Overseers won't be able to deny the facts. And then we can show them the truth."

"The ruby we replaced wasn't real?" she murmured.

"It was a glass replica. So Gramps would still see a red glow."

"So the real ruby is where?" she asked.

"Safe and sound in the attic of the townhouse."

She couldn't find words to express how brilliant he was.

"Oh, and by the way, Shutterhouse," Mark reached into the pocket of his coat and pulled out a perfect tangerine. He held it out to her. "Happy C-day. I meant to give this to you yesterday, but things got rather out of hand."

"Thank you." She gazed at him and then at the precious citrus fruit in her hand. She had nothing to give him in return, not even a lemon. And she wanted to give him so much. If he asked her, she would give him everything, no matter how forbidden.

While Elspeth was still contemplating the future and the part Mark might play in it, she saw the brown car skid off the road and plow into a snow-covered bank. Mark motored to a stop, and they both jumped out and ran forward. The doors of the brown vehicle swung open.

"Are you all right?" Mark called. He dashed to the passenger side of the car, most likely to see to the safety of his wife. Elspeth slipped and slid to the driver's side, where she assumed she belonged. She wished to show a little respect for the man who had not forced her into the wedding bed.

"Thomas?" she ventured. A booted foot popped out of the car. And then a very tall, broad-shouldered man rose from the seat and scrambled out of the vehicle. Elspeth stared, not believing her eyes. She stood in the snow, the wind blowing her leather jacket around her knees as she glanced from one brother to the other.

Mark and Thomas were identical twins.

"Are you okay?" she stuttered.

"I'm fine, thanks." He shot a cool smile at her and then glanced over the top of the car. "Darling, are you all right? I should have been more careful."

Madame Lipstick waved and patted Mark on his shoulder. "Just shaken up a little, dear," she called back.

Darling? Dear? Thomas was married to Madame Lipstick?

What did it mean? It couldn't mean…did that mean that she—Elspeth Shutterhouse—was the wife of Thomas' younger but startlingly similar brother?

Elspeth was more than shaken. She was stunned. She could feel the color draining from her face and her knees giving way in utter shock.

"Ace mechanic going down!" Mark exclaimed, laughing, as he dashed toward her.

When Elspeth came to, she found she had collapsed in a snow bank and that Mark was kneeling at her side and in the process of picking her up.

"Do you have a habit of this?" he asked.

"What do you mean?"

"Fainting."

"I've never fainted in my life until I met you." She struggled to get up on her own, but he pulled her securely into his arms. He looked down at her, his eyes serious.

"Are you sure you're all right, Shutterhouse?"

"I'm fine!" she shot back. Then she realized she would never be right, and she would never stop fainting and worrying until she knew the truth. She pushed against his chest. "Just tell me one thing, Ramsay. Are we married? I mean, to each other?"

"Technically."

"But you don't want to be?" Her fingers retracted into curls as her heart flopped in her chest.

"I never said that."

"What *did* you say?"

He rose to his feet and set hers upon the ground, but still held her close. "I said I do."

"And what did I say?" she asked, not remembering a single moment of the ceremony.

"Technically nothing. That's when you fainted." He began to dust off the snow from the back of her coat.

She loved the way he looked after her—had always looked after her, come to think of it.

"So we never made it official?" she asked, her heart racing.

He straightened and cocked a brow. "In what way?"

"With a kiss."

"I intended to wait for that, until you were fully conscious. And maybe even willing in the bargain."

"I'm *more* than willing, Mark." She placed her hands

on the sides of his warm face and drew him down. She had waited for what seemed like forever to feel his firm mouth close upon hers. He kissed her as tenderly and then more fully than she ever dreamed a kiss could be, gathering her up in his arms and pressing her into the fire of his chest. His kiss spoke of love and appreciation, but she had to know for certain how he felt. She needed to hear him say it.

"So you *do* want to be married to me?" she murmured against his mouth.

"From the moment I met you."

"Really?"

"You were unlike any woman I had ever met. Plus, I'd never seen a woman in a uniform before." He winked at her.

She pulled back and stared at him.

"You are awfully sexy in that mechanic outfit, Shutterhouse." He kissed her again and looked down at her. His expression grew serious. "But I have to know. Did you want to marry me? All I've heard from you is that marriage is the end of the world."

"I could be persuaded to alter that opinion."

"Could you, now?" He grinned, no longer taking pains to conceal his joy.

"Yes." She beamed. Her heart was glowing with so much love for him, she thought it might burn right through her chest. "You're the one person who might be able to change my mind."

"Then I'm a lucky fellow."

"I can't believe how lucky we *both* were."

He pulled back a bit. "What do you mean?"

"To have wound up together. What were the odds of that?"

Mark threw back his head and laughed. "It had nothing to do with luck."

The truth dawned on her. "You switched the cards!" she gasped.

He raised one brow. "Did I?"

"You switched cards with your brother so I would end up with you!"

"I had to, El. I couldn't have you married off to anyone but me. I love you."

Her heart swelled in her chest as she realized the risks Mark Ramsay had taken for love. For the love of *her*. Elspeth Shutterhouse.

Behind them a car door slammed.

"What's the damned hold-up back there?" a crusty voice exclaimed.

"Ignore the old geezer," Mark growled in her ear. "And just kiss me, Shutterhouse."

"My thoughts exactly," she replied.

"Like I said before," he pulled her even closer. "Great minds think alike."

THE MARRIAGE MACHINE was an exploratory journey into the dystopian world of THE LONDO CHRONICLES. This series continues in a full-length novel enttitled GABRIEL'S DAUGHTER

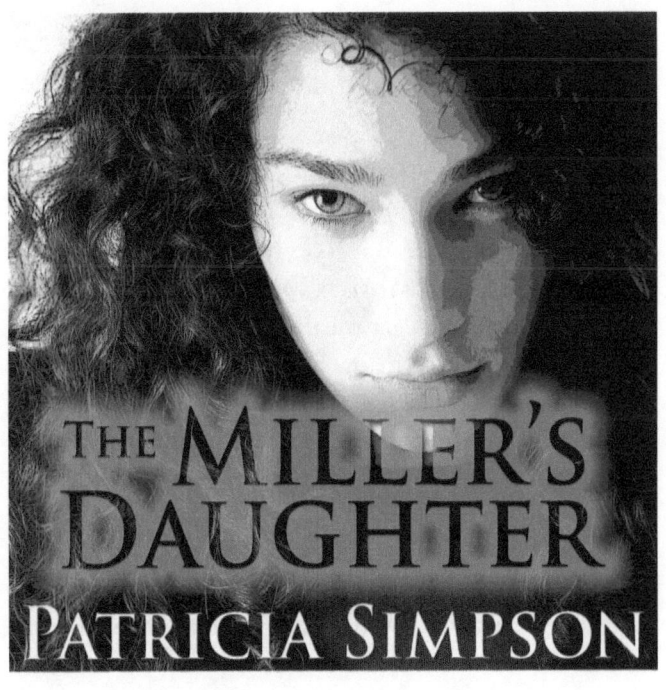

THE MILLER'S
DAUGHTER

PATRICIA SIMPSON

This historical is set in 7th century France, where not every monster is of the four-footed variety.

Chapter 1

Rouen, Neustria – AD 629

THE RAIN HAD FINALLY STOPPED, which meant the execution could be held after a delay of nearly a fortnight—not that Alaric of Soissons was in any hurry to carry out the orders of the bishop.

He walked with the witch's tumbrel from the rear of the cathedral to the middle of the town square as the late September wind plastered a flurry of chestnut leaves to his boots. After a solid month of rain, everything was wet: the leaves, the cobbled lane, the thatched cottages, and most of the villagers. Alaric couldn't remember the last time he'd been warm and dry.

But Merofled the miller's daughter would be plenty warm soon enough.

Alaric glanced back at the robed figure standing in the cart, her hands tied with coarse dirty rope, her face shadowed by a hood that covered her black hair. He had no idea who she was or what she looked like. He'd never met the woman, as she had refused the blessing of last rites earlier that day. And since he'd just arrived in Rouen a month ago, he had no idea whether her heart was as black as he'd been led to believe or as innocent as he feared. Nevertheless, he had been ordered to subject her to a gruesome death.

With one callused hand wrapped around the halter

of the donkey and the other holding his crucifix-topped staff, Alaric guided the beast down the lane toward the main square. Three dogs followed the cart, keeping close to the wheels instead of sniffing each doorway or lifting their legs at every corner as curs were wont to do. He thought it was odd how fixated the dogs seemed to be on accompanying the woman to her death. He wondered if they were her pets.

As his tattered parade passed through the village, goodwives and their husbands poured out of their homes, yelling at the convict.

"Witch!"

"Daughter of Satan!"

"Devil's spawn!"

The townspeople threw rotten plums and apples at the cart. Someone even poured the contents of a chamber pot from a second-story window, narrowly missing the top of Alaric's head.

God only knew what Merofled had done to incur the wrath of every man and woman in the village. He wished she had taken confession after all, as he was morbidly curious as to her transgression. What could she have done to merit death by fire?

Nothing, as far as he was concerned.

As a new acolyte of Notre Dame de Rouen, Alaric was duty bound to touch torch to faggot and remain until the end of the execution, praying all the while that every soul would be saved, including that of the witch. He hoped his prayers would be of some assistance to the young woman. He had little hope that such words would deliver his own spirit so easily. There was much blood on his hands.

In joining the church, Alaric had thought to avoid the senseless massacres he had participated in while a soldier in the service of King Dagobert and his father before him. He had been under the impression that priests copied manuscripts, grew grapes and tended to the sick. Either he'd been wrong about clerical duties or violence dogged his footsteps no matter what path he chose to take. For here he was again, about to slaughter another human being. God forgive him.

Alaric helped Merofled from the tumbrel and set her upon the ground. He refused to glance into her eyes, even though he felt her intense regard on the side of his face. He'd learned long ago not to look into the eyes of the person he was going to kill. It made the task easier if a human connection was not forged.

She didn't struggle as he led her to the pyre. She didn't weep or beg. He admired her for that. As she approached the platform, her robes whipped around in the wind, and she clutched the hood at her chin to keep it from blowing free. The crowd pressed around them, ominously silent, watching them.

With a sickening sense of finality, Alaric lifted Merofled to the platform where the executioner waited. The pyre was surrounded by firewood and uprooted rosemary bushes—the better to camouflage the smell of burning flesh. With every moment that passed, Alaric prayed for a miracle to deliver this woman from a fate he was sure she did not deserve.

In all his thirty years, he hadn't met a single bona fide witch. He doubted such a creature existed. But he was a newly-forged servant of God and now a shepherd of these people. The woman had been condemned to die, and it was his hand that would send her to her grave.

If God really did perform miracles, now was the time.

The executioner pulled off Merofled's cloak, tossed it to the ground and lashed her to the stake. Before Alaric could avert his eyes, he caught a glimpse of her proud expression and unrepentant shoulders.

She was younger than he had expected. She looked to be not much more than a maiden. She wasn't beautiful in a conventional sense. Her hair was far too dark and the wild curls overwhelmed her features, making her skin seem overly pale in comparison. He couldn't tell what color her eyes were, and didn't care to look that closely. Instead his gaze dropped to the rope that tied her to the stake, cutting across her breasts and outlining her hips in a stark X. He stared at her, caught up by the way the bonds accentuated her womanly curves.

Lust. Alaric chided himself for the wave of hunger that eclipsed his concern for the woman. How could he think such base thoughts when this poor soul faced her last hour on earth?

The executioner turned to Alaric, waiting for a sign.

Alaric reined in his wayward thoughts and cleared his throat. "Merofled," he called into the wind, "daughter of the late Corbus the Miller, you have been found to be a witch. You are guilty of unseemly communion with animals and behavior unsuitable for a child of God."

As if on cue, the smallest of the dogs raised its head and began to howl. The mournful bray made the hairs on the back of Alaric's neck rise in response. The woman glanced at the dog and lifted the fingers of her left hand. The dog ceased howling, laid its head upon its front paws and whined piteously, as if it knew what was about to happen.

"Merofled," Alaric continued. The wind blew the rough-spun cloth of her gown, revealing the curve of an ivory calf. He shifted his gaze. "What do you have to say for yourself?"

"I am innocent!" Her eyes glowed with green fire. He felt their glare like knifepoints, plunging deep into his heart.

"If you are as you claim, Merofled of Rouen, may God have mercy on your soul." Alaric crossed himself, and was about to raise his hand for the torch, when he spotted a man astride a huge gray plow horse thundering into the square.

"La Gargouille!" the man shouted.

The crowd turned as one, as if connected by the same kind of rope that bound Merofled to the stake. The executioner gaped at the man on the horse, forgetting all about the torch flaming in his hand while Alaric's heart skipped a beat beneath his robe. Had his prayer been answered after all? Had the miracle occurred? He wanted to believe such was the case, but he doubted it. His war-hardened skepticism was a callus not easily sloughed.

"La Gargouille!" the farmer yelled. Spittle flew from his mouth as he struggled to control his agitated mount. Alaric could see the whites of the eyes of both horse and rider. "La Gargouille!"

The horse reared and the man nearly slid off his back. "It's got my son!"

The crowd erupted in genuflections and gasps, drowning out the man's pleas for help. Determined to take control of the situation, Alaric shook his staff and ordered the crowd to hush.

"What are you saying, yeoman?" he shouted.

"La Gargouille," the horseman replied. "It came out of the river and trapped my son!"

"La Gargouille?" Alaric repeated, unsure of what had he had just heard. A gargoyle had come out of the Seine? The miller's daughter was a witch? To what other madness would these people of Rouen lay claim?

He strode toward the man on horseback, and the crowd stepped back to let him pass. He could feel the terror wafting off them, the same terror he had felt from his troops before a battle.

"Who will help me?" the horseman shouted. "Who will help me save my boy?"

The crowd fell ominously silent again. Alaric glanced from the man to the villagers. What was this gargoyle to evoke such fear in the people of Rouen? What type of creature was it?

"Will no one help?" the man cried.

Not a single person raised his hand. Alaric surveyed his flock, surprised to see fright had drained the bloodlust from each and every face. No one moved. All eyes were trained on the farmer.

"Please, will no one help my child?" the man repeated, his voice cracking in despair.

"I will," a woman called out.

Alaric turned at the sound, surprised that the young woman on the pyre had spoken. She yanked at the ropes that held her to the stake. "Set me free and I will help with the goji."

Alaric felt all eyes on his back. The bishop was out of town, seeing to his plague-stricken family and had left Alaric in charge. The decision to free the convict or burn her was his to make.

"You're a dead woman!" someone yelled from the crowd. "If you go after La Gargouille, you're a dead woman!"

"So be it," Merofled raised her chin. Her black hair blew across her eyes like a standard of war. "I'm a dead woman anyway."

Chapter 2

THE BLACKSMITH BROUGHT ALARIC A HORSE, the executioner untied the witch, and within minutes, the trio left the safety of the city walls and headed down the road toward the Seine. The farmer led the way, clucking at his horse to hurry. Alaric followed, the witch riding in front of him with her hands bound. He didn't trust her not to run off, even though she'd promised to help find the farmer's son. Being a stranger to the village, he had no idea if she would abide by her word or run off the first chance she got. He would play it safe until he got to know the young woman better.

As the horses slipped and slid down the muddy track, Alaric tried not to notice how Merofled's body jostled against his chest and thighs, or how warm she felt in the frame of his arms. He could not allow the witch to tempt him in any way—especially when there was a matter of life and death at hand. He forced himself to shift his focus.

Alaric scanned the wide valley below the knoll on which Rouen was built. The river took a horseshoe bend around the knoll and then meandered in a wide ribbon toward the sea. On the left side of the river stretched a swamp and on the right side rose high chalk cliffs.

When he'd come to Rouen a month ago, the river had already spilled over its banks because of a late-summer deluge. But now, as water poured into the Seine from scores of flooding tributaries, the river had swollen to a veritable lake.

"Look at that," the farmer pointed at the valley below. "The storms have brought so much water, the land will not drain until midsummer. It's like the sea has come to Rouen."

"I've heard this is the highest the river level has ever been."

"So it is," the farmer spit. "I've never seen it like this. More lake than river. There will be pestilence. Pestilence, I tell you."

The woman said nothing. The three dogs that had followed the tumbrel now trotted around her. One of them, a shaggy black and white cur, ranged ahead, his nose to the ground.

"If it keeps raining in the hills like it is," the farmer continued, glancing at the purple clouds to the east, "the water will rise even more. There's no telling what monsters will rise from such a flood."

"As to that," Alaric sidled closer to the large horse and rider, "what was your son doing so near the river? I was warned to stay clear of its treacherous banks."

"You know how boys are," the farmer frowned. "Always running off. Getting into mischief."

"But you know where he might be?"

"Oh aye. There's a cave he's been known to tarry at. Near one of my barley fields."

"But how do you know this creature—this gargoyle—snatched him?"

"Because I saw it, sir." The farmer's eyes narrowed. "It leapt down from a great height. I don't know if it jumped or flew. Everything happened so fast. It had big claws. Huge claws. And it snatched my boy and ran off with him into the brush."

"This gargoyle. What kind of creature is it?"

"No one really knows, sir."

"It keeps to itself," the young woman put in.

Alaric glanced at the side of her face, but she didn't say anything more. She stared at the distant cliffs with a stony expression as cold and pale as the chalk escarpment ahead of them.

"Keeps to itself, does it?" the farmer snorted. "What was it doing out of the swamp then?"

Alaric turned back to the farmer. "So it lives in the swamp?"

"From what I hear. But it was on my land today. My land, mind you, molesting my son! I hope to God that it hasn't eaten my poor boy!"

"But you've seen it." Alaric pressed for information, hoping to plan his attack before they arrived at the scene of the crime. "How would you describe it? Like a bear? A boar?"

"More like a dragon, sir."

"Dragon?"

"Aye. Not a hair to be seen. Great big nostrils. Ridges on its back, like a fin. Long tail. But to be honest, I was so worried about my son that I didn't get a good look."

"Understandable." Alaric frowned. He'd heard tales of men fighting dragons. He'd also heard tales about witches. But in all his years on Earth, he had yet to encounter either one. Surely the gargoyle was one of God's own creatures made more terrible by superstition and lack of information. The best thing he could do was capture the beast, get a good look at it or kill it, and put the fears of the townspeople to rest. He would bet the gargoyle was nothing more than a larger-than-normal wolf.

"What about you?" Alaric turned his attention back to the witch. "Have you seen this gargoyle?"

"No."

"Then how do you know it keeps to itself?"

"My gram told me. She knew of the beast in the

swamp."

"There is only one?"

"She spoke of only one."

"And she called it the goji?"

"Of course." The young woman shrugged. "Everyone worth knowing has a nickname."

Alaric thought it odd that she referred to a beast as if it were just another creature. "What else did your grandmother say about it?"

The witch shot back a glance dark with distrust and dislike. "I'm not here to tell tales of the goji. I'm here to save the boy."

The farmer turned around to glare down at her. "You'll do whatever the priest asks, my girl, or back to the stake with you!"

She flung back her head and looked away. The afternoon light glowed along the line of her white throat and disappeared into the thicket of her black curls. Not many women he'd met would talk back to a man as she had just done and with such authority. Alaric gazed at her, fascinated but wary of her wildness.

"Such lack of respect will not make you any friends, girl," the farmer added.

"Who said I needed friends?"

"Friends would have stood up for you."

The farmer's observation hung heavy in the air as they plodded down the muddy track toward the river.

Alaric frowned at the sky when they reached the barley field. It had taken a considerable amount of effort for their mounts to find footing along the muddy path to the Seine. Already the autumn sun was waning, and soon there would be too little light to look for the boy. He glanced at the field on his right.

The plot of land was shorn to stubble and dotted with

pockets of water. If the rains came again and the river rose even higher, the field would soon be submerged, its rich topsoil stripped away by the flood.

They sloshed along the edge of the field toward the cliffs where the river had eaten through the chalk long ago. The great river moved beside them, swirling and muddy and dangerous. Alaric glanced at the opaque water as his heart caught in his chest. He was afraid of the deep, as he'd nearly drowned as a boy. The sooner they got to the narrow strip of land at the foot of the cliff, the safer he'd feel.

Darkness encroached as they tramped into a clearing in front of a small cave at the base of the cliff.

"Is this the place?" Alaric asked, glancing around. His battle-honed senses flared to full alert. "This is where you saw the creature?"

"Aye." The farmer tied their horses to saplings and hurried back into the clearing just as Merofled let out a soft cry.

Alaric followed the direction of her stare. There on the ground among a jumble of stones were three leathery gray orbs, nearly a foot long. He stepped closer, and saw that they were some kind of egg, like a turtle egg. But someone had ruined them by piercing them with a pointed stick. The dogs clustered around the eggs, sniffing them, their tails tucked between their legs.

Gargoyle eggs. The creature had produced offspring. This was not what he had expected and worse than he had imagined.

Alaric felt a tug on the rope as Merofled sank to her knees. Before he could call out a warning to not touch anything, he saw her gently pull aside the soft shell of one of the eggs and peer inside it. Two of the dogs dipped their noses close to her fingers and whined.

"What's in there?" Alaric asked.

"Devil spawn!" the farmer answered.

"It looks like a bird of some kind. Perhaps a bat. A tiny poor thing!" She shot a look full of anguish at Alaric. "But it is dead." She scrambled to her feet and whirled to face the farmer. "Who did this? Your son?"

"You fault him?"

"Killing these young creatures who are unable to defend themselves? Yes, I fault him!"

"I didn't raise a fool," the farmer growled, his eyes glowing with contempt for the girl's soft-hearted nature. "One less gargoyle will not make me weep."

"And what has the goji ever done to you?" she countered.

"Stolen my son!"

"Maybe for a good reason."

"Nay, the beast is a killer—plain and simple."

"What does it kill?"

"Innocent people. Horses."

"Who has been killed in the village? Name someone."

The farmer glared at her. "Old Harold."

"Old Harold was a drunkard who fell in the river."

"Was dragged into the river, more like!"

"And what stock has been lost?" Her cheeks flamed with anger as she confronted him, her fists planted on her hips.

"I don't have to make an inventory for the likes of you!" The farmer swept a hand through the air, scattering her questions like so much dust. "Everyone knows the gargoyle is a killer. And that's an end to it."

"Yeoman," Alaric stepped between them, determined to diffuse the situation. "Which way did the gargoyle go when it took your son?"

"That way." The farmer nodded at a thicket of alders

that grew at the base of the bluff. "Into the brush, there."

Alaric drew the sword that he still wore strapped over his cassock and turned for the stand of trees, tugging at the witch to follow him. He squinted, searching for signs of the beast in the thicket, but the dwindling light made the task nearly impossible.

The witch came up behind him. "Cletus, go," she commanded of the black and white dog, whose nose was never far from the ground. "Find the boy."

Nose down, the dog paced the edge of the brush and then slunk into the thicket. Alaric followed, slashing a passageway through the brambles and ivy. The farmer brought up the rear, having taken a moment to arm himself with a cudgel made from a sturdy branch. They followed the dog as the night drew ever closer.

The heady scent of brambles and muck wafted around Alaric, making his head reel. He slashed onward, helping the witch step over puddles and fallen trees until they came to a stretch of water where the river branched into smaller parts. One of the streams ran close to the cliff, blocking their way. As Alaric pivoted to tell the others to turn back, he felt the saturated earth give way beneath his boots. And before he could cry out, he and the undercut earth plunged into the river.

Alaric fought for footing in the frigid water, but the river was deep. He thrashed to the surface, gasping for air, his sword still in one hand and the rope in the other. He took one gulp of air before the current pulled him under.

"Help!" Merofled fought to keep from being dragged into the river with the priest, but her strength was no match for the Seine. Before Claude the farmer could push through the brambles to grab hold of her, she toppled into the river, dragged into the water headfirst. She could swim, and could find her way out of any current, but she was tied to the thrashing priest, who obviously did not know the ways of water. She faced certain death if she did not save him—and do so immediately. Her hounds ran in circles on the bank, barking at her until she could barely think.

"Bear!" she shouted over the rush of the flood. The large black dog, never far from her side, stared at her, his golden eyes eager for a command. "Save the man!" She kicked to vault her shoulders out of the water and pointed at the priest. "Save him! Bear, go!"

The dog leapt into the water as she flipped onto her back and stroked hard with her legs to remain close to shore. She watched the dog's great head as he paddled toward the priest, intent on his mission. Why beasts did the bidding of man without thought to their own safety always amazed her. And why beasts did her bidding without question had always raised eyebrows in others. But for once, she was grateful for the unusual connection she had to animals. She saw Bear's jaw close around the forearm of the priest and knew they would be saved.

Dripping with water and gasping for breath, Alaric pulled the witch from the river as the great dog shook beside him, flinging half the Seine in Alaric's direction. Alaric didn't care. The mutt had rescued him. The dog could shake as much as he wanted, and as close as he wanted.

Hand over hand he pulled at the rope until the woman rose from the river, her clothing molded to her lithe figure, her wild hair running in rivulets around her white face. She looked like a goddess emerging from a painting. She was nearly a goddess to Alaric. She and her giant of a dog had just saved his life.

He realized now how foolish it was for the two of them to be bound by the rope in this dangerous place. She deserved to be free as well. After she was safely ashore and he had recovered his breath, he untied the thick rope at her wrists.

"We can't afford another surprise like that," he panted as he looped the rope over his arm. "We have to go back. It's too dark."

The farmer nodded and scowled at the river beyond them. "I hope to God that my son is still alive out there."

Merofled glared at the farmer and then chafed her wrist where the rope had cut into her flesh.

Shivering in silence, they retraced their steps through the brambles. Alaric hoped no one noticed how he stumbled here and there, as his legs still trembled from the effects of his ordeal. He would rather face the dreaded gargoyle than fall into that terrifying flood again.

When they finally reached the cave, Alaric glanced at the cliff above as Merofled inspected the two remaining gargoyle eggs. He wondered where the gargoyle had jumped from when it snatched the boy, and if it might be waiting there and watching them. The hairs on the back of his neck rose in alarm. But in the twilight, he could see nothing on the cliff face that looked like a ledge or a gargoyle.

"We'll make camp in the cave," Alaric announced.

The farmer looked worried. "Gargoyles like caves, I'll wager."

"If the gargoyle was around, I'm sure we would have known by now."

"The dogs would have let us know," Merofled added.

She was right. More than ever, Alaric was glad to be in the company of her animals.

"I'm going to look around," the farmer said. "And see to the horses."

"Suit yourself." Alaric unsheathed his sword with a

metallic clank—a sound as familiar to him as his own breathing—and headed for the opening of the cave.

Chapter 3

With the witch at his heels, Alaric strode through the mouth of the cave. He paused just beyond the entrance, expecting the worst: that the gargoyle would be hiding inside and would rush out in a surprise attack. But no such calamity occurred, and his eyes soon adjusted to the darkness of the interior.

He hoped the farmer's son had possessed the foresight to gather wood and store it inside the cave, where it might have remained dry enough to make a fire. Otherwise, they would be spending a cold dark night on the outskirts of the forest.

The cave was small, not much larger than the nave of the cathedral, and the rear wall did not extend very far into the earth. The floor was dry and sandy, and a tiny stream coursed along the right side and into a sinkhole between a cluster of boulders. Someone had arranged two fallen tree trunks around the stones of a fire pit. And praise the Lord, there was a pile of brush and split wood stacked against the far wall, well out of the weather. A folded brown blanket lay upon one of the logs.

"A lover's trysting place," Merofled observed, chafing her hands.

"Without a doubt." Alaric ran a glance over her graceful curves, wondering if she had ever known a lover. He guessed that she would demand much from a man in that regard. The thought of her naked atop him, her raven hair framing her pale shoulders, sent a bolt of desire straight to his loins. Sweat broke out beneath his already damp robe.

Flushed, he reached for a branch full of dried leaves, and struck a spark with his flint. Always on the march, always at war, he'd made hundreds of fires in his day. The practice was second nature to him—more familiar than trysting with a woman to be sure. He was glad to have something to keep his hands busy and his mind off the young woman.

Merofled sat on the log and fussed with the blanket while the black and white dog called Cletus trotted into the cave and settled at her feet. The smaller brown one leaned against her knee. Bear, the beast that had rescued him, sat between him and the woman with his jowls hanging open, slathering contentedly and gazing up at him. He didn't seem to mind being wet.

When the fire blazed strong enough, Alaric stood up and held his hands out to the flames. He was chilled to the bone and longed to strip off his robe, both to dry the garment and his skin as soon as possible. But respect for his female companion stayed his hand. If sheep in the field could bear wet wool, then so could he.

To add to his discomfort, Merofled came up beside him and swept off her wet cloak. She draped the cloak upon the rocks that ringed the flames and then shook her dress back and forth in front of the heat, trying to dry the wet wool.

Alaric refused to look down at her, sure that he would catch sight of her ankles and perhaps an indiscreet portion of her calves. He needed no more additions to his already dangerous level of temptation.

He cleared his throat. "My thanks to you," he said.

"For saving my life."

"Save your gratitude for prayer. It was my own skin I saved. Not yours."

Her sharpness took him aback.

"My thanks to your dogs, then."

"They are not my dogs. They just follow me around."

"But you know their names."

"I am not deaf. I have heard what their masters call them."

"And yet they follow you. Not their masters."

She frowned and batted at her damp gown with more force than necessary. "That is one of the reasons I was to taken to the stake. Dogs follow me. How evil does that make me, I ask you!"

"Perhaps the village folk think you cast spells on their animals."

"If kindness is a spell, then yes. But I am no witch." She stroked the head of the brown mutt that was never more than a step away from her. "This one was beaten so often that she shied from the slightest touch, even mine. It took months for her to trust me."

The dog thumped its tail on the sandy floor of the cave and gazed up at her with adoring eyes. "Yes, Juno, you are good. And you are safe now."

Alaric watched her slender fingers caress the left ear of the dog and wondered what it would be like to be petted by her in such a way. Though Merofled's tongue was sharp, her touch seemed gentle, at least as far as beasts were concerned.

A moment passed in silence before he realized he was staring at her hand as if hypnotized. He would soon be following her around like Bear and Juno if he didn't take care. He broke off his gaze.

"What about Bear? What's his story?"

"I found him chained to a post so tightly he could do nothing more than sit or stand up. He was starving and so covered with filth that I had to hold my breath while I freed him."

"And Cletus?"

Merofled shrugged one of her delicate shoulders. "He just showed up one day about a year ago. I have no idea where he came from or who his master was." She leveled her stare on him. "But enough of my furry companions. What about you?" Merofled nodded at the scabbard hanging at his thigh. "What kind of priest goes about with a sword?"

"I'm not a priest. I'm an acolyte."

"What kind of acolyte carries a weapon then?"

"A practical one," he replied, fastening his gaze upon the safety of the fire and struggling to slough off the effect of her voice.

She had a melodious way of speaking not often heard in women of her class. She spoke with intelligence and pride as if she'd received some education beyond cook pots and cows. She neither tittered nor gaped at him, lost for words as he'd experienced with most females. Perhaps Merofled possessed the rare quality of innate nobility, a flower that usually stemmed from a keen mind. Perhaps that's why she didn't fit in and why she didn't have any friends. Most people spurned those who did not fall within conventional boundaries. And he was sure Merofled the miller's daughter, with her sharp tongue and even sharper mind, did not.

"Why do you carry a sword?" she added. "Don't you believe your faith in God will overcome the goji?"

He shook his head. "It is a job better left to a quick blade and a stout heart." He crossed his arms over his damp chest. "God has better things to do in these dark times."

She nodded and looked down. Perhaps, like him, she had lost loved ones to the pestilence.

"Still I am surprised the bishop allows you to walk openly with a sword. He seems so strict."

"He did ask me to give up it up. Said it was an abomination and must be put aside."

"But you haven't."

"No." Alaric shook his head. "These are turbulent times, and my blade has served me well. I know the time's coming when I will have to give it up, and I will."

"When you take your final vow?"

He nodded again and clenched his teeth. His sword was the single item he'd kept from his old life—that and his hard-nosed practicality, which so far, no amount of religious instruction had sweetened. Dogged by habits formed over fifteen years of soldiering, he still kept his sword razor-sharp and his scabbard oiled. In fact, he still slept with his blade next to his cot.

The prospect of giving up his sole possession filled him with sadness.

The young woman sidled closer to him. "Do you not fear the wrath of Bishop Romanus?"

"No."

"Tread carefully, sir, lest you find yourself sharing a stake with me." She raised a fine dark brow at him, and the expression raised the blood in his loins again. Then she stooped to turn her cloak on the rocks, and her dress outlined the shapely curves of her buttocks. He watched her deft movements, incapable of speech.

Merofled had obviously seen a different side to the bishop than he had. Bishops were more lenient to fellow churchmen than they were to witches. But there was more to it than that.

"I trust the bishop won't burn a boyhood friend," he managed to blurt through his lustful thoughts.

She straightened and held her hands out to the flames. "Is that what brought you to Rouen—your connection to the bishop?"

Alaric nodded. "After the war, I went home to devastation." He thought of the empty huts, the cold fires, the abandoned fields, and the shallow graves in the churchyard. At the memory, his heart lurched in his chest. "Everyone in my village, save a handful of people, perished from the plague—all gone in a matter of weeks, so I was told."

"Your family?"

"Yes." He stared at the fire.

"Your wife?"

"I had none. I never stopped fighting long enough to court a woman."

Merofled nodded but didn't make a comment.

"Romanus was there when I arrived, seeing to his kinfolk who were barricaded in the castle keep. They were the only ones to escape the pestilence. He convinced me to come to Rouen with him." Alaric poked the end of a flaming log with his toe. "I had nothing better to do. So here I am."

"Giving your life up to God."

Her scathing tone surprised him. He shot a glance at her and caught her studying him, with her full lips curled at one corner.

"You doubt my intentions?" he challenged.

"It is your choice of vocation that I doubt." Her green eyes flashed as her regard swept over his wet robe and boots. "You don't look like any priest I've ever seen."

"And how many have crossed your path?" he retorted, put off by her derisive expression. "In all your world travels, pray?"

Her eyes raked across him, her gaze suddenly stormy and hard. "You mock me," she said.

"As you mock me." He held her stare.

"Sorry." She tossed her head. "But I don't like priests overmuch. Especially Romanus. He's a glory-seeker. All high and mighty—foisting his rules on everyone—"

"Don't worry. I have no intention of foisting myself on anyone. Especially you." But as soon as the words fell from his lips, he felt a flush sear through him. His words were an outright falsehood. He wanted to foist himself on this woman, and not for religious instruction.

"To be honest," he continued. "I joined the church to get away from all the bloodshed in my old job, all the fighting. I just wanted some peace and quiet. I thought priests copied manuscripts, grew grapes and healed the sick."

"No. They stick their noses in everyone's business. And they burn young women for no apparent reason."

She sighed and fell silent. He was highly aware of her silence and of her presence on the periphery of his vision. Her fiery words and confrontational nature had provoked him even more than her comely body.

Alaric heard a noise at the entrance of the cave. He glanced over his shoulder, grateful to see the farmer had returned.

With a single word of greeting, the farmer stomped across the cave floor to the boulders where the stream gurgled and disappeared. From the cold, clear brook, he pulled out an earthenware jug plugged with a wad of cloth.

"Drink?" he held up the jug as he retraced his steps to the logs.

"No thanks." Over the years Alaric had learned not to drink from bottles left uncorked and unsealed. He'd escaped many a night when his brethren suffered and sometimes even died from foul spirits.

The farmer did not bother to ask the witch to join him. He kicked Cletus out of the way and plopped down on the sand. The dog slunk to Merofled's side.

"Don't do that again," Merofled warned.

"What?" the farmer pulled out the wad of linen.

"Kick the dog. Any of them."

"Don't tell me my business, witch." He balanced the jug on his shoulder, tipped it to his lips and took a long swig. "I'm in no humor to listen your nonsense."

Angry, Merofled turned to confront him, but Alaric caught her wrist. She glared back at him, and for a long moment stared into his eyes. He said nothing, but his grip was apparently enough to make her think twice about accosting the farmer. She frowned and yanked free of him, rubbing her wrist as if his touch had burned her. But she remained where she was.

"No sign of your son?" Alaric asked.

"Nay. Or the gargoyle either." The farmer took another long drink. "The longer this takes, the more I fear for the boy."

"We'll find him," Alaric said. "Don't worry. For now, let's all get some rest."

He reached for the rope he had looped around his sword belt. "Hold out your hands, Merofled."

Her shoulders wilted. "You don't mean to tie me."

"I do." He found the end of the rope.

"I promise I won't go anywhere. It's dark. It's raining again. I'd be a fool to go out there tonight."

"Better a fool than a burned witch." He gave her a stern look. "Your hands, Merofled."

Scowling at him, she raised her wrists.

Chapter 4

A GROWL WOKE MEROFLED FROM A FITFUL SLEEP. Startled, she opened her eyes to discover Claude standing above her. He was backlit by the fire, the jug in one hand and his belt in another, staring down at her with hunger glinting in his eyes. Her blood went cold.

She turned to the left to alert the priest, but he was no longer propped against the log where he had been sitting when she had gone to sleep. Wild with fear, she glanced around the dark cave. The priest was nowhere in sight. He had left the cave and had lashed the rope around a branch at the end of the log to make sure she didn't get away. Bear was gone as well. Her blood sank to an even colder depth.

"Off to relieve himself," the farmer remarked. He tossed the jug aside, and it hit the sand with a soft thud. "As I aim to do right now."

Merofled jerked to a sitting position and struggled to get to her feet, but her bound wrists made the task difficult. Before she could get away, Claude shoved her back to the sand and snatched off the cloak she had pulled over her for warmth. "Stay where you are, witch." His breath reeked and his speech was slurred from the ale he had drunk for the past few hours. He yanked at her feet until her arms snapped back, pulling the rope taut and rendering her defenseless.

Cletus growled and closed in. The farmer kicked him in the haunches, sending him sprawling. Yelping, the dog scrambled to his feet and lunged forward again, but his scrawny frame was no match for the farmer. Juno backed away, her tail between her legs but her teeth bared as the farmer fumbled with his muddy hose and clamped his garlic-stained hand over Merofled's mouth.

"Don't make a sound," he warned. "Or I won't be nice."

She writhed, tossing her head back and forth under his filthy hand as he straddled her. She kicked, but his body was out of range of her feet and knees. All she could do was bite the side of his meaty palm.

"Ow!" he exclaimed. "Bitch!" He pulled up her gown and shift, yanking so hard that the linen hem scraped the flesh of her calf. He leered down at her, his lips wet and disgusting.

"Your stinking curs can't help you now."

As if to prove the man wrong, Juno started to howl. The sound rattled Merofled's ears as the farmer freed himself of his hose. Then Cletus leapt forward and grabbed the loose fabric of the man's leggings, shaking it while Claude swatted at him, losing his concentration. Merofled kicked and squirmed, determined to make herself as unavailable as possible while the dogs badgered him, buying her time. She prayed the priest would hear Juno barking and intervene before the farmer had the chance to mount her.

His hand dug into her jaw, hurting her, as he struggled to get rid of Cletus. His thick bulk pressed down on her belly, making it impossible to take a breath. Merofled closed her eyes, as her vision and her hope of rescue began to fade. Her life had been spared two times that day. Maybe she had run out of miracles.

"Yeoman!" a familiar voice shouted.

Claude thrust against her, desperate to carry out what he had started.

"Get off her!" the priest shouted.

"Wait your turn," the farmer snarled. His male flesh pushed against Merofled's belly while a wave of nausea passed over her. She had never felt more repulsed by a man or more helpless.

"I said get off her!" the priest grabbed a handful of the farmer's greasy red hair and yanked his head back so far that Merofled thought his neck would snap. She hoped it would. The man's bleary eyes went wide with pain.

He struggled for balance, waving his arms, which freed her mouth of his hand. But his male lust was hard upon him, and he roared with displeasure at being interrupted. With a grunt, he launched off his knees and hurled himself at the priest.

The men rolled upon the ground, fighting, as the dogs circled them, barking and snapping. Merofled pulled herself to her feet and stumbled to the limb where the rope was fastened. She had no faith that the priest would treat her any differently than the farmer, if given the chance. She didn't intend to provide him with one.

While her knees shook under her torn shift, she took a moment to figure out how the priest had tied the knot. Then she unfastened it with trembling fingers while Juno whined, frantic with worry about the violence all around her. By the time the priest had subdued Claude, Merofled had untied the rope, although her wrists were still bound.

"Cover yourself," Alaric spat at the farmer, whose hose had fallen to his ankles. He glanced at Merofled over the farmer's head, as the man bent to retrieve his leggings.

She returned Alaric's stare, not sure he would keep his distance, and not feeling safe just yet. She had seen male lust first hand on a number of occasions—not this close to be sure, but close enough to know that once most men sniffed rutting on the air, they could not be trusted to control their carnal desires.

"Cletus, Bear," she called, forcing assurance into her voice that she didn't feel inside. The dogs obeyed her summons and trotted to her side. They had served her well, and she might need their protection again. She shifted her wrists back and forth in the rope, determined to get free of the coarse bonds that held her. But she could see that she couldn't do it alone.

Merofled held out her wrists to Cletus' snout and visualized him pulling the rope loose. He seemed to understand what she wanted of him and snatched at the hempen line, shaking it and growling. Within moments, she felt the knot give way.

"Get over there," the priest commanded of the farmer. "To the other side of the fire."

She glanced up to see the farmer shuffling to the far side of the cave.

"And if you so much as look at the young woman again, I will run you through."

"Why trouble yourself," the farmer retorted. "No one will care how she is used. She's a witch."

Merofled's mouth went dry at his words while her stomach burned with bile. If she could get her hands on a weapon, she would make certain the farmer did not live to see daylight.

With a sharp shake of his head, the lean sheep dog freed Merofled's wrists and then wrestled the rope to the ground as if it were a serpent to be killed.

"Good boy," Merofled patted his neck. She could always count on Cletus' cleverness. "Good boy, Cletus."

The priest took a few steps toward her and stopped. He seemed wary of her and her animals. Good. She stepped behind the log.

"Are you hurt?" he asked.

"No."

"I should not have left you alone."

"You should not have bound me and left me defenseless."

He nodded and glanced at her hands. "I see that now."

"And you will not do so again." She raised her chin and stared at him. His blue eyes flashed in the darkness as he regarded her with an expression she could not read. She could pick up on anything an animal had in mind, and they her. But this man was hard to fathom—perhaps impossible to fathom. Neither kindness nor lust glowed in his sapphire eyes. All she could discern in them was guarded interest.

The expression baffled her. No man had ever looked at her in such a way. No man had cared to know what she thought or felt. She didn't know what to make of the priest. But as long as he kept his distance, he could be as mysterious as he wished.

Disturbed on a variety of levels and needing something to occupy his hands, Alaric bent for the blanket on which Merofled had been sleeping. The action seemed to alarm her, for she bolted forward.

"No!" she exclaimed.

He glanced up, surprised that she would object to being moved as far as possible from the farmer—although the man had fallen into a drunken stupor and would likely sleep the rest of the night without disturbing her again.

"I meant to move you closer to the log," he said, leaving the blanket where it was while he rose to his full height. "So I could sleep nearby to protect you."

She shot him a glance full of disgust. He wouldn't blame her for hating the entire male race at the moment, even if it included him.

"I need to get my cloak first," she said.

"As you wish."

She turned her back to him and knelt on the blanket. Her hair was a tangled mass, her robe was streaked with dried mud, and her shift was torn at the side from her run-in with the farmer. Still, he found her to be the most alluring woman he had ever met. He admired her womanly curves as she gathered up her cloak and held it to her breasts. When she stepped away, he bent to grasp the end of the blanket. He dragged it to the log, turning it lengthwise, so her body would lay parallel to the trunk. She would be protected on one side by the log and on the other by him.

"Not that I shall sleep tonight," she commented, kneeling on the wool.

"Nor I," he answered. He unsheathed his sword and laid it on the edge of the blanket.

The two male dogs sat in the sand on the periphery of the blanket, panting and watching him, while Juno curled up next to Merofled's hip. With her back to him, Merofled fussed with her clothing. Alaric regarded her hair, wondering how she would ever comb such a cloud of curls. Then Merofled turned to face him, and he averted his gaze, hoping she hadn't caught him staring at her. His hungry gaze had been as much a violation as Claude's pawing of her.

"Thank you, acolyte," she said, drawing the cloak to her shoulders.

"Perhaps we are even now." He smiled shallowly. He must strive to keep things light between them. She had suffered a traumatic assault, and he wanted to assure her that she had nothing to fear from him.

"Yes." She sighed and closed her eyes.

He felt Bear turn three times and then lie down along the back of his legs. He'd never owned a dog before, and was about to push the beast away, but then decided to let him be. Bear had saved his life. He would go easy on the mutt. Favor for favor.

He turned to find the witch regarding him, her serious eyes tired but unafraid.

"I feel strangely safe with your blade between us," she remarked, her voice soft.

"You shall be," he replied. "I promise you."

"Should you even think about touching me," she continued. "I will give you a taste of your own steel."

"Those are pretty tough words for such a young woman."

"You think it an empty boast?"

He flushed. "Not at all, miss." But just to show her how empty her threat was, he flung out his right hand for the sword. She did the same, and actually beat him to the blade. Her small white hand blazed beneath his large callused palm as she wrapped her fingers around the hilt.

Amazed by her quick reflexes and not a little embarrassed that she had bested him at his own game, he grinned and met her gaze. Instantly he realized he should never have touched her, much less smiled at her. Her eyes smoldered with warning. He retracted his arm.

"You think to toy with me," she said, her voice deadly serious.

"No," he lied.

"Do not underestimate me," she added. "Or you will regret it."

He couldn't tear his gaze away from her strange green eyes. He'd never met anyone like her. "I'll take that under advisement."

"See that you do."

He waited for her to release the weapon and roll onto her back again. But she didn't. She remained holding the sword, lying there with her eyes open, watching him.

Alaric couldn't remember a time when he'd been more unnerved, and never by a woman.

It was he who finally flipped onto his back. He closed his eyes, praying for sleep. But the events of the day vaulted through his thoughts, and the stare of the black-haired woman burned him with a fire much brighter than he had ever known. He lay in the cold sand, anxious for dawn to arrive.

In the morning he would find the boy, slay the beast and return to Rouen. The sooner he got back to the monkish routines of the cathedral, the better for his precarious state of mind.

Chapter 5

WHEN THE BREATHING OF BOTH MEN SETTLED to a constant rhythm, Merofled slipped out of her makeshift bed and stooped for the sword. She had kept her hand on it for a reason: so the priest wouldn't move it to the other side of his body where it would be out of reach. She intended to make good use of the blade.

She hushed the dogs with an outstretched hand and then crept across the sand to the fire. There she found a stick to suit her: one that was cool to the touch on one end and glowing orange on the other. She grabbed it and turned for the farmer.

He slept on his back, snoring at the ceiling of the cave, while spittle dripped from the corners of his mouth.

Merofled stood to the side of his head and gazed at him for a moment, fighting off the urge to plunge the blade into his mouth. Then she stuck the stick in the sand and with both hands holding the heavy weapon, lowered the sword to his right eyelid. She gave his brow a little prick with the tip of the blade.

His red-rimmed eyes flew open.

"Don't move," she warned, glaring at him. "Or I won't be nice."

The farmer struggled without rising up, as if trying to escape and thinking better of it when the sword at his eye didn't waver.

"That's right," Merofled said. "I have no qualms about killing you." She didn't. Knowing she faced the stake on her return to Rouen had freed her of many restrictions, including subservience to males.

"You'll hang!"

"Do you think I fear hanging? I'm going to burn anyway." Her lips drew back in a mocking smile. "Isn't that your philosophy?"

"Priest!" the farmer called, rolling his eyes for a view of the other man.

She jabbed the tip of the blade into his eye socket. "Not another word, Claude."

He glanced at her, his lips twitching in fear.

She nodded at the brand stuck in the earth. "Take it."

"Why?"

"I said take it."

He blinked and snatched the branch from the sand.

"Hold it to your cock."

He stared at her aghast.

"You heard me."

"You can't be serious!"

Merofled pushed the blade into the hollow above his eye until he whimpered in fright. "I am dead serious," she said. "I don't want you bothering me again, Claude."

"I won't!"

"I don't believe you." She curled her lip. "Now do it. Or so help me God I will plunge this sword into your brain."

"Okay, okay!" he blubbered. The stick trembled wildly as he directed the tip to his crotch. When it got close enough, Merofled lifted her foot and brought it down on the wood with enough force to clamp it to the farmer's body. The glowing tip burned through two layers of clothing and the most sensitive part of the male anatomy.

"Bitch!" the farmer bellowed. No longer caring about his eye, he rolled away and lumbered to his feet. Screaming in pain, he galloped for the river.

Merofled threw the brand into the fire and turned. Her work was done, and she'd derived a great deal of satisfaction from it. She was sure the brute would never bother her again.

She retraced her steps to the blanket and found the priest watching her approach. He didn't say anything. Maybe he thought she might do the same to him. Maybe he thought the farmer deserved what had been done to him. Maybe if accused later, he would say that he had been asleep when she'd burned the farmer. She didn't care what his motives were, as long as he kept his comments to himself.

"Go to sleep," she said.

"I am asleep," he replied.

She thought she saw him smile, but in the darkness she couldn't be sure.

Hours later, Merofled decided she could finally take a breath. The warrior priest had finally fallen asleep. The farmer was nowhere in sight, and was probably sleeping with the horses. The dogs seemed content. She could rest.

Merofled sighed and released the hilt of the sword that lay once again on the blanket. She was relieved. To be honest, she had not expected the priest to leave her alone. As Claude had said, she was a condemned woman and not a soul would care what happened to her. Not one person in the village would come to her defense, no matter how she was mistreated—except perhaps for the stranger sleeping next to her.

She allowed her gaze to wander over the priest, inspecting him freely now that his glittering blue eyes were not making her lose her train of thought. When those eyes looked at her, it was as if he could see right through the walls she had constructed to keep most people out. His eyes could disarm her in a glance—which was why she had been forced to throw up her guard around him.

Still, this priest seemed to be interested in more than just sex and sorcery. His gaze held more curiosity than lust or judgment, which in her experience with men was a rare occurrence.

When she'd seen him for the first time yesterday, leading the donkey toward the rear door of the cathedral, her heart had flopped in her chest. Had she not been headed for the stake and preoccupied with her impending death, she would have examined him more closely, for she had never seen a finer looking man.

He was rugged and craggy, with coarse ruddy skin, as if he'd spent his days outdoors and his nights on the ground. His hair was like an autumn field ripe with every kind of grain: wheat, flax and barley, with undertones of the richest loam.

But what she liked more than anything was his mouth.

He had an expressive mouth, with a wide lower lip and a generous upper lip that stretched over startling white teeth when he smiled or grimaced. Maybe he'd been formed in the womb in a special way, or maybe he'd been kicked in the jaw and it had healed a bit crookedly. But when he smiled, his jaw moved forward and flared below his ears in way that lent his smile more charm than she had ever seen in a man. She found his jutting, lop-sided grin irresistible.

When he had smiled at her earlier, she had nearly melted into the blanket on the floor of the cave. Had she not been traumatized by the farmer's assault, she would have flirted with him and done everything in her power to make him stray from his path and kiss her. Instead she had lashed out at him to keep him at a distance, as she still didn't trust him.

Like the gentleman he was, however, he had left her alone.

It was the last thing she wanted now.

"Wake up!"

A boot nudged Alaric in the backside. "It's out there!"

Not quite lucid, Alaric creaked to a sitting position, his hips aching from the cold night he'd spent in the sand. He could hear the dogs barking in the distance. He glanced through the opening of the cave to discover that dawn had finally arrived. Pearl-colored light filtered through the wet silhouettes of the trees. His head reeled.

"What did you say, man?"

"Something was out there, sniffing around those eggs." Claude pointed behind him with a thumb. "But the accursed dogs ran it off."

Merofled stirred beside Alaric. He glanced at her, and a strange feeling passed over him. How right it felt to have this woman wake up next to him. Seeing her rise onto one hand while she pushed back her mass of curls with her other seemed achingly familiar to him. Or perhaps it was because he desired her so much that he experienced such a rush of emotion. He broke off his stare and jumped to his feet.

"Follow the dogs," he commanded, fastening his sword belt around his hips. He picked up his sword without catching Merofled's eye. "The beast will lead us to the boy."

Alaric grabbed the rope and trotted out of the cave, looping the line around his elbow as he ran, fully awake and happy to have a fresh path to follow.

Chapter 6

Mist rose from the saturated earth as Alaric and his companions crashed through the woods at the edge of the river. All three dogs raced ahead, barking and braying.

"There!" the farmer shouted, pointing with his cudgel.

Alaric strained to catch sight of the beast in the fog. He saw the flash of a golden eye, the glint of a tail, and then the creature was gone. He could hear it crashing through the undergrowth as it barreled toward the river.

Still, he'd seen enough to realize the gargoyle was enormous—probably twenty feet tall at the head. He'd never seen a creature that tall. The prospect of fighting such a beast made his heart catch in his chest. He drew his sword, but for the first time in his life, the blade seemed inadequate for the task ahead.

The path they were on was the same one they had blazed the previous evening. In a few minutes they would come upon the branch of the river where he'd fallen in. His heart did another flip-flop. This time, however, he was aware that the bank was undercut, and he could see much more of the landscape now that the sun was up. While he trotted alongside the river to the base of the cliff, he kept a prudent distance from the edge.

Then he saw what they had missed the previous night. Had they traveled another half mile, they would have found the boy. He skidded to a stop as the witch and the farmer caught up with him.

"Look," Alaric pointed at a mound of dry land in the middle of the stream. "There he is!"

"Louis!" the farmer shouted.

The boy must have heard the dogs, for he had walked to the edge of the tiny island and was waving his arms at them. The fork of the river at their feet was not wide, but it ran deep and was clogged with branches and brush. Anyone who got swept into the snags would certainly drown.

"Papa!" the boy yelled. His reedy voice barely carried over the roar of the water.

"Hold on, son!" the farmer called. "We're going to save you!"

Alaric was surprised at the age of the lad. He hadn't asked for details and had surmised the farmer's son was fairly young—five years or so. But from the look of Louis's shoulders, he had already reached puberty. Alaric guessed he was at least twelve. He probably used the cave for drinking and wenching, just like his father.

For a moment, Alaric paused, reconsidering. He was about to place his life in jeopardy for the farmer's family— for a boy who had proved to be destructive and a father who had proved to be a lecher. That he might lose his life or sacrifice a limb for these two stuck in his craw.

But he was not here to judge anyone. He was here in the employ of the bishop of Rouen to do a job in the absence of his master. Alaric sheathed his sword and reached for the rope.

He turned to Merofled while the farmer paced back and forth, impotent.

"Can you get Bear to swim to the boy with this?" He held up the rope.

Merofled eyed the hemp cord and glanced at her huge

shaggy dog.

"The current is swift here." Her voice was sharp with concern. She put her white hand on the dog's great head, as if to protect him. "It would be dangerous."

"If Bear starts upstream, the current will work in his favor."

"But what about the return trip?" she glanced at the pile of rubbish that clogged part of the stream.

"He's the boy's only chance."

Merofled bit her lip and glanced upriver. "We could go back to town and get a boat."

"And let that monster eat my boy?" The farmer spat in protest.

Merofled glared at him. "If the goji wished to eat your boy, she would have done so by now. I doubt she has even harmed him."

"Oh, so it's a she now, is it?" He curled his lip. "Sticking up for your own kind, are you?"

"I haven't encountered any male animals that can lay eggs," Merofled answered, turning her back to the man.

"It is your decision, Merofled," Alaric put in to break up the spat once again. "It's your dog that will be put in danger."

Merofled studied the current, looked at the boy and then planted her hands on her hips. She was just about to announce her decision when a sharp cry rent the air. A shadow raced over the clearing. Alaric heard a thunderous flap of wings and looked up.

He couldn't believe his eyes.

Not twenty feet above his head soared the largest flying creature he had ever seen. It wasn't a bird. It was more like a giant lizard with wings. He could see the gleaming ridges of its ivory underbelly and the bulging veins on its leathery green wings. It—she, as Merofled had accurately pointed out—was a blue-green color on top with yellow dots bordering her sides. Her neck was at least eight feet long, ridged with spikes and topped by a head shaped like that of a horse, except for the horn sprouting out of her forehead.

He was looking up at a dragon—a living, breathing, and dangerously close-flying dragon.

Before he could snap his gaping jaw back into place and arm himself, he saw the gargoyle turn and swoop low, coming back at him in a nimble maneuver that was awesome in its deadly skill. He saw her golden eyes then, blazing at him, and her round, flaring nostrils, so large he could fit an entire fist in one.

For an instant he wondered if this is what a rodent felt like in the field when a hawk dropped out of the air—hypnotized and frozen in place, stunned by abject fear, and with no place to go.

Then he saw the beast lower her front legs, and the movement galvanized him into action. He ducked, missing her talons by mere inches.

"Jesus Mother Mary!" Alaric gasped. He grabbed his sword and staggered back. "Into the trees!" he shouted. "Get back!"

Even the dogs dashed for safety, leaving Alaric alone in the clearing.

The gargoyle circled, flapping her wings and coming around again.

Alaric stood at the edge of the clearing and waited until the beast soared into range. Then he ducked to avoid her knife-like claws and pivoted to slash at her wing as she went by. The gargoyle bellowed in pain and veered toward the river, her right wing tilting downward.

"You got her!" the farmer crowed.

"It was but a scratch." Alaric watched the gargoyle flap crookedly and circle back. "Here she comes again."

This time, however, the gargoyle pulled up at the water's edge and flapped her wings in a reverse motion, until she lowered her long body to the ground in a terrifyingly graceful descent. She would be no clumsy prey on land. Alaric backed toward the trees, his sword at the ready and his heart hammering in his chest.

Hissing, the gargoyle slithered forward with her tail swatting the beach back and forth and her head lowered. A fin flared up on her spine, marked in a riot of yellow and green circles. Another flared behind her head, red and yellow and edged with spikes. She looked even fiercer than before. Alaric raised his blade, wondering how he would ever get near enough to such a creature to inflict more than a superficial wound.

The gargoyle crept closer. Alaric held his ground, searching for her weak spot and waiting for his opportunity to strike her. When she got within ten feet of him, she opened her mouth and hissed again. Strings of mucous sprayed out, landing on the rocks and brambles and setting the leaves to smoldering.

Alaric stared, sure that the gargoyle spittle had burned the vegetation. What would it do to human flesh? He backed up a step, intending to keep out of range of her strange bile.

Then she raised her head and trumpeted to the sky, rattling his ears until he thought he would go deaf from the noise.

Alaric hurried to the other side of the clearing, hoping to draw her away from the others. She swung her tail across the sand and gravel and lunged at him, nearly catching him with her snout. He jumped back.

"Faith!" he gasped.

She straddled the ground with her massive back legs and much thinner front ones, while she watched him circle her. He kept his distance, looking for the blind spot he hadn't discovered yet. She didn't make a move to stop him, but stayed in the middle of a patch of sand, tracking his path with her huge horned head. Her reptilian belly heaved in and out with strident breaths. The fins folded down with a clatter while she made a noise deep in her chest, like a dog growling a warning.

She would not attack him if he kept his distance. He could tell. Had he hurt her that much? He hadn't thought so. But as he circled, studying her, he noticed her green and ivory skin was streaked with scars. A lump hung at her neck, just behind her left ear. Her teeth were yellow, her claws ragged, her flesh was callused around her joints and she was definitely short of breath. Then it struck him.

The gargoyle was an old lady. Perhaps a sick old lady.

Stunned, Alaric stared at her with a new perspective. He couldn't kill a creature at the end of its days. There would no honor in carrying the head of someone's grandmother back for display in town.

Before Alaric could decide what course to take, he saw Merofled venture out of the brush.

"Merofled, don't!" he yelled. "She'll spray you!"

Merofled didn't take notice of his warning. Her entire being was focused on the gargoyle.

"Goji," she called softly.

The gargoyle tilted her head and squinted her eyes at the young woman. A growl rumbled through the beast's chest. But the creature made no move toward the witch.

"Goji, I have something for you," Merofled said, holding out her folded cloak.

The gargoyle hissed, warning the human to stay away. She shook her head and the fin behind her ears flared out.

"Get back!" Alaric yelled. "She's going to spray you!"

Frantic, Alaric circled closer to Merofled as she

deposited her cloak at the edge of the clearing, all the while holding the creature's gaze. What was the young woman doing? She was mad to think she could charm the gargoyle like she charmed domestic dogs. This was no tame animal. This was a cold-blooded monster with a cold-blooded heart. He would stake his life on it.

Then he saw the cloak move of its own accord, as if alive.

Merofled slipped back into the brush.

Alaric watched in amazement as a foot-long lizard slithered out of the woolen cloak and ambled in jerky uncoordinated steps toward the gargoyle.

"You fool!" the farmer shouted. "You saved one of the spawn?"

"It has a right to live," Merofled retorted.

"One is enough!" Claude spat.

He lunged forward, swinging his cudgel, trying to swipe at the young gargoyle before it got to its mother. The goji hissed and opened its mouth, spewing the farmer with her vitriolic spit. Momentarily blinded, the farmer staggered through the clearing, screaming in pain. As he stumbled toward the river, he struck the back leg of the gargoyle with his weapon. The creature bellowed and pivoted out of the way, bringing her tail around to slash at the farmer. She sent him flying. He hit the ground near the water's edge.

Alaric ran up to the farmer to help him to his feet. The man's tunic and face were speckled with the phlegm of the gargoyle. He couldn't waste a moment and allow the strange bile to eat away at Claude's face. He dragged the unconscious man to the river and rolled him into the shallows. He splashed water on his face, doing his best to wash away the burning slime. Claude moaned and came to his senses.

"That witch is mad!" he exclaimed. "Damn her to

Hell!"

Alaric shot a glance over his shoulder at the gargoyle. She nudged her baby with her nose and seemed to be ignoring them for the moment.

"There's no time for worrying about the witch," he said. "She can take care of herself."

"Because she does the Devil's work!"

"Go back to town and get a boat. I will deal with the woman."

"Aye." Claude sat up and grimaced.

"And take the other horse back with you."

"Sir?" Claude lumbered to his feet, panting.

"I don't want the animal to get eaten or killed, especially when it doesn't belong to me."

The farmer waded out of the river. His clothes were singed and tattered, and it was difficult to discern where the effects of human vengeance ended and the goji defense began—better for Claude that way when he explained the state of his attire. His burned crotch blended in with the rest of his singed clothing now. But his face would be scarred for life.

"I'll be back!" Claude yelled to his son. "I'm going to get a boat!"

At the sound of the farmer's voice, the goji bellowed and swung her head around to face him. Her neck fin flared.

"Get out of here!" Alaric shoved him in the shoulder. "Before she decides to come after you."

"Aye." The farmer limped away.

"If something happens and we are not here when you get back," Alaric called after him. "Don't look for us. Save the boy."

"You don't have to tell me twice," the farmer shouted over his shoulder. He broke into an uneven trot and disappeared into the brush.

"Priest!" Merofled exclaimed behind Alaric. Her voice had a strident ring to it.

Expecting the worst, he turned around. Merofled pointed to the sand in the middle of the clearing. For a moment, he couldn't make out why she seemed so excited. And then he saw the orbs moving in the earth.

More gargoyle eggs. The creature had laid eggs in more than one location and had come back to protect them as they hatched.

Chapter 7

"HOLY MOTHER OF MARY," ALARIC SAID, easing closer to the gargoyle. He edged around the perimeter of the clearing, careful to keep his distance. The beast curled her body in a crescent around the eggs. He could see her left leg bleeding where the farmer had struck her with the cudgel.

He could attack the gargoyle now, when she was occupied with her hatchlings. But he just couldn't bring himself to do it.

Alaric padded over the sand and gravel until he had joined Merofled and her dogs. Bear came up and nosed his hand.

"Tell me all you know of the gargoyle." Alaric wiped his slobbery hand on his thigh. "Now, or I will finish what the farmer began."

Merofled shot him a dark glance. "You would not!"

"If I think that animal will endanger the villagers, I have no choice. So tell me what you know."

She clamped her full lips into a straight line as she considered his threat.

"All I know of the goji is that they live in the swamp."

"They, meaning there is more than one of them?"

"If there are fertilized eggs, that would mean there was a male at one time."

She was right, of course. Alaric watched one of the eggs tear apart and a small olive-green head poke through. "Do you think the reason we are seeing them now is because the flood has displaced them?"

"Yes." As she contemplated the gargoyle, Merofled stroked Juno's head. "As my grandmother said, they keep to themselves." She nodded at the giant lizard. "You see that she doesn't attack us when we do not provoke her."

"She is distracted with her young at the moment." Alaric propped his hand on the hilt of his sword. "It's hard to tell what she would do if she didn't have young to worry about."

"But why is your first thought to kill her?"

"Because she and her brood could become a big problem."

Merofled sighed and hugged her chest. "What do your brethren teach us?" She studied the creatures emerging from the eggs. "To every thing there is a season? And a time for every purpose under Heaven."

"In reference to man, Merofled."

"As you interpret it. But I think all creatures have a place on this earth and a right to live. And that God made them for a reason." She turned and cocked a brow at him. "Is not my interpretation just as valid?"

Alaric gazed at her. When she raised her fine eyebrow at him and looked at him with her large hazel eyes full of fire, he forgot all about scripture and gargoyles. All he could see was her.

He forced his thoughts back to the problem at hand.

"Is that all your grandmother told you of the gargoyles?"

"That and they are said to bear young only once every hundred years."

Alaric raised his own brows. "So this brood will not reproduce until we are gone?"

"Long gone," Merofled added.

"And this one is at least a hundred years old?"

"Probably a great deal more."

No wonder the gargoyle bore so many scars. Alaric stared at the beast with a new appreciation. He was looking at the most ancient creature he would ever encounter.

"Why haven't people seen the young ones?" he mused. "How have they been kept a secret so long?"

"My grandmother believed the young go to sea."

"To live in the ocean?"

"Or perhaps on an island somewhere?" Merofled crossed her arms over her chest. "But that she couldn't prove. She could never convince a fisherman to take her to look for them."

Alaric glanced at her. "So I assume you have come from a long line of witches."

"Witches?" She raised her proud chin. "That is not how we refer to ourselves."

"Of women connected to God's creatures then."

"Interested in them, yes. Connected?" She shrugged. "It is one thing to read the mind of an animal. It is another to know their ways so well that you can predict what they will do."

"And yet you sent Bear to rescue me."

"He has been bred for such things. It is his nature to want to swim toward a struggling man."

Alaric studied her profile, wondering what Merofled's life had been like. Being strong and good-natured, he had always been accepted by others. She, being strong-willed and peculiar had obviously not. He wished it were not that way. He wished he could do something to bring Merofled and her fellow villagers to a common ground. If she helped to save the boy, she might be taking the first step toward acceptance. But another glance at her full, firm mouth made him wonder if she would value the acceptance of the townspeople.

Merofled nodded at the gargoyle, which now encircled three young ones. "Remember, priest, your mission is to rescue the boy," she said. "Not to kill the goji."

Alaric doubted his mission could be completed without killing the beast, especially since the farmer had been injured. Claude would insist that someone or something pay for his pain and disfigurement. When it came down to it, Alaric knew it would be the goji or the girl. He didn't plan on allowing Merofled to take the blame. In fact, once this was all over, he would do his best to keep her from being burned at the stake.

As for now, all they could do was wait for the farmer to return, and make sure the gargoyle didn't harm the boy—or them. But waiting for the farmer was not good enough for Merofled. She heaved a large sigh, as if she had decided something, and stepped away from him. He should have known she would have an alternate plan.

Merofled's heart pounded in fear as she walked away from the priest and knelt on a rock in the clearing. She held out her hands and made a chirping noise, the same noise she had heard the little lizard make when calling for its mother at the cave. The gargoyle's huge head rose and cocked to one side as she listened to the human mimicking the cry of her young. The hatchling that Merofled had saved also turned toward her and stared.

"Come, little one," she called, holding out her hands. She made the sound again. She hoped that the baby might confuse her with its mother, as she had been the first one the little lizard had seen when it hatched. Sometimes ducklings attached to the wrong mother when they beheld a creature other than their mother upon hatching. She hoped it would be the same with gargoyles.

The mother gargoyle watched her. The beast's huge

golden eyes didn't blink, but the pupils narrowed to black slits, making her look like a deadly snake. Merofled held her ground, holding back the waves of fear that threatened to choke her when the goji stared at her like that.

The priest put his hand on the hilt of his sword, ready to spring into action.

"What do you think you're doing?" he hissed.

"I am taking this family away." She made the chirping noise again. "You can stay with the boy and wait for the farmer if you like. But for me and the goji, waiting is a death sentence."

She turned her attention back to the small lizard. "Come, little one," she cooed. She held out her hands and chirped again. The baby lizard skittered across the beach toward her, his thin body making quick crisscross movements.

"You are mad!" the priest unsheathed his sword with a clank.

At the sound, the gargoyle swung around and growled at him. The fin behind her head flared out.

"Don't!" Merofled exclaimed. The priest could ruin everything if the goji thought he threatened her young. "Put away the sword! Now!"

She shot a hot glance at him, pinning him in place with her will as she clasped the squirming baby to her chest.

The priest stared at her, his sword arm frozen in the air.

Bear, sensing the danger, appeared at the priest's knee and started to bark at the giant lizard, defending his newfound friend. Juno whined and Cletus panted, watching all three possible sources of trouble: his mistress, the priest, and the gargoyle.

"Bear!" Merofled cried, worried that the gargoyle would panic and fling her bile at them.

Someone had to make a move, and she decided to make it.

Holding the baby lizard to her breasts, she scampered along the edge of the clearing, away from the priest. The goji bellowed behind her, and the sound echoed into the sky, frightening Merofled to her bones. But she wouldn't look back. She counted on the lizard's motherly instincts to save her young. While she held the baby, she prayed the goji would not harm her and might possibly follow her.

She heard a rustling behind her and a disgruntled growl. Merofled ran downstream, past the logjam and into the brush, headed toward the sea, with her canine companions not far behind.

A few moments later, the goji lumbered to her feet and limped after the witch, dragging her back leg and bellowing. The two other babies scampered alongside, chirping and running in circles.

Merofled's heart leaped with joy. Her plan was working!

Merofled had been gone only a few minutes when Alaric decided to follow her. He would be dealt with harshly if he let the witch escape. The boy was in no danger on the island and could wait by himself until his father showed up with the boat. After all, the boy had spent the night alone. Another hour or so wouldn't matter. He took off at a jog.

He caught up with the wounded goji, but kept a prudent distance behind her. He could see Merofled hurrying along the riverbank up ahead, following the old cliff road.

Suddenly the dogs started to bark at something in the distance. Alaric drew his sword, ready to dash past the gargoyle and risk being sprayed with bile. Just as they turned a bend in the road, they came face to face with four riders and a coach with large wooden wheels. Alaric recognized the coach immediately as the bishop's. The low road must have been flooded, forcing the bishop to take the perilous cliff road—a trail that wound down the face of the chalk escarpment and onto the narrow bank of the treacherous side of the river.

Seeing the humans, the gargoyle bellowed and struggled toward the river. But she was in bad shape. Bleeding and panting, she staggered halfway down the bank and then collapsed, wheezing, with one wing half-open.

Merofled's pale face turned a new shade of white. She darted to the river and put down the baby.

"Go!" she cried.

The little lizard looked up at her and then at her dying mother. She chirped. The two other gargoyles skittered over to join the older one.

"Go!" Merofled urged, pushing the first one into the water.

The coach door opened, and the bishop appeared in the doorway.

"What have we here?" he demanded.

Alaric watched his superior step down to the ground, aided by a coachman, even though the bishop was not much older than Alaric.

Alaric strode forward. "It's the gargoyle, sir."

"And isn't that the witch who was to be burned?"

"She offered to help find the gargoyle, sir. It had trapped a boy in the river."

"I leave for a fortnight, and this is what happens?"

The bishop swept past him, not even waiting for an answer. His narrow face was grim and hard. All must not have gone well at the house of his family.

"Get this witch in hand at once!" he ordered to one of his horseman.

The priest jumped off his horse and headed for Merofled.

"As for this beast," the bishop stared at the struggling gargoyle, his hands on his hips and his feet planted wide. "I'm glad to see it is not long for this world. It's a menace to the village!"

"Romanus," Alaric began, coming up beside him. "The gargoyle's injured and sick. It's not going to hurt anyone."

"No, it won't." The bishop slanted a cold look at Alaric. "And we shall make certain of that."

"Father Paul," he turned to gesture at another of the horsemen. "Tie this beast to the coach. It shall walk back to Rouen. There it shall be burned, and we will have a celebratory feast."

"No!" Merofled exclaimed. "You can't!"

"Silence!" The bishop barked at her. "When I want your opinion, girl, I shall ask for it."

Alaric met Merofled's terrified eyes as the men looped a rope around the neck of the gargoyle and tied the other end to the back of the coach. He wanted to do something—anything—to keep the gargoyle from being dragged to her death. But he could not disobey his bishop. Besides, if he were going to save his favors for something, he would save them for Merofled.

An hour and a half later, the gargoyle was dragged into the city square. Alaric walked beside her, not sure if she still lived. He couldn't see her breathing. His heart was sick. Merofled rode behind one of the priests, her arms lashed to her sides. Alaric marveled that she hadn't fallen off the horse, as she'd ridden up the hill to Rouen without having had anything to cling to.

News of the capture traveled quickly, and soon the town square filled with villagers cheering and whooping for joy. The bishop descended from the coach and waved at the crowd in a regal gesture that he had practiced since childhood when he and Alaric had played a game they called "Pope."

"My good people of Rouen!" the bishop exclaimed in his best sermon delivery voice. "I have captured the gargoyle!"

Cheers and clapping echoed off the walls of the square.

"Today the monster burns!" he crowed. "And tonight we celebrate!"

Another cheer went up.

"Brother Alaric," the bishop looked over his shoulder. "See to the burning of this beast."

"But sir—"

"I will hear no protests. You heard my command. Carry it out."

Heartsick, Alaric swallowed back his words of entreaty on the goji's behalf. He couldn't look at Merofled. He knew the expression on her face would devastate him.

He and three other priests stacked wood around the gargoyle. Then, before the torch was set to the faggots, Alaric drew his sword and stepped up to the gargoyle's head.

"I am sorry," he said, not sure if she was still alive and could hear his voice. He thrust his blade into her, where her spine met her skull. He hoped he had hit her brain and put her out of her misery. Her tail flopped and that was her only reaction. Then Alaric stepped back, and the grim event of the day proceeded as the bishop had decreed.

When Alaric was certain the gargoyle was roasting well, he tramped out of the square and headed for the back of the cathedral. The dogs were there, lying at the rear entrance of the church. Bear jumped up to greet him.

"Hi there, Bear," Alaric ruffled his neck. "I'll see what I can do about your mistress. Don't worry."

Bear panted happily, his big jowls hanging with strings of drool. He looked completely confident that Alaric could do anything. Alaric wished he shared the dog's sentiments.

Chapter 8

WITH THE DAY HANGING HEAVY ON HIS SHOULDERS, Alaric trudged through the door of the church and headed for the cellar where the priests stored ale, food and prisoners. He gathered an apple and pear from the larder and then proceeded to the dungeon—the part of cellar farthest from the stairs and light.

In the gloom he looked into every cell until he found Merofled. He peered through the small barred opening in the door and could just make out her slender shape huddled on a bench. All he could see of her head was a tumble of raven-colored hair. Her knees were pulled up to her chest and her arms were wrapped around her shins. She looked as if she were shivering. He wasn't surprised. The autumn afternoon was dank, the dungeon was cold and she hadn't had anything to eat for two days.

He slid back the wrought iron deadbolt and opened the door.

She looked up, and when she saw who stood in the doorway, she rose to her feet.

"Here," Alaric held out the fruit. "You must be hungry."

"How can I eat, smelling that smell?" She hugged her chest and stared at the stone wall, as if she could see what was happening in the square.

Alaric set the fruit on the wooden bench, which was

the only furniture in the cell. Then he sighed and studied her.

"I'm sorry, Merofled."

She shot him a glare, distraught. Pain and heartache streamed from her clear green eyes, which were like beacons in the darkness.

"The gargoyle was bound to die anyway," he added gently.

Merofled hung her head, and her hair hid her expression. But Alaric could tell she had begun to weep by the shaking of her shoulders. Seeing the proud young woman weeping fractured something inside him. He had thought he merely lusted after this woman. But witnessing her breaking down, he realized that his feelings for her ran much deeper than desire.

He longed to give her solace. In fact, he wanted to take care of her and make certain she did not suffer in any way. The revelation startled him. He could feel his loyalties shifting and the underpinnings of his life giving way, as the riverbank had given way under his feet.

"Merofled," he said. His voice cracked, betraying deep emotions that were better left buried. Aware that he was about to take a step that could never be retraced or retracted, he reached out for her and gathered her into his arms.

She didn't protest. She collapsed against him, while her body trembled with sobs. She clung to him, her arms around his chest and her fingers digging into his shoulder blades. He'd never felt so stricken and so aroused at the same time.

"Merofled." He put his hand on the riot of curls at the back of her head. Her hair was softer than he had imagined it would be. He stroked her head, much like she stroked her dogs, and held her firmly but chastely—not in the way he longed to caress her. "You did your best. You saved the little ones."

"Maybe," she blurted through lips swollen with tears. "But maybe they drowned. Your precious priests wouldn't let me look."

"They won't have drowned. The will to survive is strong. In all of us." He pushed back the hair at her face and urged her to look up at him. "You did everything you could, Merofled. Everything."

She gazed up at him, searching his face as if looking for the truth, as if he knew the answers.

Then, before he could say anything more, her mouth seemed to grow closer of its own accord. And before he knew it, he was bending down to kiss her.

His world exploded. He had never wanted to kiss a woman more than he'd wanted to kiss Merofled. Her mouth was moist and hot from crying, and her arms hugged him fiercely as she kissed him back with a fervor that amazed and thrilled him. He tightened his grip, crushing her breasts into his chest and running his hand down her supple spine to her firm, rounded backside. He moaned, desperate to be close to this strong unusual woman, to feel her naked body against his own naked flesh and to break down all barriers between them.

"Alaric!" she whispered against his lips.

He wanted her. Desperately. But he could not have her in this place. Someone could come into the cellar at any moment to get preparations for the evening feast. Moreover, he was a fledgling priest. Chastity was one of the virtues championed by Bishop Romanus. According to the bishop, refusing all associations with the fairer sex was the only way a man could concentrate on his calling.

Alaric had to break it off before he lost his last shreds of self-control. But in doing so, he denied himself the one thing he wanted more than anything in the world. Merofled.

Sighing raggedly, he kissed her one more time upon the lips and then urged her to step back by unlinking her arms and drawing them away from his torso.

"We can't do this," he said. "Not here. Not now." He released her wrists in front of him.

She nodded and swallowed, and hugged her arms around her chest again.

"At the feast, I intend to beg for mercy for you," he said. Gently, he squeezed her left shoulder. "Don't lose hope, Merofled."

She nodded again, her eyes brimming with tears.

"You have a friend in me," he said.

She reached up to touch the side of his face. As the warmth of the connection poured over him, he knew what it was like to be cherished by Merofled the miller's daughter. Like Bear and Cletus and Juno, he melted beneath her caress.

That evening the village celebrated the demise of La Gargouille. Rough tables and benches ringed the burned corpse, and at the raised head table in front of the cathedral sat Bishop Romanus and twelve of his priests, one of which was Alaric. He'd been given a place at the left end. The number of men and position of the bishop was not lost on Alaric. This was certainly the last supper for the goji.

He couldn't look at the poor creature. He also couldn't eat, even though he hadn't had any food since the gargoyle hunt had begun. He sat through the festivities barely sipping his ale, waiting for the right time to speak, and thinking about what he wanted to say on behalf of Merofled. Her life depended upon his words and his ability to sway the opinion of the townspeople.

While he mused, he saw the executioner approach the head table.

"Pardon the interruption, Your Excellency," he knelt in front of the bishop.

Romanus stopped gnawing on a chunk of ox they had roasted for the feast.

"Yes?"

"The beast hasn't burned all the way. If you look at it, Your Excellency, you will see that the neck and head refuse to burn."

The bishop glanced at the charred gargoyle. "So I see."

"The farmer, Claude, wants to chop off its head to make certain the beast will not rise from the ashes."

"I see no harm in that." Romanus waved him off and grasped the shank of meat in both hands again. "Do as you wish."

Alaric scanned the crowd for the farmer and saw him standing near the head of the gargoyle, with his red-headed son at his side. He had changed his clothes, so no one could see what Merofled had done to him. But his face was a red expanse of pockmarks where the gargoyle bile had burned him.

The executioner lumbered back to Claude and gave him the axe. The eager smile on the farmer's face sickened Alaric, but he couldn't look away. He watched Claude raise the double-edged axe above his head.

"Go back to hell, gargouille!" he shouted. Then with a powerful swing, he severed the gargoyle's neck. The head bounced and lay still.

Whooping, Claude snatched up the head by the horn, and held it aloft. The crowd cheered, egging him on. In triumph, he glanced at the bishop and then seemed to see something behind the table of priests. He strode to the huge double doors of the cathedral while everyone watched, hushed and curious as to what he was about to do.

Claude jumped up and smashed the head of the beast onto the hook that usually held a wreath.

The crowd went wild. Nothing pleased them more than to see the head of the monster on display.

Proud of himself, Claude wiped his hands on his tunic, smirked at Alaric, and then disappeared into the crowd.

As darkness fell over Rouen and the bonfires blazed, the townsfolk poured the bishop's ale down their gullets, emptying cask after cask. By nine o'clock, most of the villagers were well into their cups. Still sober, Alaric decided the time had come to make his move. He rose.

"A toast!" He held up his tankard. "To Bishop Romanus, slayer of gargoyles!"

"To Romanus!" the crowd roared, rising to their feet.

The bishop, basking in the glory he loved so much, nodded and smiled at the villagers. It was just like the times the two of them had played "Pope": Romanus hauled around in a small wagon, waving at an imaginary congregation, while Alaric paid homage to him and carried out his every command so he could earn a sacred wafer. He had gone along with Romanus only for the treat, as sweets had been rare in his struggling household.

"May your days be many," Alaric continued. "May you live to be as old as Methuselah."

"Methuselah!" the crowd echoed.

"And may we commemorate this day with a special dispensation."

Romanus' head jerked around in his direction. Alaric continued, undaunted.

"Bishop Romanus, may you pardon one criminal each year on this day in honor of what Merofled the miller's daughter did for the city of Rouen."

"The witch?" Romanus leaned on one elbow to peer at Alaric. "Are you suggesting I pardon the witch?"

Alaric addressed the crowd. "Merofled is no witch. Without her and her dogs, we never would have found the gargoyle or the boy. She is the reason this beast lies here before you, dead!" He raised his tankard. "To Merofled!"

"Merofled!" the fickle crowd echoed, almost in a frenzy now, just where Alaric wanted them. "Merofled! Merofled!"

The bishop's eyes blazed at Alaric. He obviously did not want to pardon the witch, but if he didn't make the gesture now, he would look like a bastard in front of his admirers.

"So be it," he grumbled, adjusting his miter. He rose and urged the crowd to hush as Alaric took his seat.

Romanus looked to the heavens and raised his arms wide. "From this day forward, we shall pardon one criminal a year, to remember the great feat that was accomplished here today. And by so doing, we will never forget the day the terrible gargoyle was vanquished." He gestured toward the church behind him. "And by hanging the beast's head upon the door of our great church, we will let any and all gargoyles know that Rouen will not suffer monsters that threaten her. Any monsters! We shall slay them in their tracks!"

"No monsters!" the crowd erupted in cheering so loud, the noise blotted out the thunder of the fires.

Alaric sat back, glowing with happiness. He could relax now. He had saved Merofled. He couldn't wait to tell her. But he knew he must be patient in that regard.

Alaric watched the bishop finish his third goblet of wine and then stood up and walked to the side of Romanus' chair. As he approached, two pages served the bishop yet another chunk of meat and glass of wine. Romanus must have fasted during his journey back from Soissons, or adulation had whetted his appetite.

"Your Excellency." Alaric waited until the bishop looked up at him.

"Yes?" Romanus' voice was tight with impatience.

"It has been a strenuous couple of days for the young woman, Merofled," Alaric continued. "I ask your leave to free her or take a meal to her?"

"You shall do neither," the bishop snapped, setting down his jewel-encrusted goblet with a thunk that conveyed his annoyance. "She must suffer some punishment, lest she fail to learn her lesson."

Alaric's buoyant mood sank. "What kind of punishment?"

"I intend to make an example of her," the bishop said. "It is no small matter to pardon a criminal. The accused must do something in return for such a favor. They must display their gratitude to the church as well as show the proper amount of contriteness."

"In what way?" Alaric's joy frayed even more. A public display involving Merofled would not go well. She would never show the proper amount of contriteness. In her mind, she had done nothing wrong. "What kind of example?"

"I am not certain yet. But you may be sure that I will come up with a fitting penance."

"And she must starve until then?"

The bishop nodded. "It will be good for her soul. Perhaps hunger will make her reflect on why she is hungry and what sins she committed to have placed her in such a predicament."

Chastened and worried, Alaric fell silent.

"Will that be all, acolyte?" the bishop asked, gazing at the smoldering corpse of the gargoyle as if he were bored.

"Yes."

The bishop glanced up at Alaric and narrowed his

eyes. "She does not deserve your concern."

Alaric frowned.

"And I will brook no interference from you, Alaric. It was enough that you pressured me into pardoning her. You sorely test the boundaries of our friendship."

The voice of the bishop faded into the background as Alaric stared at the crowd. Who were these people he had decided to call his flock? Who was the man he had followed to Rouen and now called his master?

After the loss of his family, Alaric had clung to anything familiar—even if that familiar thing had never really been his friend. He saw now how poor a decision he had made in coming to Rouen. He had chosen a path not suited to him, just as Merofled had said at the cave.

The cave. It seemed so long ago now.

"Brother Alaric?" the bishop prodded him with the shank of his meat, nudging him out of his dark thoughts. "Did you hear what I said?"

"Yes. I heard you." Alaric glanced down at the bishop, seeing him now with Merofled's eyes. Gone were his childhood memories of the games they had played and the boys they had once been. He saw Romanus for what he was—a self-absorbed and self-righteous little man. "I bid you goodnight, Your Excellency."

Romanus stuck out his hand. Alaric knelt and kissed his ring, hating every moment he must show fealty toward the man. Then he strode out of the town square, his stomach burning and his spirits at an all-time low.

In case the bishop saw fit to send one of his spies after him, Alaric did not go directly to the cathedral. Instead, he took a circuitous route to the church, sticking to the shadows and making certain he was not followed.

When he got to the rear of the church, he noticed Cletus standing at the door, listening with a cocked head. His hackles were up. Juno trembled at his shoulder, whining. Bear padded up to Alaric and pushed his head beneath his hand. Even Bear's bloodshot eyes looked worried.

Alaric's funk turned to alarm. He told the dogs to stay and hurried down the steps to the cellar.

As he turned for the dungeon, he heard someone cry out, "Leave me alone!"

The voice belonged to Merofled.

Alaric dashed toward her cell.

Chapter 9

THE OUTRAGE THAT HAD BEEN EATING AT ALARIC flared to an inferno when he saw Merofled's cell open and a man standing in the doorway, holding a club.

"You there!" Alaric shouted.

The man turned. Even in the darkness of the cellar, there was no mistaking the yeoman's red hair and pitted face. Claude had decided to take matters into his own hands and seek revenge on the woman who had shamed him and most likely maimed him.

"Here to defend the witch again?" Claude taunted, tapping the end of the club in one of his beefy hands. "People will get the wrong idea, priest."

"I care little for what people think."

"You should." Claude's pale blue eyes glittered in the darkness. "When the townspeople sober up, they'll demand a burning. If not the witch, then most likely you."

"Then you have not heard." Alaric treaded closer, his hand itching to unsheathe his sword, but he checked his natural inclination to arm himself. He hoped to talk Claude out of his revenge. "There's not to be a burning. The bishop has agreed to pardon Merofled."

"He's going to pardon me?" Merofled gasped, her eyes round.

Alaric spared a glance at her. When he saw the hope shining in her eyes, he had to look away. The expression was like a cleaver, splitting him in two. He couldn't believe how strong his attachment was to her. He felt her emotions as if they were his own. He wanted to rush to her, take her in his arms, kiss her and tell her that all would be well. All she had to do was play along with Romanus and all would be well.

But she would never play along with Romanus. And that's what he loved about her.

There would be no embracing. No kissing. Not just yet. Claude stood between them, expecting to exact his own form of justice. But the witch he intended to kill now had a friend as well as a champion on her side.

"Step away from the door, yeoman," Alaric commanded.

"I don't have to obey the likes of you." Claude retorted. "I saw the bishop tonight. I could tell what was on his mind. If this witch never sees the morning, Bishop Romanus won't shed a tear. Maybe he'll even reward me."

"You are a fool to second guess the bishop."

"No, I'm not. I know the man well. You're the stranger to Rouen, priest. And you have much to learn about what goes on here."

"If that is true, it's time for a change."

Merofled stepped toward Alaric as if she agreed with his declaration and had decided to stand by him.

Without warning, Claude turned and rammed the end of the club into her abdomen, knocking her back into the cell. Crying out in pain, she fell to the floor, holding her stomach and writhing.

Alaric lunged forward to help her, but Claude backed into the doorway, using his bulk to block the way.

"Don't think you can charm your way out of your troubles this time, witch," Claude barked. "I'm not some lovesick puppy that has fallen under your spell."

Alaric flushed. He wasn't sure if the farmer referred to Merofled's dogs or to him. But he was sure of one thing: no man would ever hurt Merofled again.

He grabbed Claude's arm and spun him around. Enraged, he slammed his fist into Claude's nose, breaking it.

Claude yelled and fell back as blood poured over the fingers he held to his face.

Alaric wasn't done with the farmer. Far from it. He wouldn't draw his weapon on a man who was not equally armed, but his fists and knees were nearly as deadly as a blade. He took another step and plunged his right fist up and under the man's ribcage. Claude staggered back and fell to his knees, gasping for breath.

While Claude struggled to his feet, Merofled took the chance to scurry out of the cell.

Claude growled and raised his club. He obviously had no qualms about using a weapon against an unarmed opponent. While his nose ran with blood and his mouth grimaced in pain, he bashed Alaric in the hip.

Alaric reeled from the force of the blow. But before the farmer could swing his weapon away, Alaric grabbed it and wrested it out of his hands.

Though Claude was fit from tilling the soil and harvesting his crops, he was no match for a warrior who had fought in hand-to-hand combat for the last fifteen years. Much to Alaric's regret, the one thing he excelled at was fighting and killing people. He knew all the moves. He knew what the enemy would do.

But he was done with killing. He would not crush this man, however much he wanted to.

With a roar of fury, Alaric tossed the club away and lunged for the farmer, grabbing him by the waist, and barreling forward. He knocked Claude into the cell where Merofled had been imprisoned. The farmer crashed against the bench and fell forward, onto to the floor on his hands and knees. Before Claude could lumber to his feet, Alaric sprang away and slammed the door. He slid the bolt across, locking the farmer inside.

"Witch-lover!" Claude yelled, pounding at the door. "Demon!"

Without making a retort, Alaric grabbed Merofled's hand and dashed for the stairs, leaving Claude to shout profanities from his prison cell.

Not until they had passed through the south gate of the city did Alaric speak.

"Where is your home?" he asked as they hurried along the rutted path that followed the river.

"To the east."

"Do you have anything of value there?" he asked. "Anything or anyone you can't leave?"

"I have some fowl. But they can fend for themselves. They roam freely."

"No family?"

"My grandmother died last winter. She was my only kin." She tilted her head and looked at him with eyes that were wise beyond her years. "Like you, Alaric, I am alone in the world."

He glanced down at her. The full moon illuminated her face, lending her pale skin an unearthly glow. She was like no other woman he had ever seen. He knew he would never tire of looking at the soft planes and shadows of her face.

"No keepsakes?" he added, entranced by her ethereal beauty.

She shook her head. "My world has been unremarkable. Until now."

"Aye. It's not every day a person gets burned at the stake."

Her brows knitted. "I was not speaking of my supposed sorcery. I was referring to you."

"Me?"

"My life changed when you came into it. You showed me that I am not alone."

He regarded her, his heart pounding in his chest.

"Now I know there is another person in the world that understands me," she continued. "You understand me, Alaric. And you can't know how much that means to me."

Alaric thought it was high time that she touched him, to reveal what he meant to her on an emotional level and seal the decision he was about to make. But she simply kept walking beside him.

Merofled had been mistreated and misunderstood most of her life. Her experience had turned her into a warrior, just like him: crusty and hard. She would need gentle coaxing to help her emerge from her shell.

Alaric was ready for such a challenge. He could be gentle. He had infinite patience when it was required. He would have to let her come to him in her own time. She had revealed enough of her sentiments with her passionate kiss in the dungeon. He could not forget the kiss. Even now, the memory sent a frisson of desire through him.

He knew if he gave her time, she would kiss him again. And more.

He stared down at her, knowing he was about to take the final step into a strange new world. And he would take it willingly and joyfully.

"You can't stay in Rouen," he said.

"I know. Do you have any suggestions as to where I should go?"

"Paris. You will like it there."

"It's along the south road." She glanced at the horizon. They were headed south. The fact must not be lost on her.

"If you like, I could take you there."

"But what about the church?" she countered. "Will you not be punished for helping me escape?"

"I've reconsidered my choice of vocation," he replied. "You were right, Merofled. The life of a priest is not for me.

"Then," she glanced at him and smiled for the first time. "It is Paris. For both of us."

Her smile was all he needed. It filled him with bliss. His chest felt as if it would burst with happiness. He had only known this woman for a handful of days, but he was willing to gamble that she was the perfect mate for him.

He had reached a crossroads. There was no going back. No more Rouen for him. No more Bishop Romanus. There was only Merofled and a future in a faraway place.

"Then let's head south." He took her hand. "And put bishops and gargoyles behind us."

"Yes!" she squeezed his fingers.

He'd never felt more empowered or more optimistic. It was as if his bloody past had been swept away. He had found his peace and his path at last.

They walked a mile in companionable silence, the dogs ranging ahead of them in the moonlight and Alaric enjoying the warmth of her fingers clasped in his.

"So what is your nickname?" he asked, after a good long silence.

"My nickname?"

"Yes, what did your grandmother call you?"

"She called me Mero. Why?"

He glanced down at her. "You once said that anyone worth knowing has a nickname."

She smiled again, and the expression bounced into

his heart and settled there with a wonderful glow. "I did, didn't I?" She looked pleased that he had remembered.

"So, Mero it is." A new name for a brand new life.

"Yes," she replied, clinging to his hand and tipping her tousled head against the top of his arm. "Mero it is."

Patricia Simpson is a writer, artist and dog lover who lives in the Bay Area of California. When she is not playing trivia with her beloved beagle mix at their favorite Irish pub, she is busy renovating houses, painting tropical fish (just on canvas, not the actual fish) or traveling with her Scottish husband. You can find more information at *http://www.patriciasimpson.com* or on Facebook at *Patricia-Simpson-Author.*

Author's Note

When I was asked to write a story about a gargoyle, I had to do some research. I knew what gargoyles looked like and what their architectural function was. (They serve as rain spouts.) But some gargoyles on the skylines of France are different. They hover over the rooftops, looking out. Why? And what inspired the medieval sculptors of Europe to create such monsters? My mind raced with possibilities.

Perhaps the sculptures were based on actual beasts that existed in the ancient world—but are now extinct. That planted the first seed of my story.

My research also produced an account of the very first gargoyle, the legend of the gargoyle:

The Legend of La Gargouille

Long ago at Rouen, on the left bank of the Seine ranged swamps where there was a terrible monster that devastated the area, devouring men, killing horses and corrupting the air by its pestilential breath. The terrified people of Rouen called the creature The Gargoyle. When Saint Romain decided to confront the gargoyle, the only person who volunteered to go with him was a condemned man who had nothing to lose. When they arrived in the territory of the monster, Saint Romain drew a cross on her body, which induced the beast to lie at his feet. Then he used his scarf as a halter, and brought the gargoyle to the city where

*she was burned at the front of the cathedral (or thrown into the
Seine, depending on the version). Her head and throat would not
burn, so they hacked off the creature's head and hung it from
the wall of the cathedral to ward off evil and other monsters
that might try to terrorize the people. This legend is the origin
of the "privilege of Saint Romain" where each year the bishops
spared the life of a man condemned to death. This privilege
disappeared with a few others, the night of 4 August 1789.*

I took this legend, considered the many accounts
of Nessie sightings in Loch Ness, depictions of winged
lizards on Egyptian tombs, as well as medieval paintings
of knights fighting dragons, and came up with a possible
explanation of what a gargoyle might have been when
it walked the earth so long ago. Then I gave the legend
a modern twist, with a forward-looking woman who in
our day would have been a biologist or an animal rights
activist instead of a witch.

I hope you enjoyed the interpretation!

www.ingramcontent.com/pod-product-compliance
Lightning Source LLC
Chambersburg PA
CBHW031542240626
47153CB00002B/348